THE BETRAYED

JJ ANDERS

GRAYTON

THE BETRAYED

DIGITAL ISBN: 978-1-945100-45-1

PHYSICAL ISBN:

Published by Grayton Press

SUMMARY

After a horrible attack on the royal family, Princess Caylee is left alone to rule Genoa. Seeking any explanation about where her family has disappeared to, Caylee finds help from her family's trusted friends. When Wizard Col discovers something that might give her the answers she seeks, Caylee embarks on a quest and plunges headfirst into exhilarating travels on Genoa's vast ocean. However, Caylee soon finds that travels on a ship are far more treacherous than she believed, and Captain Rouen's ship might damage more than her ego. It might just damage her heart.

Captain Bryce Rouen has always lived life to the fullest, yet he's maintained a strict code of honor—never touch the merchandise. It is a code he now finds hard to follow.

Faced with a royal quest filled with dragons, wizards, and a princess, he now doubts his pathway. Discovering the mystery behind the quest is only one of his goals. The other is to seek the secrets that hide behind the witching green eyes of the royal princess.

To McKenna. You have a deep well of muchness. I hope you never forget it.

MAP

Full-size map available at www.jjanders.com

AUDIOBOOKS

Enjoy listening along. Grab a copy of The Scholar, The Warrior, and The Queen on audiobook. Narrated by Marnye Young.

Links:
Amazon
Audible

PREFACE

Caylee stopped running suddenly as her boots skidded along the narrow pathway. She listened for any sounds of her quarry, her heart pounding in her chest.

The forest around her grew quiet as a gentle afternoon breeze blew the leaves from the branches. The harvest season was in full swing, and the crisp air stirred her long dark hair as she swung her head left and right.

"Where are those boys?" she hissed, stomping one of her feet against the path.

At twelve seasons—or years, as the people of Genoa now called them—she was quite tall. She wore her training uniform still and was grateful she hadn't changed back into her evening dress. Tracking down her brother, Zander, and his best friend, Corbin, was proving harder than she thought.

She had seen the two leave the wizards' training yard only moments ago, their heads bent close together—one blond and the other bright red—no doubt plotting a great adventure without her. This fact had infuriated her, and she had slipped from her own lessons and had followed the pair.

But they hadn't gone to the village of Tharian like she had thought. Instead, the two had headed right out of the schoolyard and into the forest.

Hearing a noise to her left, she quickly started running again. Thoughts of catching up with her brother made her feet fly. The tall trees of the forest kept her sight of the way forward limited, but that didn't slow her down.

When she came to a dip in the path, she almost lost her footing and tumbled. A quick leap had her back on the path, but she slowed. The afternoon light showed no signs the trail had been used recently.

"Drat, where are they?" she hissed to herself as she spun around to look back in the direction she had just come from. That's when she saw the first cat.

The large black creature was bent over the trail about twenty feet from where she stood. The monster was over five feet tall at its shoulders, and its horns were another two feet above that. Its massive jaws opened once, sending shivers down Caylee's back. She could tell it was a female, as the large second row of horns of a male cat was missing.

When the creature gave a low growl, she heard an immediate response on her left, then another on her right. She was surrounded. Before panic could set in, she bolted for the closest tree.

She ripped her sleeve and felt blood drip down her arm as she gained the first branch. Well before she gained a height of ten feet, she was bloody and bruised and terrified.

Cats in Genoa were never a good thing to encounter, even if you had a full brigade of warriors. Here she was, a fool of a girl who had wandered into the forest by herself. All for what? To chase her brother?

"*Food.*" She felt the first cat's thoughts of hunger cry out to her through her magic.

"*Food*," a second hissed as they neared the base of her tree and started to circle its trunk.

Her royal magic was still newly discovered, but it was powerful, even though she was only twelve. Closing her eyes, she held on to the tree's branch and tried to focus past her fears and down towards the large cats.

"*Here*," the first cat hissed at the others.

"*Food*."

She took a deep breath, swallowed once, and looked down at the three large cats that surrounded the base of her hiding place.

"I am not food," she stated, her words mixed with her magic. "I am Caylee."

"*Food*," was the only response.

"No, I am Caylee. You will not harm me." She pushed her magic harder at the three large beasts.

"*This one knows our words*," one of the cats hissed.

"*Food*."

"No, not food!" Caylee screamed as tears of fear leaked out of her eyes. "Caylee!"

"*We hunted you, we eat you, little Caylee. You will be a small meal, but a meal*," the first cat hissed.

"No! You will not. You will need to find something else to eat." Her magic was strong, but so were her fears. She squeezed the branch so hard, she felt fresh blood trickle down her fingers.

"*No, we hunted you*."

"No!" This time, Caylee could see the wave pattern of her magic float down towards the cats. She took some courage when she saw one of the creatures cringe in pain, but then its glowing eyes glanced back up at her, hunger in their yellow depths.

"*Caylee, we climb,*" the cat said as it started to inch up into the tree.

Panic filled her now, a deep darkness that turned her pale green eyes black and her magic dark. She felt herself losing control of her fears, and she opened her mouth in a scream.

What came out was sheer magic. It ripped into the closest creature as it was clawing its way towards her. As her magic hit the cat's flesh, it boiled and twisted. Red slashes cut along the black fur. Its hair singed, and it emitted a short growl before it hit the dirt, dead. Caylee then turned her magic on the other two cats. Before the second cat lay dead, her dark magic was following the third as it tried to race away from the burning destruction of its fellow creatures.

A tear seeped from her eyes, which were once again turning soft green, now that the last cat finally lay dead.

THE START

"Caylee!"

The voice drifted into Caylee's dreams. She didn't want to wake; the dream was so lovely. The orange sun was touching the water as it sank lower in the sky, giving her a feeling of joy. She could hear gulls crying out to each other as the sea's spray kissed her cheeks.

"Caylee!"

Erica's voice drifted finally into her unconscious, and she dug deeper into her pillow as the dream floated away from her.

Giving a small moan, she opened one eye and saw her best friend standing at the head of her bed. Her friend's head only reached three feet above the raised mattress, but the stern look the wind nymph gave her had Caylee rolling to her back and giving a large stretch. Even at only four feet and eight whole inches, Erica still could be intimidating.

"Oh, is it time already?" Caylee asked sleepily as she stretched her arms way over her head and stifled a yawn.

"Well past it," Erica said, and Caylee could hear her friend tapping her small foot on the soft carpet.

"I was having a lovely dream," Caylee stated as she sat up. She saw the room was still dark and pouted a little when she thought of the early hour. Erica had lit the sconces already, and her bedroom was filled with a soft glow. Blue and deep purple rugs and tapestries filled her rooms, her two favorite colors. The thick blue curtains leading to her balcony were still shut, keeping the early morning light out, but a low fire was burning in the fireplace to ward off the night's chilling temperatures.

Caylee gave a quick sniff of the air and smiled when she smelled her favorite tea. She cast her eyes towards the small table near her hearth and saw steam rising from the pretty blue pot.

"Your slippers are here when you want to join me," Erica said quietly. She moved over to pour tea for them both.

"I was on the ocean," Caylee said as she slipped her robe on and found her left slipper with her foot. "The sun was setting."

"I know you miss it, and once the council has approved, you can return to the tribe for a few weeks," Erica stated as she set two small cakes on a plate and handed it to Caylee, who sat in one of the soft chairs.

"Mom says we might get to go earlier than that," Caylee said. She took a dainty bite of cake before she took her first sip of tea. "I hope we can go before summer is over."

"Do you want to hear your schedule?" Erica asked, already lifting her pad and pen. Erica's white hair was already tied back in a soft bun at the nape of her neck. Caylee always had to remind herself that, despite looking like a small child, Erica was the same age as her, twenty-one.

"I guess," Caylee responded. She tried to hold in another yawn.

"The queen will be making the dinner preparations for today, but you will need to ensure the goodwill boxes are set for delivery. That will be your evening chore," Erica stated, and Caylee saw her mark an item off the list before continuing. "After breakfast, you are expected to join Counselor Bree-Nest in the great portrait chambers. She needs to get approval to hang the most recent portrait of the family."

"Oh, is Master Dow finished then?" Caylee asked. She took some fruit from a pretty white bowl and placed the food on her plate.

"Two days ago. It has been drying and was only approved by the master last night. He framed it and is quite pleased with himself," Erica said.

Caylee saw a frown pass over her friend's face. "Oh, don't be like that, Erica. You know Master Dow is new to living amongst humans." Caylee thought of the gentle sprite whom she and her family had sat for. "Besides, he let me peek at the painting last week and it was marvelous."

"Yes, well, after the portrait chambers, there was a request from Counselors Ray, Blake, and Fielder to review the new encampment for the trolls. I hear there is a dispute regarding the water locations."

"Oh, not again," Caylee hissed. She took a rather large bite of cake in frustration before she remembered her manners. "Very well."

"Then you are lunching with the book club in town. I will have the carriage waiting, and if your meeting runs long—"

"You will come and save me," Caylee said with a smile.

"Yes. Once the lunch is finished, I thought a bit of shopping would be in order. The local seamstress has some new material, and the midsummer ball is fast approaching. Then while we are there, inspections of the south battalion are long overdue."

"Oh, can't Zander do this?" Caylee asked, trying not to frown too much as she poured herself a second cup of tea.

"Today is the first Gunya day. He is training with Reyleen on the dragons," Erica said with a frown.

"Oh, can't I do that too?" Caylee asked as she quickly sat forward.

"Your lessons are next week," Erica advised her and then continued her long list of the day's events. Afterward, Caylee moved into the bathroom to wash and dress for the day.

Erica had chosen a soft green dress for her, but after one look, Caylee changed instead to the blue dress with hints of gold woven in the lace. Then Erica helped her brush her long dark hair and tied and twisted it into piles that sat on top of her head.

When her thin crown was set amongst the braids, she added jewelry around her neck and wrists. She studied the outcome in her mirror and nodded with approval. She still thought her forehead was a bit too wide and her nose a bit too short, but she enjoyed the way her green eyes shone in contrast to the blue fabric. She was adding a little lip rouge and slipping into her soft shoes when the door to her room burst open.

"Caylee!" Charlotte cried as she rushed into her room.

"Charlotte," Caylee said, smiling at her younger sister.

"Did you see it?" Charlotte asked as she moved over to grab a thin slice of cake from the plate on the table.

"Have you eaten?" Caylee asked with a shake of her head. She bent over to dish Charlotte a plate.

"I have, but this is my favorite," Charlotte said with a mouth full of lemon cake. "Have you seen the painting?"

"I was just heading there myself," Caylee stated with a sigh.

"Oh, it's so lovely," Charlotte said. Her braids whipped out as she gave a quick spin. "Dow did a great job!"

"Charlotte!" Caylee scolded and tapped her foot against the floor. "I've told you not to use that nickname."

"Oh, he doesn't mind," Charlotte said with a giggle. "Besides, he's not here." She sent a smile and a wink towards Erica, who returned the smile softly.

"That isn't the point." Caylee chided then smiled. "Have you seen Grant?"

Charlotte frowned slightly, but then she turned her back towards her and ate another slice of cake. "I haven't seen him today, yet."

"I guess I will see him later," Caylee stated. She turned to leave.

"If you have to."

Caylee turned and studied her sister again, a frown on her face.

Her temper rose quickly, last night's argument with her parents still fresh on her mind. Their harsh words and strict orders had caused her head to hurt.

"Don't start that again," Caylee urged with a frown. "You know Grant has been nothing but patient with you all! Even Mom and Dad have acted intolerably towards him."

"That's because we don't like him," Charlotte mumbled.

"I'll see you later," Caylee said sternly and, without a backward glance, she left her sister in her room.

She didn't know it would be the last time she saw or spoke to Charlotte for a long time.

The portrait chambers were in the western wing of the castle, and Erica kept pace with Caylee as they made their way down the hallways. Caylee saw several servants bustling along the wide walkways. All were on their way to or from duties, much like she was. She spoke to several and stopped to chat with the head florist, Mrs. Longstone, about a special arrangement for her mother.

"I will write out a card after I see to the portrait," she told the woman, trying not to feel too guilty about the harsh words she had screamed at her parents the previous night.

"I will wait until then," the woman replied. She gave a small bow before continuing on her way.

"Don't tell me you lost your temper again," Erica asked, and Caylee saw the disappointed look on her friend's face.

"It was inevitable," Caylee said with a pout. "Dad and Mom both want to move the date back again."

"Good," Erica said with a nod, running to catch up to Caylee as she continued walking.

"Not you too," Caylee said. Without glancing backward, she moved to walk into the hall.

"Yes, me too," Erica said, quickly moving to block her way forward. For a small nymph, Erica could move quickly when she wanted to. "There is a reason your whole family, and I, don't like Grant Worthington."

Caylee tried to move around her friend but was blocked by her small body once again. The frown on Erica's pale face made Caylee narrow her eyes.

"Grant told me that you had warned him about continuing our relationship. What did you say to him?" Caylee asked, her thoughts of rushing past forgotten as her friend took a defensive stance and then tapped a foot.

"I told him I didn't like him," Erica explained with a nod of her head. "And I warned him."

Caylee didn't mean to laugh, but just the thought of little Erica going up against Grant had a smile crossing her lips. Grant was much taller than Erica. What was the nymph going to do, kick him in the shins?

"I threatened him with your brother!" Erica explained. Caylee stopped laughing. "Zander would love to throttle the man."

"He wouldn't dare," Caylee said with a hiss. "My brother knows I would never speak to him again if he harmed Grant."

"Oh, there are other things Zander can do that don't leave a mark," Erica said with a wicked smile.

Caylee sighed dramatically. "Oh, for goodness sakes." She shook her head at her friend, then quickly moved past her and entered the portrait chambers.

There was a procession of people already waiting for her. Master Dow and Counselor Bree-Nest were there along with Grant. Caylee perked up when she saw her fiancé standing with the others.

"Oh, Grant," she exclaimed, quickening her steps across the vast room. "I didn't know you would be here."

"Darling," Grant Worthington said, and a broad smile crossed his handsome face as he opened his arms to let Caylee greet him.

Grant was only taller than Caylee. After grasping her hands and giving each a kiss, he moved back a step to remind her they weren't alone. His pale green eyes moved from her to Erica.

Today, Grant was dressed in a stiff dark green suit. He had a pale high-collared tan shirt under the jacket. Gold buttons adorned his coat. His blond hair was slicked back, and Caylee had smelled a hint of hair grease and shaving gel when he had bent over her hands.

"I am here now," Grant said, his eyes still on where Erica stood, now only inches from Caylee's skirts.

"I am not yet finished with my duties," Erica stated, and Caylee thought she heard a stiffness to Erica's tone.

"Very well," Grant replied. With Caylee's hand still in his, he turned to address Master Dow. "The portrait is quite lovely. However, there will be a need for a new one soon."

"Ah yes!" Master Dow said with a nod of his head. "A wedding portrait?"

"Yes," Grant said stiffly. "It will need to be bigger than this one."

"Yes, of course. When the queen is free, I will be happy to work out the details," Master Dow said with another nod of his head.

"I am telling you now," Grant replied forcibly, and Caylee felt him tighten his grip on her hand.

"Grant, you're hurting my fingers," she said quietly. She quickly took a step back when Grant's green eyes turned on her. She thought she saw more than anger behind them but wasn't sure. He took a small breath before he released her hand and smiled.

"Of course, I apologize. I guess I do not know my own strength." He turned back to Master Dow and his smile increased. "It is a lovely painting."

The portrait was hung on the eastern wall next to the painting of her parents on their wedding. There were three other family pictures, but since the last included her in braids as a small child, this portrait was long overdue.

"Now that this is finished, might I have a private word with you?" Grant asked, steering her towards the hallway.

"Sorry, Grant, I have a meeting now with the counselors," Caylee advised him. She tried to pat his hand away as he attempted to lead her towards the doors.

"That can wait," Grant stated as he continued to guide her.

"No, Grant. Sorry, but I am already late for the council meeting." She tried again but Grant's right hand was clamped over her arm now.

"Caylee," Erica suddenly stated from the doorway. Caylee caught one last glimpse of her friend before Grant had her turning a corner.

"Grant, what is this about?" Caylee exclaimed as she tried to tamper down her frustration. If she missed this meeting, it could cause her to miss her lunch in town, something she was really looking forward to.

"Can I not have a private conversation with my woman?" Grant asked, frustration lacing each word.

"Yes, but now is not the time," Caylee urged as they finally came to a stop two corridors away from where they had started.

"I do not like it," Grant hissed as he finally let go of her. "She has to go."

"Go?" Caylee asked as she rubbed her arm where Grant had gripped her.

"I will not continue this way. She goes today, or I do!" He balled his hands and pounded them against his thighs to emphasize his point.

"Grant, please calm down and tell me who we are talking about," she pleaded.

"That little nymph!" The words exploded out of him; his face turned red as he confronted her.

The fierceness of his gaze caused her to step quickly back. She had seen him angry before, but never this mad. His usually pale complexion was beet red, and his green eyes flashed with anger or hatred, she couldn't tell which.

"Erica?" she asked as she grasped her hands together.

"Yes, Erica!" Grant hissed, pounding his hands against his thighs again. "She undermines my authority and belittles me at every turn."

"I'm sorry you feel that way," Caylee started but when Grant's angry eyes turned to her, she found herself taking another step backward. "Look, I'm late for a meeting, but I'll have time later to discuss this."

"See, she has you doing it too," Grant hissed with a shake of his head.

"Grant," Caylee soothed as she closed the distance between them quickly, then placed a hand over his balled fist. "No, I mean it, I want to hear what you have to say. It's just I am already running behind for this meeting. And I still have to drop this note off to Mrs. Longstone so she can deliver it to Mom with the flowers."

She saw him narrow his eyes at her, but after a moment, he nodded and relaxed his fists. She didn't know she herself was holding her breath until he smiled and took her hand again.

"Darling, I can deliver your note to Mrs. Longstone and meet you after the meeting." His smile was quick and genuine, and Caylee relaxed.

"That would be helpful. Thank you very much. Mrs. Longstone's office is next to the east entrance. She already has my specifications on the flowers I want in the bouquet."

She handed him the note already inside its envelope, then turned when Erica quickly came up to them.

"My lady," she stated, and Caylee gave her a nod.

"Will I see you later?" she asked Grant, but he was already turning away with the envelope in his hands.

2

THE FAMILY

Caylee's mind wandered as Counselor Fielder droned on about the location of the troll's new encampment. He worried it would be too close to the tree sprites' home, but Counselor Ray worried there might be issues with drainage if it was too near the river.

Instead of focusing on the map, she found her mind wandering to Grant's earlier reaction and his demand. He had been adamant that she dismiss her friend. But Erica was not only her best friend, but she was also the one she relied upon to keep her rooted in her duties and reality. In truth, Caylee knew that without Erica, her world would come crumbling down around her ears. Erica kept her work schedule and kept her personal life organized, and she was always there as a friend.

"Your majesty?" Ray said close to her ear, and she realized all three counselors were looking to her, no doubt waiting for an answer to a question she hadn't heard.

"Sorry, what was the question?" She felt her cheeks go pink with embarrassment. Luckily, the room was empty except for her and the three counselors.

She knew her duties, at least for this month. She and Zander took turns with their royal duties and this month was hers. Charlotte would join them when she turned nineteen, but that wasn't for another two years. Until then, she and Zander had agreed to trade off this duty with training. And yet it seemed Zander always found reasons why he couldn't complete a full month of the chore.

She didn't mind though. Many of the royal duties included socializing with the townsfolk, something she loved to do. The job kept her busy, and she found it to be satisfying.

Zander was still trying to obtain a higher level in the dragon tribe, but Caylee was more interested in dragon caregiving and her archery. She had several awards and for each one she obtained a higher standing with the tribe, something she enjoyed.

"We think the plains along the northern border of Pinewoods might be the best. There is a new trail that the trolls can use to reach the town, and water can be delivered daily," Ray restated, his dark eyes studying her as he spoke.

"What does King Clagk think?" she asked.

Counselor Blake tugged on his yellow mustache. His odd orange eyes blinked once and then he smiled.

"Clagk—"

"*King* Clagk," she said. She got another blink from Blake.

"Ah, yes, King Clagk is concerned about the access to water. It appears they use it to build their homes."

"How many homes are they hoping to create?"

"Well, there are quite a few who wish to move here." Ray cleared his throat once before he continued. "It is estimated over a hundred will be making the trek."

"That many?" She looked up from the map when the

doors to the chamber burst open and her twin, Zander, strode in.

"Morning," Zander said with a nod.

"Brother," Caylee stated as he drew near to her, slightly annoyed when she saw Grant waltzing in behind Zander and Seth. "We are in council at the moment."

"I have just been advised by Seth that Mother and Father are missing," Zander said. He turned to look at Seth. "Please tell us."

"It is true. I had just left their private council room and forgot my pack. When I returned to the room to gather it, they were both gone," Seth stated, concern written all over his face. "Ray, I smelled magic."

"Magic?" Ray stated as one of his hands reached up and his fingers brushed across his mustache. "Where is Belent?"

"I left him in the training yard. He is helping Rey gather a battalion. We have had news from the pass," Zander explained.

Ray's fingers continued to brush the hair on his upper lip as he listened to the newest report. When Caylee stood, Zander walked over and placed his hand on her arm. She felt herself shaking at this news but tried not to panic.

"Don't panic. We don't yet know what the mist is, but it's my intent to go find out," Zander said as he embraced her.

"Darling, don't worry about that. I'm sure the prince has things well in hand," Grant said as he pulled her from her brother's arms and hugged her. "Go. I'm sure you can take care of the pass most efficiently."

She nodded once. Zander narrowed his eyes, but then he immediately turned to Seth.

"Seth, please find Belent and have him meet us outside my parents' chamber."

Zander gave her a stern but comforting glance before he, Counselor Ray, and Seth left the chamber. Fearing for her parents, but knowing what her duty was, she pulled from the embrace and turned to Counselor Blake.

"Counselor, please fetch the others and ask a runner to fetch the trans rock for both Wizard Leian and Col. I feel they should be advised of the situation immediately." She turned and sat once again on her throne.

"Darling," Grant started, but Caylee held a hand up first and turned to Counselor Fielder.

"Counselor, would you please call for the lady Erica. I require her services," Caylee said, her eyes on the grey-haired counselor until he bowed and quickly left the room. When six royal guards took up station at the room's doors, she noted their presence and then finally turned to study Grant.

"I fear my day's plans have been altered," she said. She saw annoyance on his face but convinced herself it was concern. "I fear our private talk will have to wait."

"Of course." He drew closer to her. "I do not think—" Whatever he was going to say was interrupted as a runner came in bearing the trans rocks, which were kept only three rooms away in a storage room.

"My lady," the lad said as he produced two boxes, one labeled "Col" and another labeled "Leian/Shiarra."

"Thank you." She first picked up Col's box. She told him about the possibility of her parents' disappearance and, as predicted, he immediately wanted to journey to Castle Pines.

"No, please wait until the search is done. If nothing is discovered, then I will need you here." After getting Wizard Col's agreement, she reached for the other box.

Wizard Shiarra and Wizard Leian were of the same

mind. They wanted to travel immediately, but she urged them to wait.

"I will let you know the results of the search. I think I hear Zander now. I'll contact you soon," she said. She had just replaced the stone inside the box when her brother rejoined her.

"No sign of them," he said as he sat next to her and grasped her hand in his. "Caylee, there was magic in the room."

"Magic?" She felt her brother squeeze her hand.

"Belent says it's dark magic. He thought the room was no longer of Genoa," he whispered to her.

"No longer...?" She tilted her head closer. "What does that mean?"

Zander shook his blond head. His deep green eyes turned to study her.

"I don't know, but one thing is clear. Mom and Dad are missing," Zander explained as the royal counselors all rushed into the room.

The headache was trying to settle behind her left eye. Caylee could feel it threading its evil way outwards as her vision throbbed with each heartbeat.

The two large thrones to her and Zander's left were empty, and she felt a vacuum settle where her parents had once sat.

"*Where are they?*" she asked. Her mind wandered to all

the dark possibilities as the royal counselors continued to argue before her and Zander.

"We must enact law forty-two!" Counselor Blake shouted. Two more who flanked the sand sprite nodded their heads at his statement.

"There is no proof of death," Counselor Derlop, a rather old water sprite, shouted. Several more agreed to this statement.

"There have been plans in place for such an act," Counselor Ray said calmly as he stood before the group.

"No offense, but are the children ready to lead?" Counselor Blake demanded. His long hand reached up and touched his orange and yellow mustache as his odd orange eyes blinked.

"Hey, now!" Zander objected, but he quieted when Caylee rested a hand on his arm. She knew his temper and, despite feeling the injustice of being called a child, didn't feel that arguing the point now was beneficial.

"Gentlemen," she spoke. "The discussion of who rules is not yet needed. We are here to decide where to look for the queen and king first."

"Begging your pardon, Your Highness, but even that decision must be made by one of authority," Counselor Blake replied.

"Then we will make it!" Zander interjected, and Caylee heard the refined anger build in her twin's voice.

"Where is Charlotte?" Caylee asked Seth, who stood to her right, suddenly aware that her sister was missing.

"I was told they were unable to locate her." Seth's reply had Zander standing quickly.

"Not her too?" He started to head towards the door, but Counselor Ray stopped him.

"No, you must remain here. I will have Seth and two

guards search for her now." He patted Zander's shoulder as fear built in Caylee all over again.

"Probably somewhere in the library, hidden in a corner with a book," Caylee heard Seth mumble, but she saw worry filling his face before he quickly left the room.

"Look, there are three of us to divide Mom and Dad's responsibilities," Caylee started. She held up a hand when Zander opened his mouth as he approached her. He sat back down. "I know the mist blocking the pass needs to be inspected. However, with the attack on our family, we must remain here, where it's safe," she pleaded, hoping someone would confirm the castle was indeed safe.

"But here isn't safe," Zander quietly said. He grabbed her arms as her eyes grew wide with fear. "I know the mist is connected; maybe I can find out who or what is causing this. And in discovering this, we might find where Mom and Dad are. Caylee, we know the mist is at the pass, right now."

Her internal struggle lasted a whole minute. Her fear was so vast that a black mist crept around her vision. She finally took a small breath to prevent herself from passing out.

In her mind, she saw Zander traveling up to the pass, discovering the mist and her parents, safe and well. But then she also saw herself, left alone in the castle while she was surrounded by a fiery red haze, and fear enveloped her once again.

Then she thought of her parents, the strength they had instilled in her through her upbringing. She had a fleeting second to remember being trapped in a high tree while large cats circled below but quickly cast that out of her mind as she stiffened her spine again, resolved to never be a victim again.

"What shall we do?" she asked softly as the advisors continued to argue around them.

"What they raised us to do," Zander stated strongly and gripped her small hand in his. "And what they themselves would do." The smile on his face was one of determination as he looked up at the counselors' faces staring back at them. "I go to the pass and hunt the red mists to find my parents."

"I will help you," Sorcerer Belent stated with conviction. Zander nodded and turned to look at her. "Sister, Genoa counts on your wisdom to govern. I ask that you remain here, safe with the royal guard to protect you and Charlotte. When I find Mom and Dad, I will return them to us."

His conviction strengthened her, and she raised her pointed chin a little higher and gave him a nod.

"Very well but know this. If you do not return within ten days, I will depart to track you down." Her green eyes narrowed at him as if daring him to disagree with her statement, but he just smiled.

"Agreed," he said with a nod. "Belent, please tell Rey we will take a full regiment of men."

"Take Corbin and Sash with you," Caylee pleaded as she grabbed his arm to prevent him from turning immediately from her.

"And Seth," Zander agreed with another smile, "for entertainment." He smiled down at his sister. "As soon as possible, send word to Wizard Col and Timmons, maybe even to cousin Calob in Matera. Heck, might as well tell all the others too. They will come."

She nodded at his words and then turned to leave.

As the doors closed behind her brother, Caylee felt the weight of the royal seat for the first time in her life. So much sat upon the decisions held by the office. So many lives were affected by what the queen and king decreed. How had she assisted all these years in her princess duties and never known the weight of the office?

Suddenly, she felt so alone.

Turning, she saw Erica standing only inches from her and reached out to grasp her friend's hand. When Erica squeezed her fingers, she felt a new strength in the small fingers and stiffened her spine once more.

"Page." She turned and saw the young boy named Maxwell. "Maxwell, please fetch the rocks for King Malicky and Uncle Calob as well." He bowed once and then turned on his heels and ran out of the room.

"Do you think that is needed?" Grant said, startling Caylee at how close he was. Turning, she saw him standing in front of Zander's throne and frowning down at her.

"Grant." She lowered her hand from her throat where it had flown seconds before when he had startled her.

"Why are you calling for them?" he demanded, and she saw the counselors still present cast their eyes at him.

"I will discuss this later with you. For now, I need to adjourn to the council chambers." She stood and glared at him when he moved to block her way. "Later," she hissed at him, narrowing her eyes when he didn't move.

"Later," he said, and she thought she detected a warning in his voice.

Turning, she left the main council hall as the royal guards surrounded her. Erica, who carried the other two boxes holding the trans rocks, followed a few steps behind. The guards took her to one of the private chambers her family used. She noted it wasn't their personal chambers and assumed that was the room now filled with a red mist.

Instead, it was chamber room three, or as she called it,

the blue room. Blue rugs, light blue tapestries, and tan chairs surrounded a wide oak table.

"Here, place the stones here," she told Erica. She turned to the guards. "Two remain outside, the other four can stand inside. Don't forget the balcony," she warned, but the men were already positioning themselves against the locked glass doors.

"What else do you need, my lady?" Erica asked, her small frame standing close to the table.

"Just the other boxes. Can you retrieve them from Maxwell?" she asked. She moved to open the box with Col's name on it again.

"Right away," Erica said and immediately turned to find the boy.

Turning, she picked up the pale golden rock and warmed it with her hands, waiting for Wizard Col, or Uncle Col as she knew him, to respond to her summons.

3

———

SUPPORT

"Poor little bird!" Aunt Shiarra said, calling Caylee by her childhood nickname. She quickly rushed across the room to hug Caylee.

Shiarra and Leian had appeared in a puff of blue haze caused by their trans rock. Breaking the communication stones allowed instant transportation to the other half of the magical rock, which is why the wizards of the queen each kept one.

Shiarra and Leian, married now over twenty years, had settled in the wizard's town of Tharian, far northeast of Castle Pines. They had three children. Their oldest was Breanna, who was a professor at the wizard's school and was six years older than Caylee and Zander. Their son Otis, who had recently become a wizard, was twenty-two and helped run the school. Their youngest, Penn, was still only eighteen and a student.

It had been over three years since she had visited Tharian herself, but her mom and Shiarra were still very close. Shiarra and Leian were the queen's children's godparents, but Caylee and her siblings always called the couple uncle and aunt instead.

With Shiarra's caring arms around her, Caylee finally felt the shock and dismay overwhelm her. With her parents' disappearance, and now the uncertainty of her sister's location, she had been left alone. Zander and his battalion had taken flight only minutes ago and yet a feeling of foreboding overwhelmed her.

"Is there any news?" Wizard Col asked as he drew near and patted Caylee on her shoulder while Shiarra continued to squeeze her in a tight hug.

"No," she squeaked, her face wet with tears. "Nothing."

"I think we need to take a look at this room ourselves," Leian said. He and Col disappeared quietly as Shiarra pulled her back at arm's length to study her.

"Come. I think some tea is needed. Have you had lunch yet?" She clucked her tongue when Caylee shook her head no. "Well, at least we can start with a meal. Then we will talk."

Shiarra rang and Erica quickly rushed into the room, her pale face drawn and her eyes wide with concern.

"Erica, it's good to see you," Shiarra said with a smile. "Could you be a dear and have tea and lunch delivered. I think this room will do nicely for now."

"As you wish," Erica said and with a small nod. She turned and rushed from the room.

"Poor girl, she is worried for you," Shiarra said as she directed Caylee over to a soft chair near the empty hearth.

"She wouldn't leave my side until you arrived," Caylee said as she sat and shifted her skirts. "Grant also wanted to stay, but I urged him to check on the search for Charlotte for me."

Busy with her skirts, Caylee didn't see Shiarra wrinkle

her nose at this last statement, but by the time she looked up, her aunt had settled in the chair across from her.

"Caylee, do you know, have there been any threats against your family?" Shiarra asked.

"Oh, Aunt Shiarra, I wish I knew," Caylee said with a shake of her head. "Since discovering the disappearance of Mom and Dad I've been trying to think back. The red mist has been spotted in several villages; I believe it has even killed several families." She shook her head again and sighed. "Honestly, Zander was taking care of these reports, and I left all the details to him." She wiped at her eyes again and tried to think about those reports but came up with only a smattering of information.

"We will save the details for later. Right now, tell me about this morning," Shiarra said. She leaned forward and patted Caylee's hand encouragingly.

Caylee told her aunt about her morning. She didn't know why, but just talking to Shiarra calmed her down. Before she had gotten to the part about hanging the portrait, Wizard Leian and Col rejoined them. Both men remained quiet as they took seats next to the women.

When she was finished with her telling of the morning's events, Erica had set the table with a vast lunch and steaming tea.

"Here, let's eat while we tell you what we discovered," Leian said, moving to help Caylee up from her chair.

"The room stinks of magic," Col said as he scratched his bald head once and shook it. "The mist is gone, or faded, but there is still the feeling of dark magic."

"The room had not been disturbed," Leian said. He took a bite of cheese. "The small table had fresh flowers that were undisturbed, but two chairs were disturbed. One was on its side, as if it had been knocked over."

"You didn't go inside?" Caylee asked quickly.

"No, we just looked from the doorway," Col said, patting her hand quickly.

"The flowers, was it a bouquet of Purfla and dragon's breath with Mom's red roses?" Caylee asked.

"Yes, set in a crystal vase," Leian stated as he stopped eating to study her.

"My flowers were delivered," Caylee said with a nod of her head.

"Flowers?" Shiarra asked as she set her cup of tea down again. "What flowers?"

"Last night, I had a terrible fight with Mom and Dad," Caylee said as dread and regret filled her. "I said the most horrible things to them." Unable to sit still, Caylee paced as she thought back to her words from last night and felt ashamed. "Oh, I was horrible," she said with a sob.

Shiarra quickly stood and rushed over to embrace her again. "Shh..." she said, trying to comfort her.

"No, you don't understand. They wanted me to delay my wedding. They requested I delay until next summer. Oh, Shiarra, I was so horrible," Caylee said with a sob.

"I know your parents love you," Shiarra said and hugged her tighter.

"But I was yelling at them. Oh, Shiarra, what if it's the last time I ever see them?"

"Now, do not talk like that. Remember, your parents are strong. You must have hope that we find them." She hugged Caylee again.

"Your mother is a strong dragon warrior and your father too," Col said sternly.

"But..." Caylee started to say, but she was interrupted when Grant walked into the room.

"What is all this?" he said accusingly.

"Oh, Grant! Have they found Charlotte?" Caylee asked quickly, rushing over to him.

"I searched her rooms personally. I found a hidden doorway behind an old wardrobe in her closet. I fear she has been abducted from this," Grant said. He placed his arms possessively around Caylee's shoulders.

"Narnia!" Caylee said with a smile. "No, she wasn't abducted, she escaped!"

"What?" Grant demanded.

"It's a story Mom told us about when we were young. The hidden passageway was known only to my family. Charlotte wanted a secret tunnel from her room to the forest and so Mom had it built years ago. But she hired only one person."

"Me," Col said with a smile. "And I never told anyone."

"Uncle Col built it at night," Caylee said as hope bloomed inside her that Charlotte was safe. She didn't speak of the other tunnels Col had also built. That was still her family's secret.

"If she is not here, where could she be?" Shiarra asked, and Caylee felt dread fill her again.

"I will ask Captain Adams to start his search where the tunnel comes out." Col quickly left the room.

"Have you informed your cousin about your parents' disappearance?" Leian asked, speaking of cousin Calob, who was king of Matera. Calob and his wife Arianna ruled with their six children.

"Yes, and King Malicky too," Caylee said with a nod. She turned to study Grant when she felt him stiffen a little. "Cousin Calob is sending Aiden, and Malicky is going to send Svlain and Zain, but I fear they won't be here for well over a week."

Disturbed by Grant's stiff behavior, Caylee moved to sit

back at the table. Grant crossed the room to stand next to the fireplace as she turned her attention back to Shiarra and Leian.

"The council will request a meeting soon," Shiarra said. She stood and tugged on Leian's arm, so he too stood. "We will go and see about this."

"What? Now?" Leian asked as he was pulled from his chair. "But I was not finished eating."

Caylee smiled slightly as the two left the room, leaving her alone with Grant, who still had his back to her.

"I am glad they came," she said with a sigh.

"Why?" Grant said quietly.

"Excuse me?" Caylee asked, unsure she heard him correctly.

"Why?" he said again, turning.

Caylee was shocked to see anger on his face.

"Why did they come? Why did you call them here?" Grant hissed as he bunched his fists again. "You do not need them."

"Yes, I do," Caylee said, unsure why he was so angry. "They are family. I need them."

"No, you do not!" Grant shouted this time.

Shocked and confused, Caylee studied him. Grant's face was red with anger. His pale green eyes flashed with it while his body shook.

"Grant? What is wrong?" she asked, unable to comprehend why his anger was directed at her.

"You should not have called them here without telling me," Grant hissed, taking a step towards her.

"Excuse me?" Caylee said, her anger rising as he moved closer to her.

"I should have been consulted," Grant said, his anger blinding him to her rising fury. "I went looking for the little princess just like you asked, and then what? I come back to a cozy lunch where you had already called three wizards to you? You did not even tell me you were going to do this!"

"Look here!" Caylee said, finally standing. Her own hands were fisted in fury as she glared at him. "I don't need your permission to do anything!" Anger blocked her vision as she neared him. She gave his chest one hard poke with her finger. "My family was just attacked, and you say I need your permission—*PERMISSION*—to ask for help." She emphasized the words as she shouted at him. "I don't need anything from you, nothing! And right now, I don't need to see you," she shouted, not caring if the whole castle heard her.

Grant stood his ground. Then, his face still flushed with anger, he nodded once and turned to leave. Not caring if he left the room or the castle, Caylee spun on the spot and kicked the leg of the nearest chair. When she felt her middle toe hit and snap, she hissed in pain. After a few choice words, words her father favored while angry, she sank into the chair. The anger drained from her as her toe throbbed in pain.

Erica had to wrap her toes together so Caylee could walk into the council chambers an hour later. Caylee felt foolish for having lost her temper, again. But Grant's words and attitude had shocked her more than anything.

Even as she sat upon her throne listening to the worries and demands of the council, she thought back to how her fiancé had looked earlier. She had seen him lose his temper before, but never so severely, nor directed solely at her.

When she felt her temper rising at remembering Grant's words, she turned her attention instead to Col's latest news. Su Na had been discovered missing. Her mother's dragon was always where her mother was located, and they knew the queen hadn't taken him. After discovering the golden dragon was missing, Caylee and Col quickly agreed that Charlotte must have taken him. Somehow this discovery eased her worry for her little sister a bit. Su Na would do all in his power to protect Charlotte, the daughter of his mistress.

"My lady." Counselor Blake's words broke into her thoughts, and she turned to study him. Blake, the only sand sprite she had ever met, stood tall before her. His orange and yellow hair shone in the afternoon light, which was filtered through the room's windows. She saw him brush at his mustache and knew he was annoyed he had to repeat himself.

"Sorry, counselor." She leaned forward a bit.

"Yes, well, given the circumstances, I completely understand." He turned to the other counselors. "We feel the need, given the recent attack on the royal family, to deploy a specialized battalion strictly for your security."

"A whole battalion?" Caylee asked. "Twenty-five guards? At all times?"

"My lady, there will be two shifts. This will allow full and complete safety," Counselor Blake advised.

"And a wizard with you at all times," Counselor Ray added with a nod of his head.

"Agreed." Counselor Derlop and Fielder seconded the request.

"Will they join me in the bathtub too?" Caylee asked,

standing from her chair. "Twelve is too much. No!" She sliced her hand in the air before her, cutting off any objections as she quickly continued. "I feel six is sufficient. Remember, we didn't know an attack would happen. Now that we do, we know what to look for. I will agree to six guards who will clear a room before I enter, and will guard its entrances and exits. I will also agree to the wizards, if they agree."

"We do!" Shiarra spoke up from the back of the room.

With a nod, Caylee turned to address the counselors again. "I will also agree to remain inside the castle until my brother returns from the pass."

"Agreed," Counselor Ray said quickly, and it was a few minutes before another seconded his agreement.

"Now, let's discuss the search for my parents and sister," Caylee advised.

The discussion was long and frustrating. Soon Caylee knew all the missing details of the previous sightings of the red mists. She heard details of the missing or dead families, including the state of the remains, which caused her stomach to sour.

"Parian is only a day's ride from here," she said in shock. "What relief have we sent to the village and families affected by this tragedy?"

"Relief?" Counselor Blake asked.

"Counselor Bree-Nest, please see that aid is sent tonight to the town, include healers and food if needed," Caylee stated. The woman nodded and left the room quickly. "Counselor Fielder, please see that Captain Adams join us. I wish to hear about ensuring protection for the city as well. It appears we might need to expand our patrols."

Within the hour, she had more guards stationed around the city and had sent two wagons of food, medical supplies, and blankets to the small town of Parian along with the royal family's condolences regarding the tragedy.

The council meeting was just breaking up when a runner came into the vast room and approached Wizard Col. Caylee saw the wizard's face go pale as he turned to look at her.

"My lady," he said and quickly approached her. "There has been news from the pass."

"Zander?" Caylee asked as she grabbed the side of her chair tightly.

"Half his battalion disappeared in a red mist inside the circle stone," Col said quietly. Chaos erupted inside the counselors' chambers.

Sorceress Io Maltesea stirred the blood and bent her deformed shape over the bowl, which was carved out of bone.

After it turned a deeper red, she hissed the magical words and saw her minion's face peering up at her.

"Report," she hissed.

"All were sent, but one got away."

"The little witch!" Io Maltesea hissed.

"Yes."

"Fool! Of all, that is the most dangerous."

"What now?"

"Hold. Wait for my orders." In her anger, the sorceress swept the bowl off the altar with her bent arm.

The little witch was going to be more trouble than she

thought. She would have to ward against her magic, this little Charlotte.

A smile cracked the ugly face as evil plans came to her mind.

"Yes, I think we must expect the little witch soon." Io Maltesea called to her minions, who hovered and cowered near her. "Bring me the Entanglement Crystal!" she hollered as her smile widened to show cracked yellow teeth. "Yes, that will do nicely." She laughed with glee over the chaos the crystal would soon engender. The echoes of her cackle vibrated all the way down to the prisons where her latest conquests still slept.

4

DELAYS

"I'm not waiting!" Caylee hissed. She tried not to stomp her foot again as she stood near the fireplace in her private rooms. Her foot throbbed with pain, but she ignored it and focused instead on her anger and frustration. The soft glow of the low fire cast shadows out in the comfortable room, but its warmth and light show gave her no comfort that night.

Her brother was gone now too. Frustrated and angry at her predicament, she fisted her hands and tried to stop the tears from falling.

"I know, little bird," Shiarra crooned from her place in the soft chair before her. "But Col and Leian want to check out the pass first."

"But Zander too!" Caylee hissed, sinking back into her chair. "Oh, Shiarra, what am I going to do?" she wailed.

"I don't know," Shiarra replied. Caylee heard frustration in her aunt's voice, which matched her own. She took comfort in the fact that she was no longer alone.

"When will they be back?" Caylee asked as Erica filled her teacup one more time.

"Col and Leian? Tomorrow. They ride through the night. Without dragons, it will take them until tomorrow morning, but they will ride the dragons back to us. Col's dragon Tu Lenas will fly out at first light to retrieve them," Shiarra advised as she rubbed the base of her neck in worry.

"They said it was the mist," Caylee said with a shake of her head. "And they increased my guards."

"Good," Erica stated as she returned the teapot to the warmer. "I have already canceled any outings outside the castle."

"But even the castle isn't safe," Caylee said. She immediately regretted her words when her friend paled.

"Then we will make it so," Shiarra said. "I have already secured your private rooms. Before the morning, I will secure the throne and council chambers."

"That will take all night," Caylee stated, looking over at Shiarra. "Tomorrow will be soon enough. I promise I won't leave this room until you tell me." She leaned forward and patted Shiarra's hand gently. "Stay with me. We both need each other."

After receiving a nod of agreement from Shiarra, Caylee turned to Erica and smiled. "That goes for you too."

"I am not going anywhere," Erica said. She sat on the rug near the fire.

The night was long and stressful, but it was made more bearable by the company Caylee kept.

Around midnight, Caylee received a private message from Grant, apologizing for his prior behavior. It was delivered with a single deep pink Laither blossom.

Unsure if she was willing to forgive him yet, she set the blossom on her nightstand and returned to her chair by the fire to worry and think.

She was still hurt and confused by Grant's words. He

had talked to her like she was a child, someone who took orders from him. Someone who needed his guidance in a duty she had been raised to complete.

When she felt her anger build again, she turned her worried mind to her parents and Zander. She wondered if they were dead.

She didn't think so. After all, no trace of them had been found and several of the dragon warriors that had been with Zander said they had disappeared, as if they had been pulled out of Genoa, not blown apart. Their description of the attack had encouraged Col, and even Leian and Shiarra had been encouraged by the description of the red mist.

"I think we should try a finder's spell," Caylee suddenly said. Erica's head had dropped down onto the pillow against the back of the couch.

"What?" Shiarra said quietly.

"A seeking map," Caylee said. She felt stupid for not thinking of it before.

"Yes. That is a great idea." Shiarra stood so quickly that she woke Erica with her fast movement.

"What?" Erica said as she jolted to her feet.

"Go, fetch something of the queen's. A hairbrush or something. Quickly, I will find a map." Shiarra asked two guards to step in while she and Erica left for a moment.

Caylee felt odd having two guards standing inside her room, but since she knew both, one who was married to a pretty maid from the first floor, she smiled and asked if they wanted any tea.

"No, my lady, we just came on duty from the barracks," they said. Before much time had passed, Shiarra and Erica were back.

"Here, on the table," Shiarra said as she unrolled a large

map. I brought more than one. I even got one of Earth. I think your mom and Leian saved it from their time there."

Caylee had never seen the Earth maps, but she recognized the maps of Genoa, along with the ones of the dark tunnel called the Kylix and the distant land Midzark.

"Do you think they could have been sent here?" she asked as she studied the Midzark map.

"I don't know, but we will try the spell on all of the maps until we find them," Shiarra stated.

The spell was cast and after several disappointments, they decided they would try to locate Zander and Charlotte as well. Erica was sent to fetch more personal items, then once again Shiarra started to cast spells. It wasn't until they tried to find Zander that they finally had any success.

"There!" Erica cried as she pointed at the Earth map of Colorado. "There, in this city, see. A rip!"

Three heads bent over the map at the same time. The rip was small, but it was a rip.

"Denver," Shiarra stated and looked up into Caylee's eyes.

"Earth!" Caylee said with a smile. "Not dead!"

The three women danced and cheered with excitement so loudly that the guards came rushing in with their swords raised. It took a while for the women to convince them they were excited, not under attack.

"How do we get them back?" Caylee asked, and the previous excitement drained away. They sat at the table and pondered the problem.

"Cats!" Shiarra said. "Earth!"

"The Orick!" Caylee exclaimed hopefully, but Shiarra shook her head again.

"The last of the Fin Crystals were used to get your

mother back. It would take five years to make more," Shiarra said sadly.

"Shiarra, if Zander was sent to Earth, do you think Mom and Dad are there as well?" Caylee asked hopefully.

"I don't know. They are not showing up on any of the other maps I have here." Shiarra shook her head.

"Maybe another place then?" Caylee asked hopefully. She spent the rest of the night studying the cut in the map that indicated her twin.

"The pass felt different than the room," Leian explained the next morning as he and Col sat around Caylee's fireplace eating breakfast.

"It was the same, yet Leian is correct, it was stronger," Col advised as he took a bite of flat cake.

"That's because he was sent farther," Caylee hypothesized quickly.

They had shown the two wizards the map of Earth and where Zander's tear currently was, in what appeared to be a library.

"Never could get him to read here, but the first time he's on another planet, he heads right to the books," Caylee mumbled as Col studied the map again.

"My guess is he or Belent are trying to find a talisman that will allow them to return," Col said with a nod. "Of course..."

When the wizard didn't continue, Caylee sighed a big breath and finally spoke up.

"What? Of course... what?" she demanded.

"It has been years, but... No, I will need to do some research before I say anymore." Col shook his bald head.

"Next time don't say anything then," Leian hissed with a shake of his head.

"But what of Tresstéanna and Kriston?" Shiarra demanded. "Why don't we see them on any of these maps?"

"It could be because they are not in any of these locations," Col replied sternly. He took another bite of bread.

"Then where are they?" Caylee demanded.

"We only have maps of known Genoa places. Maybe they are in another location," Col replied.

"So, we should consult the goddess?" Shiarra asked, indicating the goddess who had created all life on Genoa, which was named after her. Genoa's corporeal body was located down in the vast tunnel called the Kylix. Tresstéanna and Kriston went on an expedition to return the stolen globe of the goddess years before Caylee was born.

"Not yet. I think I should do some research first," Col advised.

"Oh, just tell us now. If what you say turns out to be bad, we will forgive you for it," Leian grumbled. Clearly, missing a night's sleep made him grumpy.

"Very well," Col replied. He set his fork down next to his breakfast plate. "Years ago, when I was an apprentice, before we split your mother into parts..."

"Yes?" Caylee said impatiently. She waved her hand, indicating Col should continue. She didn't want him to retell the entire story of how he and three other wizards separated her mother in their attempt to save her from an evil king, who happened to be Caylee's dead grandfather.

"Well, it was the reason Wizard Orden chose Earth,"

Col continued as he scratched his head. "He had come from the islands and spoke of a hidden mirror. One that allowed the looker to see anything their heart desired."

"A mirror?" Shiarra asked in confusion.

"It is unclear exactly, but Orden said he had once looked into the mirror and saw Earth," Col finished with a shrug.

"Where is this mirror? Will it show me my family?" Caylee asked excitedly.

"Again, I will have to do some extensive research before I answer any of those questions," Col scolded.

Frustrated and tired, they all finished breakfast. After they left, Caylee settled down to sleep. Erica, who refused to leave her, lay down on the couch near the fire.

When Caylee finally slept, she dreamed of being chased by a red mist. It chased her over all of Genoa and, finally, it followed her across the vast ocean far to the east.

Around dinnertime the following day, Caylee was allowed to journey to the council chambers. But after five minutes inside the vast room, she wished to be anywhere but there. New demands and worries troubled the counselors so much that soon she found her guards doubled yet again.

Word of thanks had been received back from Parian. The townsfolk and their Sayer sent concern back regarding the king's and queen's disappearance.

"Panic might ensue if we do not let the people know you are safe," Counselor Blake insisted.

"What would you have her do? Go on display just to prove she hasn't disappeared?" Counselor Ray demanded.

"We could move up the wedding?" the sand sprite suggested.

Caylee didn't know why, but just hearing the words

wedding now caused her stomach to kick and flip in a very unpleasant way. Something had changed inside her since her argument with her parents only two nights ago. Now, the thought of marriage to Grant frightened her and caused a deep panic inside her.

"No, there will be no need for that," she interjected sternly. "I will not wed until my parents return safely."

"A wise choice my lady," Counselor Ray Fielder said from beside her.

Glancing over to Ray, she caught a flash of a blond figure disappearing out one of the side doors. Dread quickly replaced her panic.

"Grant?" she whispered, realizing how harsh her previous words had been. Her concentration was once again directed towards the council meeting, and she had no more time to think about Grant and her argument with him until well after dinner, when he sought her out.

"Princess, Mr. Worthington would like a few words with you, if you are available," the guard stated from the door.

Erica quickly stood from her place beside the table. After receiving a nod from Caylee, the small woman quickly disappeared into the adjoining bedchamber to give the couple some privacy.

"Very well. Thank you," Caylee said to the guard. She stood to retrieve another cup for Grant and poured him some tea.

"Caylee," Grant said as he strode into the room, his arms filled with flowers of every variety and a pitiful look on his handsome face. "Caylee, please forgive me."

She studied him for a minute and then smiled and set the cup on the table. "Grant, what lovely flowers."

"Please, I was a fool. I was distraught over not finding

your sister. I was completely upset by that when I spoke to you. I am so ashamed by how I acted," Grant pleaded as he stood there, the flowers still filling his arms.

"You aren't upset by my godparents nor Wizard Col's appearance?" Caylee asked doubtfully.

"No, of course not!" Grant replied and lifted the flowers higher. "I brought you these as a peace offering. Please, forgive my previous anger."

"I got the feeling you didn't want them here," Caylee said as she walked across the room and took the bundle of flowers from him. "I'm glad I was mistaken."

"Of course. All is forgiven," Grant replied, confusing Caylee with his choice of words. "Ah, tea!" Grant settled down in one of the chairs, then turned to her with his pale brows uplifted. "Are you going to pour, or shall I send for a servant?"

"Um, let me just put these in some water," she stated. She turned to find Erica already standing next to her with a vase.

"Here, let me do that," Erica stated. She set the vase on a nearby side table, then took the large bundle of flowers from Caylee. Seeing her small friend disappear in the colorful blossoms made her smile. She thanked Erica and returned to the table to pour Grant a cup of tea.

"So, is it true you discovered the location of Prince Zander?" Grant asked as he added two servings of sugar to his tea.

"Earth. Yes, that is correct," Caylee replied with a frown.

"What a shame," Grant absently replied. He took a sip of tea, then added another spoon of sugar.

"At least he's not dead," Caylee said quickly. "Wizard

Col has an idea that might help us get in contact with him or my parents, but he has to do a little more research."

"Wizard Col?" Grant asked as he stopped stirring his tea to study her. "What idea?" he demanded.

"Oh, something about a mirror," Caylee replied. She was distracted by Erica, who was behind Grant's back, waving her arms in a wide circle.

"Erica, is there a bee in the flowers?" Caylee asked, not entirely understanding why her friend was behaving oddly.

"Yes, my lady," Erica said quickly as Grant spun in his seat to study the wind nymph. "Would you mind helping me take them into the other room. I fear it might sting you. We could place the flowers by the window and hope the bee flies away."

"Grant, if you will excuse me," Caylee requested. Without another word, she walked over and helped Erica with the flowers and vase. She didn't see the bee but still followed her friend into the other room. "Well, what is it?" she asked when Erica had firmly shut the door behind them.

"Don't tell him anything!" Erica hissed. She quickly moved across the room, away from the door. "I don't trust him, and you shouldn't either!"

"Erica," Caylee scolded, but then her sleeve was quickly grabbed by her friend, and she was dragged down to Erica's level.

"Please! I beg you, tell him no more until the wizards are done with their investigation," Erica pleaded, her eyes wide with fear and concern. "Please, Caylee."

Caylee saw how upset her friend was, and after a moment she slowly nodded. She didn't think it would cause any harm to refrain from telling Grant anymore about Col's idea. After all, Col himself had been hesitant to tell her.

"Very well. I will speak no more about Col's idea, for now," she said. Erica relaxed.

The flowers were set on Caylee's night dresser and then she returned to the main room. Grant cast an accusing look at Erica but said nothing until the nymph closed the door, leaving them alone again.

"I still do not see why you keep her around," Grant stated quietly and leaned forward a bit as he continued. "She cannot even carry a vase of flowers; how can she do anything else?"

"She may be small, but she is most valuable to me," Caylee replied with a smile.

As she settled back in her chair, she felt a small headache starting to form. Before an hour had passed, she made an excuse to him. She wondered if she would feel guilty later for feeling relieved when Grant finally left.

5

TIME AFTER TIME

"I should be back within the week," Wizard Col said the next morning as Caylee, Shiarra, and Leian ate breakfast outside on Caylee's private balcony.

"Are you sure you searched the whole library?" Shiarra asked as she buttered a slice of toasted bread she had stolen from Caylee's plate. "Maybe you missed something."

"I had all the helpers looking too. No, Castle Pine's library is just not as large as Valorna's," Col said soberly as he stood and walked over to look past the handrail.

Caylee saw him sigh once and quickly cast her eyes out to the vision beyond. The morning was warm, which is why she had decided to have her morning meal outdoors. However, most of the castle still hadn't been protected, which left her with a picnic on her balcony.

When Wizard Shiarra and Leian had joined her, she had perked up and sent Erica to fetch more food. Wizard Col had followed Erica back in, then quickly joined them with his latest news.

"There is mention of a mirror in a book here, but not by

name, nor any location is discussed. I need to consult the older books located in Valorna," Col continued.

"What if you do not find any reference, what then?" Leian asked, helping Erica set another chair at the table.

"Let us start there," Col said. He frowned when Erica moved to leave. "Are you not eating with us?"

"Please join us," Caylee asked, then got up to get another chair for her friend. "You are family. I need you here."

"Very well," Erica replied, her cheeks slightly pink. Caylee wondered if she had embarrassed her friend with her request.

As they ate, Col explained his plan to fly his dragon north to the queen's home in Valorna, which held the land's largest library.

"Leian and Shiarra will protect you and continue to cast protection spells throughout the castle," Col said as he heaped a pile of oats onto his plate. "No bacon?"

"We are vegetarians here," Caylee said sternly, squinting at Col. "You remember."

"Yes," Col said with a sigh and then smiled at her. "I remember. I just miss bacon is all."

"Our little bird had the whole castle go vegetarian a while back," Shiarra stated with a stern look at Col. "Her magical gift of communication with creatures prompted this, so stop teasing her."

"An old man needs his bacon," Col mumbled, but he lowered his head in defeat.

"Oats are healthier for you," Caylee explained as she passed the jar of honey to the wizard. "Here, pour some of this on your oats and you'll never want to go back to bacon again."

"Doubtful," he muttered as he drowned his oats in the sweet honey.

"Have rooms been made ready for the others?" Caylee turned and saw Erica reply with a small nod of her head.

"Yes, we will have the prince set up in the suite three rooms down from Zander's quarters. The Bremens are in the room three down from you," Erica said. She looked up quickly. "Do you think their son will be joining them?"

"I don't know," Caylee answered, and her thoughts turned to Svlain and Zain's son Brett. She knew her friend had a crush on him and tried not to smile. Brett was half land nymph and was quite tall, like his parents.

"I'll prepare the green room next door to them, just in case," Erica stated with a nod. She pulled a small pad out to make a note.

"I want protection spells on these rooms as well," Caylee advised.

"I can do that while you and Leian are in meetings," Shiarra confirmed. She smiled when Leian wrinkled his nose.

"I thought you were going to go to the meetings." Leian sighed.

"I'm sorry you both have to do this," Caylee stated, grabbing Shiarra's hand. "I promise to keep the meetings short."

"We know." Shiarra smiled at her. "My husband just does not like politics."

"It is not politics I do not like, it's politicians," Leian grumbled, causing Caylee to laugh.

"Then we have something in common," she replied.

The dragon yard hadn't yet been protected, so she couldn't go down to say goodbye to Wizard Col. Instead, she had to settle for waving down at him from one of the castle's high windows while she was on her way down to the blue room.

All council meetings had been relocated to a more private, secure location until the threat was over. As she walked, she wondered if the kingdom would ever feel safe again. She knew people were scared. Hell, she was scared too.

Townsfolk had started to lock their doors and windows, even during the day. The army's patrols helped a little, but most people had stopped traveling far from their homes. Most were safely locked in their homes well before dark. This was something Caylee understood as she, herself, was limited to a handful of rooms inside her own home.

What she didn't understand was where the threat was coming from. This morning's meeting might shed some light on this question. Captain Adams would be joining her with further details. However, until her family was located and safely returned home, Caylee doubted she would feel safe again.

She neared the meeting room and held in a groan when she saw Grant standing outside the door. She wasn't in the mood this morning for more demands or complaints from him. Quickly adjusting her features, she smiled as she drew near.

"Good morning." She stopped a few feet from him. Already the guards were set outside the room, and one turned to open the door for her.

"These two wouldn't let me in!" Grant complained with a scowl on his face.

"And they were right," Leian said quickly. "I have not yet cleared the room." With that, the wizard quickly approached the door. He nodded to the guards then entered with his hands outstretched before him.

"Captain Adams is taking my safety very seriously," Caylee said with an apologetic smile. She felt the eyes of the guards on her and secretly wished Leian would come back to say the room was safe.

"I did not think I would be denied entrance," Grant said sourly, turning his green eyes on her. "You look horrible."

The comment took her by surprise. A quick 'humph' escaped her lips before she raised one eyebrow and glared at him. Despite being confined to her rooms, Caylee wasn't sleeping well, knowing her family was missing. She worried about her parents, her brother, and her little sister. She also worried about her own safety. Sleep had eluded her for the past two nights, and she found Grant's comment distasteful.

Studying him, she realized he looked like he was getting enough sleep. It appeared Grant had no worries other than being denied entrance into the chamber. His light grey suit was pressed and clean. He wore it over a blue shirt. His short blond hair was slicked back and his gaze was clear, though it showed his annoyance.

"Thanks, that's what every woman wants to hear," she mumbled. Without Leian's approval, she walked past Grant into the room.

She heard the guards follow her in and hoped Grant had stayed in the hallway. When she felt his hand grab her arm, her annoyance grew.

"I would like a few minutes with you before this meeting," Grant stated. His tone made his words sound more like a demand than a request.

Turning, she saw his focus wasn't on her. His green eyes were on where Leian stood against the closed windows. The wizard's long arms were raised high as he studied the locks, looking for hidden magic.

"Sorry," Caylee replied, shocked to hear the harsh tone

in her voice. "I'm slightly busy trying to run the kingdom. Try back later."

"Caylee..." Grant hissed. "We need to talk."

"Not now!" she growled, yanking her arm away from him. After seeing a worried look on his face, she softened a little. "I might have time later, but right now I'm busy."

"Maybe after lunch," he urged with a nod. He left as four more guards piled into the room to take up their posts.

Caylee didn't find any time that day, nor the next. In fact, it was three days before she had time to talk to Grant again. Even then, it was a short conversation filled with his demands and suggestions on how she should be running the kingdom.

Firing several key staff was first on his list of demands, along with the proposal of a quick wedding to appease the counsel. Since Caylee had no intention of doing either, the conversation resulted only in an argument followed by a headache.

Five minutes into the conversation, Caylee cut Grant off and stated she was late for another meeting, despite her not having any. She left in such a hurry that the guards had to scramble to catch up with her.

"Su Na is back!" Shiarra announced as she rushed into Caylee's rooms the fourth night after her family's disappearance.

"What?" Caylee asked as she quickly stood from the

couch. Erica and she were going over the next day's schedule and having a late-night snack at the same time.

Shiarra's long hair was braided as if she had been in bed. She wore her slippers and robe and held a note in her hands. Her cheeks were flushed with excitement.

"He is back!" she restated.

"Charlotte?" Caylee asked instantly, trying to rush past the wizard.

"No!" Shiarra said, blocking the doorway. "Leian is on his way. Her rooms have not been cleared yet."

"Oh, Shiarra!" Caylee said with a smile. "Has anyone seen her yet?"

The wizard shook her head and held the note out for Caylee. "They found this on Su Na's saddle." Caylee grabbed the paper and returned to the couch, where the lamp light illuminated the dark room. Excitement filled her when she saw her sister's handwriting, but then it was replaced with fear as she read the letter.

Dearest Caylee,

I don't have much time. Everything is happening faster than I expected. Be on your guard; there are moles all around you.

Keep close to S&L and take Col with you when you leave home. I go to find Mom and Dad. I fear my journey will be darker than yours. Know this, you will be in great danger from one whom you trust.

Love, Charlotte
P.S. Trust your heart!

.   .   .

"What does this mean?" Caylee asked as she shook the note in the air. "What does she mean?"

"I don't know," Shiarra replied as she walked over and knelt next to her.

"Shiarra, she says she's going to find Mom and Dad," Caylee stated, then looked at her with fear in her eyes. "Shiarra, you don't think she's going into the red mist?"

Caylee saw Shiarra's face turn pale a second before she stood and bolted from the room. Caylee tried to follow but Erica was there, her small frame blocking her.

"No! You can't leave!" Erica screamed. She threw her small arms out to block the doorway. "It isn't safe! Let the wizards handle it."

"No, I have to find Charlotte!" Caylee started to move her friend aside when Erica sent a blast of cold air at Caylee's face.

Erica didn't use her natural powers often, and as the cold wind blasted Caylee, she felt shocked that her friend would attack her in such a manner. Then she felt proud. It took guts for a smaller woman to stand up to a larger one.

Glancing down, she saw determination mixed with anger on Erica's face. Her pale blue eyes dared Caylee to try and push past again. Her arms were still held stiffly out, blocking the door.

"It isn't safe!" she shouted again, and Caylee felt another blast of cold air hit her. It was the second blast that successfully calmed Caylee. After taking a defeated breath, she nodded and returned to the couch.

"Oh, Erica," Caylee murmured. As she sat, she saw her friend was still blocking the door. "Oh, come over here. I have been successfully chastised. I won't leave, I promise you."

After nodding, Erica walked over and sat on the couch

next to her. Then, seeing the note still in her hands, Erica grabbed it and read it.

"What does she mean, when you leave home?" Erica demanded and turned her blue eyes back to Caylee.

"I don't know, I don't understand most of it," Caylee admitted, feeling Erica pat her hand in comfort.

"What is a mole?" Erica asked as she handed the note back to Caylee.

"That I do understand," Caylee said as she studied the closed door leading out of her room. "It appears there's a spy inside the castle."

"Here?" Erica asked quickly. She stood once again, stiff and ready for another fight.

"Oh," Caylee said with a smile, "not in this room. But, yes, inside the castle." Her friend was small, but when it came to protecting the ones she loved, Erica was fierce.

"I knew that," Erica replied, sitting back down. "But who could it be?"

"I don't know, but if Charlotte says there's a mole, we have to find out who it is."

They were interrupted when Leian came into the room. He wore red slippers and a robe over his bright green sleeping gown. He ran a hand through his silver and blond hair as he entered.

"Where is Shiarra? She was supposed to come and tell you..." He stopped when Caylee stood and held a hand up.

"She was here, but I thought Charlotte may have gone to the chamber room where Mom and Dad disappeared," Caylee explained as Leian's face turned red.

"I am a fool!" He quickly turned on his heels to rush out of the room. He drew up short when Shiarra came into the room before he'd gotten two feet towards the door. Her hair was escaping from her braids, and her cheeks were pink from running.

"Leian!" She put her hands up to stop him. "She is not there." Shiarra directed her last statement to Caylee. Caylee plopped back down onto the couch next to Erica with a large sigh of relief.

"Are you sure?" Caylee demanded. Shiarra nodded in reply.

"At least there was no sign the magical seal we put on the chamber's door was disturbed," Shiarra stated.

"The door?" Caylee quickly stood once more. "But what about the secret passageway?"

"What passageway?" Leian demanded.

"I'm the fool!" Caylee exclaimed and quickly rushed across the room towards the door again. "Follow me!"

"No, is it safe?" Erica asked as she quickly rushed after the group.

"No time." Caylee threw these words over her shoulder at her friend and rushed down the hallway with the two wizards, six guards, and one very small wind nymph quickly following her.

6

SECRETS

The odd company ran down the castle's long hallways, and the lamplight threw their shadows across the walls as they went.

Caylee led the race, her small feet eating up the distance. The pale blue folds of her dress were caught in her hands so she wouldn't trip. She passed down hallways and stairs leading to the castle's northern entrance. The castle was set so each main wall faced one of the points of a compass—north, south, east, and west. Since the town of Pinewoods was on the southern side, the castle's main entrance was there. The practice yards were on the western side, with training yards to the north. On the east, where Mount Lehar's massive peak rose, was their mother's garden.

"We need to go outside," Caylee shouted. Three of the guards finally passed her as they raced ahead. "To the eastern wall." She felt the first stitch of pain in her left side as she ran.

She felt completely out of shape by the time she

reached the castle's door. She stopped finally as Leian grabbed her arm.

"Where?" he demanded in between breaths.

"The wall in the guard's stand. There's an extra-thick back wall," Caylee answered.

"Stay here," Leian demanded, reaching for the castle's door.

"But I have to show you how to unlock the door," Caylee said quickly. "It's tricky."

"Fine, but we clear the garden first," Leian demanded. He quickly walked out with three of the guards, leaving Shiarra to guard her.

Six minutes later, he was back, holding a large lantern. "It is dark out, but Crisp lit the torches."

"Here, let me hold that," Shiarra said as she took the lantern from her husband.

They walked in silence, Erica next to Caylee and Shiarra and Leian walking in front. Eight guards now surrounded the group.

When they reached the guard stand, Caylee shook her head at them.

"There's not much room in here. Let the wizards come with me and then the guards can come in when I've opened the passageway," Caylee instructed. She stood aside as Leian went into the guard stand first.

It was a small building made from the same bricks that formed the castle's outer walls and fences. Large white stone lined the small building and a green metal roof arched above them as she entered the wooden door.

"Where is the entrance?" Leian asked as he studied the small room.

A single chair and table sat against one wall where a

port opened to the garden. A little fireplace sat on the opposite wall to keep the guards warm during cold days.

"Here." Caylee walked over to the empty fireplace. On the back wall of the fireplace, carved into the stone, was a picture of a mermaid, a beautiful woman with long hair covering most of her upper body. She had an alluring smile on her lips, and her long tail was curved and wound about the stone.

Bending down, Caylee smiled at the carving and placed her right hand on top of the figure's left hand. She gave it a little twist, and the entire back wall of the fireplace dropped back an inch and silently slid to the right.

"Oh!" Shiarra exclaimed from behind her.

"It's all right," Caylee said with a smile. "Here, hand me the light."

"I go first!" Leian demanded. He placed his hand protectively on her shoulder. "Then, after I see the way is clear, you may follow."

The passageway was long and twisted. Each guard carried a lantern, as did Shiarra and Erica. There were no side tunnels for the first fifty yards, then they approached a branch tunnel on their left.

"That leads to a dead end. It ends in a chamber where the training yard well sits, but there's no way out of the tunnel from there," Caylee explained as she waved the group forward down the right-hand side.

"When we get to the end, I want you to fall back with the guards," Leian instructed.

"Is there any sign that Charlotte was here before us?" Shiarra asked from behind them.

"There are tracks here," Leian said, his voice sounding grim. "Small prints and another set, much larger."

"Do you think she was followed?" Caylee asked as fear for her sister filled her.

"No," Leian said as he stopped and peered down at the dust on the tunnel's floor. "I think they came here together."

"Who would be with her?" Shiarra asked.

"I don't know," Caylee said with a shake of her head. "Why, and to where, would she take Su Na and then return? With whom?"

"All good questions, but for now, let us make sure she is not just ahead," Leian said as he stood once more.

"The tunnel ended at a round staircase. Col had set an arch stone staircase in place using his magic several years ago. The stones were oddly shaped but as they climbed the staircase, each step felt sturdy.

"At the top is a small landing," Caylee explained as she tried to remember this passageway's secrets. "It's been years since I used this one, but I always loved the mermaid. Beyond the landing you will see a door. To its left is another smaller one," she explained as they climbed.

"Smaller one?" Leian asked from above her.

"It's a portal you can use to look out into the room," Caylee explained. "I want to have a look into the room."

"No," Erica hissed from somewhere below her on the steps. "It might not be safe."

"That's why I want Leian to look first," Caylee answered. "I promise, I won't look if he says it's not safe."

Five very dizzying flights of stairs later, they finally reached the landing. Six of their group could stand comfortably on it while the others had to remain on lower steps.

"Here, do you see the latch?" Caylee asked, pointing to the left of the larger door.

"Stand back. You three please move so she can stand at

the back," Leian instructed as three large guards moved to shield Caylee as he approached the latch.

Several silent moments later, she heard Leian whispering to Shiarra. Their words were quiet, and their heads were bent close together, but when they finally broke apart, she was called forward.

"It is safe, but we can only look through. We will not be going into the room," Leian said sternly.

"Agreed," Caylee replied as she moved forward to peek into the room.

This exit was identical to the entrance in the guard station with one exception—the peek hole utilized a painting on the side of the stone fireplace. The painting depicted her mother returning the goddess to the cradle, in mermaid form, while her father fought off the crab creatures.

Using the wooden stool that stood below the portal, Caylee stood on her toes and peered out at the dim room.

"I can't see much. It's too dark," she complained.

"Here, let me stand there a minute. I can light some of the lanterns from here," Shiarra said quickly.

After the lamps were lit, Caylee peered into the room again. She saw the familiar room and its furnishings and immediately missed her parents. The soft leather couches with their bright red pillows reminded her of her father. The little doilies and knickknacks her mother favored sat on the side tables, while beyond the couches stood the vast table surrounded by chairs.

She saw the overturned chair and crumpled papers on the table and frowned. When her eyes landed on the dead flower bouquet, she held in a cry of dismay. Then her eyes fell upon an empty purple envelope next to the vase. It had been ripped open.

"Where is my note?" she asked, looking harder.

The papers around the vase were all large. Some were maps. She didn't see any bright purple stationary lying around the vase and quickly looked down at Shiarra and Leian, who stood next to her.

"My note, it's gone," she exclaimed.

Back in her private chambers surrounded by Leian, Shiarra, and Erica, Caylee stewed about the missing letter she had written her mother.

"I don't understand," she said for the tenth time.

"Maybe it disappeared along with your mother?" Erica asked.

"But how and why?" Shiarra stated from her spot on the sofa.

"Caylee, why does this bother you so much?" Leian asked from his spot next to the fireplace.

"Don't you see?" Caylee stood from her spot to pace back and forth in front of them. "The flowers and envelope were still there, but not the note itself. What if it was used to deliver the weapon?"

"Weapon?" Erica asked. Her eyes quickly darted to the doorway, as if she expected someone to barge in and blast them out of the room.

"We know Seth was in the room with Mom and Dad only moments before. Then, when he left, something happened to them. The only thing I can think of is that Mom opened the letter. My letter," Caylee said miserably.

"You do not know this," Shiarra said as she stood and embraced her.

"But Aunt Shiarra, Seth said no one entered the room while he was gone. He was still in the hallway only ten steps away before he turned back." She felt tears forming in her eyes and quickly closed them as she laid her head against her aunt's shoulder.

"Hush, little bird," Shiarra murmured and patted Caylee's back.

"Who delivered these flowers?" Leian asked after several moments of Caylee quietly crying into Shiarra's shoulder.

"Mrs. Longstone would have delivered them," Erica supplied. "I will go fetch her myself."

By the time Erica returned with Mrs. Longstone behind her, Caylee had refreshed her composure. She had spent time in her bathroom sprinkling cold water on her face and combing her hair. Shiarra had stood next to her, speaking words of comfort and support.

"Here we are," Erica said. She moved to put a pot of water on for tea.

"Mrs. Longstone, thank you so much for coming at such a late hour. Please, have a seat." Caylee motioned to the empty spot next to Shiarra.

"My lady," Mrs. Longstone said. After a small curtsy, she sat on the edge of the couch cushion. She was an elderly woman with pure white hair and a wide smile. Her plump figure spoke of a fondness for cakes, while her hands spoke of her love for gardening.

"These are my godparents, Wizard Shiarra and Leian Balzac from Tharian," Caylee explained.

"Ah, yes. I believe I met you several years ago," Mrs. Longstone stated with a polite smile at the two. "Of course, mistress Caylee was only a child then."

"Yes, I remember you," Shiarra said with a smile. "I have yet to see an equal to your bed of Purfla and Morgan hair blossoms."

"Oh, you do me an honor," Mrs. Longstone replied, blushing handsomely.

"Mrs. Longstone, the reason we pulled you away from your bed so late is because we have an urgent question for you," Shiarra stated as Erica came forward and poured the steaming tea for them.

"Mrs. Longstone. My note to my mother, the one I asked you to deliver with the flowers..." Caylee asked, but when she felt tears threatening again, she cast a look at Shiarra for aid.

"Was the note with the bouquet?" Shiarra asked quietly.

"Of course. The note Mr. Worthington handed me was placed in the center of the bouquet. I hand-delivered them to the queen myself as she and the king were heading to their private chamber room," Mrs. Longstone said. Her smile faltered as she leaned forward to look at Caylee. "I have been distraught since your parents went missing, my dear. I just know they will be found and pray to the goddess each night for their safe return."

They finished their tea with Mrs. Longstone, and Caylee thanked her for rushing to the impromptu meeting, apologizing profusely for the late hour. As the plump gardener left, Caylee's hope and energy seemed to leave with the woman.

Shiarra and Leian went back to their rooms while Erica once again slept on the couch out in the outer room. As Caylee crawled into her bed, her thoughts turned once again to her little sister.

"Oh, Charlotte." She sobbed and hugged her pillow to her. "Where are you?" she whispered as she fell asleep.

The sound awoke her first. It was a deep growl mixed with a high-pitched yell. Startled awake, she lay in her bed a second before a loud crash from her outside sitting room had her up and moving.

"Stay away!" she heard Erica scream, and she quickened her pace across the room.

When she flung open her bedchamber door, the sitting room was almost in total darkness. Hearing a crash on the far side of the room, she did something she didn't normally do—she brought magic to her hands.

The red glow of magic faintly sputtered to life. It illuminated a large figure bearing down on the childlike body of her best friend. She saw the flash of a blade and panic filled her.

"Erica!" she screamed as her magic grew in intensity.

"Stay back!" Erica screamed as the large castle guard turned away from her friend and faced her.

She knew the man; he was a regular palace guard named Tolech. Young and friendly, he was normally assigned to guard duty for her parents, but since their disappearance, he had joined the regiment assigned to her watch.

"Tolech, what is the meaning of this?" she demanded as her magic faded upon seeing a friendly face instead of an enemy.

"Don't come near. He has a knife!" Erica's scream had Caylee glancing over at her friend until the man suddenly jolted towards her.

Two things happened as Tolech came rushing towards her. First, the door to her private chambers burst open. Several new guards rushed in, having heard the commotion. Second, Caylee's magic blasted out of her in a red deadly arch, much like that day in the forest above Tharian years ago.

When her magic hit Tolech, it wrapped around the man as it had the cats. Red, killing ribbons of fire twisted and snaked around Tolech's head, arms, and legs as it burned him.

No scream, no sound of shock or pain came from the man. However, since he was facing Caylee, she saw what her magic did to him. Flesh burned and hair singed as her killing magic encircled him. She saw the man's eyes go wide with pain as they turned from a red to a soft blue before the light of life was snubbed from them.

"Caylee!" She heard a firm voice and felt a light touch on her arm as Shiarra talked gently to her, urging her to turn her magic off. "The danger is passed, little bird, shut it down, shut it off," her godmother crooned.

"You four, secure the other rooms!" Leian ordered as he helped Erica up from under the chair, which had been thrown upon her by the attacker.

"There, there," Shiarra said softly. Caylee's arms were shaking as Shiarra lowered them, and the magic died from her fingertips. "Sit down, I will fetch something cold to drink."

"No, don't leave me," Caylee urged as Erica, with the help of Leian, rushed over and buried herself against Caylee's right side in a tight hug. "Are you hurt, friend?" Caylee asked, her eyes burning with tears as she still looked upon the smoldering mess that had once been a man.

"I think she has a hurt arm," Leian stated as he stood and blocked the dead man's body from her sight. "I called for a healer and more guards."

"Here, drink this," Shiarra urged, handing both Caylee and Erica a drink.

It was strong ale from a bottle that sat upon her sideboard for guests. She drank the whole cup and took a deep breath as tears fell from her eyes. It was then that she smelled what her magic had done. She choked from the smell and bent over quickly as she was sick on the pretty blue carpet of her sitting room. Then she fainted.

7

ADVENTURE AHEAD

"No!" Captain Adams shouted as he stood his ground in the royal chamber room fifteen days later.

Caylee, now surrounded by dragon warrior guards, kept her seat but tensed at the captain's raised voice. It wasn't often that the leader of the queen's army shouted, so when he did, everyone understood it was already too late, he had already lost his temper.

"Captain," Wizard Col said calmly as he stepped forward. "The means to find the other royals are assured. We only need to reach out and grasp it."

"If the means could be obtained without putting our one remaining royal in harm's way, I would be the first to reach out and clutch at it. But Col, you of all people should know that taking Princess Caylee into the unknown, just to hunt down a fabled magical mirror that may show us the location of the missing queen and king, whatever it is called..." Captain Adams looked over at Wizard Leian, who provided him with the term *Trillium*. "This Trillium, then we must find another way."

"But there is none," Caylee spoke up as the captains' angry eyes turned upon her.

She'd had very little sleep since the incident. Her nightmares haunted her, and visions of Tolech's death kept her awake. Nothing anyone said could calm her or change the fact that he had been killed.

Two other guards also lost their lives that night, Tolech had killed them to gain access to her rooms. This fact still didn't ease her conscience. She saw the man's dead eyes every time she closed her own. Even now, surrounded by the royal counsel in broad daylight, he haunted her.

"I have no doubt you agree to this reckless adventure," Captain Adams said as he shook his head. His silver hair was buzzed short. His intense blue eyes studied her as he reached up and brushed his thick mustache.

"I have to admit, it has been a hardship being confined to only part of the castle, but since Cousin Aiden arrived, I feel Wizard Col's plan can work," Caylee said as she leaned forward in her chair. "The prince will sit on the throne while I locate this Trillium. Wizard Col informed me that the one seeking the lost must be the one to glance into the mirror. Once we locate my family, then we might be able to rescue them."

Caylee turned to study her second cousin Aiden. He had dark green eyes that spoke of family, but there was also a hint of his mother's fairy blood showing in the upturn of his eyes and the point of his chin. Caylee had been pleased when Aiden had arrived three nights ago from his home of Matera, where his father Calob ruled.

Aiden, the youngest of four, was only nineteen but had already served on the Matera counsel for three years. He seemed far older than his young years. She trusted him and his guidance, and with Wizard Col's return the night before, he had agreed with her plan.

Since the night of her attack, she and Captain Adams had disbanded the royal guard until further review of the attack could be completed. Instead of having royal guards, she now was surrounded by the dragon warriors. Each held a rank of four or higher, and she knew each of them personally. Seven were from her mother's tribe, Draydon, while the other five were from a southern tribe called Nereis.

Six women guarded her during the night while six men made up the day guard duties. All had trained with her brother and her. Their families had known her mother since she was a child living along the cliffs of Faro, where the dragon tribes lived.

Pren and Tonkee were the two highest ranks and the captains of their patrols. Pren was a large, tanned man of thirty with a bright yellow dragon tattoo covering most of his face and bald head. He led the group of six male warriors who guarded her during the day. Tonkee, a female of only twenty-five, was a fierce warrior who led the female guards. Tonkee and Caylee had trained together and were close friends but as different as night and day. Tonkee had flaming red hair that curled excessively when near the ocean. She also had freckles over most of her pretty face. Both these warriors had a high tribe level of eight.

Caylee only held a low rank of one, finding that she never enjoyed training to be a fighter at a young age. Instead, she used her magic and skills to study to be a caregiver, one who looks after the dragons.

Her dragon, Pin-O, was a rather small red and black dragon who was extremely fast. Caylee loved riding Pin-O along the shores of the ocean and cherished the time her family spent along the coast.

Knowing these warriors most of her life, and trusting the dragon tribe's training, it had been easy for her to quickly replace the royal guards with dragon warriors. Especially since, after the attack, the council insisted guards be posted inside her private rooms.

It had been that last demand that had Caylee scrambling to find an acceptable solution. She was already a prisoner in her own home, unable to freely walk about the rooms or even the gardens without a cluster of guards. But when the council demanded that six guards remain inside her private chambers at all times, she had drawn the line.

Finally, after three days of arguing, they had all agreed upon having six female dragon warriors stay in her private day room and use the male guards for the day shift. With this decision, Caylee saw her freedom and privacy slip away from her.

Wizards Leian and Shiarra were also on double duty. Leian remained by her side during the day, while Shiarra slept in a cot inside her bedroom. Erica also joined them each night. Since Erica's arm was still in a sling from her injuries, Caylee had requested her mother's lady, Kenna, assist. Kenna, a pretty blonde of forty-four, had served her mother since before Caylee had been born.

Caylee knew and trusted those she now surrounded herself with. Captain Adams had complained at first, but since the attack had been from one of his men, he agreed to this change. What he didn't agree to at the moment was allowing Caylee to leave the castle on a quest to find the Trillium.

"The council also has concerns," Counselor Blake interjected as he stepped forward to stand next to the large captain.

"I know and understand your concerns," Caylee said as

she rose from her throne. "However, I have made up my mind." She quickly raised her hand to stop any more arguments and took a step down from the dais. "I will, however, agree with the council regarding the number and members of my party." She saw Counselor Blake's odd eyes study her for a minute before he nodded slightly.

Turning, Caylee saw the land nymph Svlain and her son, Brett, step forward. Svlain nodded slightly, her slender face sincere as her green eyes continued to study Caylee. Svlain, who had gone down with the queen into the dark cave called the Kylix, was one of her mother's oldest friends. The trip had taken place years ago to return the goddess, Genoa, to her resting place. Svlain had even assisted in freeing the smaller slaves of Midzark from the giants in the foreign and distant land.

"If you all will excuse me, I need to confer with Svlain and Brett," Caylee said dismissively. The council members all bowed and left.

As the door shut behind the last council member, Caylee smiled and walked off the dais towards Svlain and Brett. Leian joined her and, after welcomes were said and hugs were given, they walked out of the room and into the blue chamber room Caylee now referred to as her private office.

"Welcome," she said as she poured the tea Kenna had set on the table. "How was your journey?"

"It was long," Brett stated. He was a man of twenty-three and bore a striking resemblance to his father, tall of build with handsome features and a deep dimple in his chin, but his coloring was all his mother's. Green eyes, green hair, and a long, narrow nose.

"I fear that this may be the last quiet time you have,"

Wizard Leian said as he grabbed a biscuit from the tray and then continued his pacing around the room.

"I imagine it will be," Svlain said with a shake of her head. "Zain will join us shortly. He wanted to speak to the head of the dragon tribe here at the castle first. Caylee, I had a vision of our journey."

The land nymph's last words had Caylee leaning forward in her chair. "What did you see?" she quickly asked.

"Caylee, danger still surrounds you. Three nights ago, as we were passing the Maylin River, I had a waking vision. I saw a red glow surround and settle inside the castle. It was a dark red and it reached out to swallow those you love, your family," Svlain explained. She reached to lift her teacup to her lips, but her hand shook too much, and she quickly set it back down on the table. "Caylee, the red engulfed your family but did not surround you. I saw you out at sea. A vast ship lay beneath your feet as the red glow snaked aboard. It hovered on the deck and snapped at those nearest you."

"A ship?" Caylee asked, both excitement and fear filling her with Svlain's words.

"The ship appeared as a slender woman," Svlain said with a shake of her head. "Sorry, my vision showed the red glow more than anything."

"Mother almost fell off Dad's dragon," Brett said with a shake of his head. "Luckily, she was tethered onto Llis's back."

"Svlain, I asked you and your family here because I need your help," Caylee said after a moment of silence. "I was hoping your visions could guide me."

"Caylee, both Brett and I had visions," Svlain advised, turning to look at her son.

"Mine was shorter and more intense," Brett said as his

mother reached over and grabbed his hand in hers. "I saw you, Caylee. I saw you die."

Caylee pondered Brett's words as she neared her private chambers that evening. She didn't understand most of Svlain's vision. It was Brett's that worried her the most.

"*I saw you jump from the deck of a ship,*" Brett had told her. But when pressed for more details, he shook his head and was unable to provide much more.

"Caylee," Grant said, startling her, as she drew near to her door.

Pren, the large dragon warrior, quickly blocked Grant's way to her, but Caylee nodded at him, and Grant was allowed to draw near. Grant appeared worried. His usually pressed clothing was disheveled and there was a black smudge near his right eyebrow and along his lower jaw.

"Grant, what have you been doing?" she asked, reaching up to wipe at the mark.

"Oh, just a misunderstanding." Grant quickly pulled a handkerchief from his pocket to wipe the dirt away. "Caylee, dear. I must talk with you."

"I supposed so," Caylee said. She waved a hand towards her chambers.

When they entered, she was shocked at the state of her outer rooms. Usually, the sitting room was where she saw guests, both family and friends. It was also where she had most of her meals of late, as only a few rooms were deemed "safe" for her.

With this thought, her eyes landed on the spot where Tolech had died. The vision of the man caused her heart to speed up, and she quickly averted her eyes to where Erica was sitting on a chair in one corner, her arm resting on a pillow. Three of the female dragon warriors were trying to return the couch to its normal spot near the fireplace.

Soot and ash, along with a half-burnt log, littered the room. The side table appeared to have been knocked over, and her favorite tea set lay smashed on the spoiled rug.

"What has happened here?" Caylee demanded as her guards rushed into the room with their weapons raised.

Kayla, the second in command of the female warriors, turned and drew her weapon with a scowl on her dark face. "Why do you not ask that one?" she hissed and pointed the sharp end of her sword towards Grant.

"Grant?" Caylee asked as she faced him once again. The movement stopped in the room, and all eyes turned on her fiancé.

"I told this woman I wanted to see you," Grant said, still trying to rub the soot off his face. "And then she attacked me!"

Feeling a headache form, Caylee took a deep breath and rubbed her left eye. "Grant, the council informed you of the recent protocol."

"I know, but I refuse to submit in writing a request to see my fiancée!" Grant hissed. He gave up on cleaning his face. "I came here thinking we could have tea together. I even brought your favorite set, and then I was attacked!"

"That was very thoughtful of you." She placed a hand on Grant's arm. "I already had tea in my meeting, but would love a walk..." When she saw Pren shake his head no, she turned and saw the balcony doors open. "How about we enjoy the balcony instead." She received a quick nod from her guard.

"I suppose that will have to do," Grant said. He held his arm out for Caylee to take it. "You mentioned a meeting? Was this another council meeting?"

When the fresh air hit Caylee, she smiled and took a deep breath. It had been two days since she had enjoyed the outdoors, but to her, it felt like years. The potted plants on her private balcony were filled with flowers and their mixed scents hung in the air. The sky was stark blue above the town far below. Beyond that, the distant Highman Plains bloomed. Grasses of all colors waved in the afternoon heat, with flowers dotted amongst them.

From this distance, she couldn't hear any of the town's noises. Sometimes she could hear a shout from kids playing in the streets or even the call of a merchant trying to sell their wares. Today, it seemed the heat had banished everyone from the streets.

"What a lovely day!" she exclaimed as she released Grant's arm and rushed to the railing. After taking another deep breath, she shielded her eyes and watched a purple bird dip its wings as it dropped into the forest far to her right. A small portion of the Deepen Forest sat north of the castle while the main part was far south of the town.

"Caylee, you did not answer my question," Grant insisted as he settled in one of the chairs around the stone table.

"What?" she asked as she spotted another bird fluttering around one of the roof peaks from the castle's southern wing.

"The meeting? Did you have another council meeting?" Grant asked, and she heard a little frustration in his voice.

"Oh, yes. When don't I have council meetings?" Caylee

stated. After one last look at the view, she sighed deeply and joined Grant at the table, making sure she was facing the view as she settled her skirts about her. "Wizard Col returned last night; he discovered an item that may help locate my parents."

"What?" Grant asked as he leaned forward.

"But it's some distance away," Caylee continued distractedly as she spotted another bird.

"So, the wizard is leaving again?" he asked as he sat back against the chair's cushions.

"Oh, not until we're ready." She stood again to get a better look at the new bird; she was sure it was a large eagle.

"We?" Grant demanded from behind her.

"Yes. It should only take six or seven days before everything is ready." Caylee turned to watch the eagle fly over the roof of the castle. "The dragon warriors, Captain Adams, Wizard Col, and I will be going on dragon back first. Then it appears we need to procure a boat. I haven't been on one since I was a child. We had to learn how to evacuate the tribal town. Those drills were fun! I got to stay up all night, and we had a cookout the next morning on the islands." She was so lost in her thoughts; she didn't see Grant's expression of annoyance.

"Caylee," Grant barked, causing her to turn from the view to study him. "You cannot go."

Stunned by his words, Caylee stood where she was.

"You cannot go on such a dangerous mission, not with your family already missing, not with the counsel depending on you and a kingdom to run," Grant walked over to her and put his hands on her shoulders. "You should not put yourself at such a risk. Think of the danger you will be putting yourself in," he urged.

"But Grant, it's my family," she explained. She saw the worry in his green eyes.

"But they are gone." He squeezed her arms. "You are here, you are safe, here. Stay here, stay with me."

She shook her head and took a step back, but his hands held her tight. "Grant, don't you see? I must try. I have to find them," she pleaded. She reached up and placed her hands on top of his, which were still resting on her arms.

"I only see you," Grant said, his voice low. "I fear for you."

"I have to go. Wizard Col says I am the only one who might be able to locate them using this mirror."

"Then take me with you," he requested suddenly. "If you must go, take me."

"She must be stopped!" the voice hissed from the vast distance.

The red mists swirled as the sorceress Io Maltesea growled in response to the impertinent tone of her minion. She kept the ball of mist formed between her hands, but her fingers flexed with her anger.

"This is your problem," she snarled in reply.

"No. If she discovers this mirror, she may be able to locate her parents," the voice came back.

"What if she does?" Io Maltesea asked, not concerned, and even becoming bored with the conversation now.

"The discovery might lead to a rescue attempt. If that happens, my plans here will be overthrown," the voice responded. "And if that happens, your plans for Genoa will fail."

"Impertinent!" Io Maltesea hissed. Her anger sparked her magic into little flashes of fire.

"Think, witch!" the voice boomed. "Think of all that is at stake. Send the Lanart. It can cause a delay. It might even cause the little princess's quest to fail if the right person is targeted."

"Who is your target?" Io Maltesea asked with a smile at the thought of blood.

"The wind nymph," the voice grumbled. "She sees too much. Have your creature kill her."

8

RIGHT AS RAIN

To her dismay, Caylee's adventure was delayed by three days. Heavy rain had come to the plains, completely locking the dragons to the ground as an unusual cold spell settled over Castle Pines. On the morning of the fourth day, the sun shone bright and warm, and the quest could finally be started as soon as they were all packed and ready.

"I can go!" Erica insisted as she pounded her small foot against the new sitting room rug. Her arm was still in a sling, but her pale cheeks held a nice pink hue to them, as she had taken to resting out on the large balcony during the day.

"I know, but Shiarra thinks your arm will heal faster if you remain behind," Caylee replied sweetly at her friend.

"I am going!" Erica insisted, placing her good hand on her small hip. "With or without your approval, Your Majesty." The last word came out more like a threat, but Caylee just smiled and nodded.

"We shall see."

"No, I am telling you now, I am going. Brett and Zain

said I could, and Zain's a healer. He would know." A smile of triumph passed over Erica's face.

"You consulted Zain?" Caylee asked.

"Of course," Erica stated. She walked over to continue packing her small bag. "He is the best healer I know."

"If Zain says it's ok... but Erica, are you sure?" Caylee had worried for her friend since the attack almost two weeks ago.

"Brett is coming by to pick up our bags soon. I want all my things ready by then." Erica turned to study Caylee. "You had better go and get your mother's things."

"Cats!" Caylee said suddenly. "I'd forgotten."

Turning, Caylee rushed from the room with her guards closely following. Her mother's things were the gifts Sorcerer Belent had given Tresstéanna years ago. The pretty swan bracelet, the unicorn knife, and the dragon-carved bow were her mother's most prized possessions.

Caylee rushed down the hallway and met Wizard Shiarra within two feet of her door. Shiarra would remain behind, guarding and protecting Prince Aiden as he filled the duty of the throne while she was gone. Wizard Leian, however, had been called back home with word that their youngest son, Pen, had gone missing. Shiarra was worried, but Otis, their oldest son, had explained they'd had an argument several days before. Otis had been hopeful that Penn had just run off to the family's small cabin north of the city. But when Otis had traveled to the cabin to search for the missing lad, the nineteen-year-old wasn't there.

It was at this point that Otis and his sister Breanna had contacted the officials and a formal search had started. Since Leian and Shiarra had used the only trans rock to travel to Castle Pines, a messenger had been sent with this news. Leian had left the night before, assuring his wife that he would find their youngest. He also took new communication stones with him.

Shiarra wasn't pleased to remain behind and was worried for her family and Caylee, too, who would be departing within the hour. However, Wizard Col was Shiarra's senior in the wizard's society, and he had assured her that he was capable of watching Caylee on the quest for the Trillium.

"Are you heading to the vault?" Shiarra asked as she matched Caylee's steps.

"Yes. I waited to pack Mother's things until right before I left," Caylee replied as she studied the clear blue of the morning sky outside the nearest window. "I feel Mom would approve; don't you think so?"

"I do. Your mother would want you protected at all costs," Shiarra stated with a nod.

They walked down the long corridor and turned into the Exhibition Hall. In this vast room was the battlewear of both Matera and Valorna. Coats of arms were kept here along with items obtained from Matera. A black Gaura cloak stood on a wooden mannequin in the corner. Next to it was an empty honeycomb from the giant Mellifera bees. On one wall a parchment with Svlain's wanted poster hung next to a rough drawing of the Regorge Palace done in pencil.

Both women continued into the room toward its end and stopped before a rather large painting depicting a golden dragon. The painting was titled Su Na and had been painted by the queen herself. As the guards set up positions around the room, Caylee nodded once and motioned for Shiarra to proceed.

"I always liked this painting," she said, leaning forward to touch the corner of the frame.

Caylee saw her fingertips light with a faint blue magic, then the painting slid forward. Shiarra stepped into the vault first and, after inspecting the room, told Caylee she was free to enter.

"How long has it been?" Shiarra asked as she lit the lamp closest to the opening.

"I was in here two years ago. Mom wanted to give me her first crown for the winter ball," Caylee replied as she helped Shiarra light another lamp. "I think Charlotte was in here last month, but I'm not sure."

"Why do you say that?" Shiarra asked as they moved deeper into the vault.

"I don't know. Maybe it was something she said to me?" Caylee replied as she stepped over a large rolled-up rug. When she passed the Orwic flower on its pedestal, she paused for a minute, then continued. The Greilk box was next to the flower and, distracted by it, she almost tripped over a large backpack.

"Here, this case here should hold the knife," she said when she reached the corner of the vault. She held the light up.

"I do not see it," Shiarra stated, stepping closer.

"I don't either. But this is where Mom kept it." Caylee looked under the shelf. "I don't see the bracelet either." Concern flooded her as she realized both items were nowhere to be seen.

"There's the bow." Shiarra pointed to the right, above the case.

"But where are the other items?" Caylee asked as she held her lamp up higher.

A complete search of the vault resulted in only the bow. Both knife and bracelet were missing. Caylee felt defeated as she left with the bow and its quiver strapped over her back.

"Mom will be mad if she discovers her items are missing," Caylee said quietly as they relocked the vault.

"We will worry about that after you find her," Shiarra said, but her voice spoke of her concerns too.

"Col estimates the trip to be about four weeks," Caylee said as she fingered the strap of the bow. "That should give us time to sail to this Dua Sacro island and then another four weeks to return home."

"You will miss the leaves turning if you do not hurry," Shiarra said softly, and Caylee thought she heard a whisper of longing in the wizard's voice.

"I will miss you." Caylee put her arm through Shiarra's to link them together. "But I will have Svlain and Erica with me, and all the warriors too."

"But your mother had me on her prior quests," Shiarra mumbled.

They returned to Caylee's private rooms, where Brett and Zain were waiting, and Erica continued to pack. Brett kept trying to assist the small nymph but instead, in his rush, he kept knocking items over.

"Son!" Zain finally said with a shake of his head. "Sit and let her finish. Her arm is hurt but she can still manage."

"Thank you again for waiting," Erica said as she folded a lightweight raincoat and placed it in a small backpack. "I only just confirmed I would be allowed to go a few moments ago." When a stern look was thrown her way, Caylee ducked her head and picked up her raincoat to place it on top of her bag.

"I still have my reservations," Caylee mumbled, but she smiled when Erica gave a low growl. "I worry for you my friend, that's all."

After the bags were taken, Caylee changed into her travel clothes. She put on black pants and a red shirt with her riding boots, then covered it with a light cloak to block the wind.

Her last act was to place her silver circlet on her dressing table. There would be no need for a crown out at sea. This piece signified her position, and she felt sorrow when it was no longer on her head. Until she thought of getting outside the castle walls.

She had been limited to a handful of rooms for over twenty days and her nerves were on edge. She needed fresh air, the outdoors, and adventure. She needed to find her family.

Turning, she studied her bedroom, deep purple and blues surrounding her. Her curtains had been thrown open and the bright blue of the morning lay outside the windows. She felt her excitement well up inside her. Then the portrait of her family caught her attention. It was a small painting her mom had given her at the last Mid-day.

She picked it up, hugged it to her breast, and closed her eyes.

"I promise, I will find you," she whispered. She took the picture with her when she left her room.

The town of Byways sat along the waters of the Alluvion, the massive ocean of Genoa. The port of Byways was on the city's northern side. It was a quaint town and its ports bustled with activity. Everything from fishermen to furniture traders could be found there.

It had taken three days for the princess of Genoa and her troop to arrive in Byways. They landed early in the day in the western part of town where a royal guard resided in the Fort of Byways. The fort had been set over fifteen years earlier and was small compared to others. Once the dragons had landed, the royal flag had been raised on top of the fort's battlement, as was tradition whenever a member of the royal family was in town.

The captain in charge of the fort was a seasoned warrior named Brian Boorough. The good captain was now as wide as he was tall. He had grey hair and a bushy beard that he liked to stroke when he talked. He had fought in the queen's war, before Genoa had been united as one, and was said to have been the leader of the water nymphs who had helped ambush the southern soldiers on the great Highman Plains.

Captain Adams and Captain Boorough greeted each other with smiles and hard claps on their backs when the troop had arrived. Runners had been immediately sent out on Captain Boorough's orders to find a suitable ship for the princess and her crew, but the runners didn't return until later that evening.

"I would like to inspect any ship before we agree to employ it," Caylee insisted as she sat in the captain's private quarters with Svlain, Zain, Brett, and Erica. Captain Adams was also there with Captain Boorough. The room was quaint if a bit dusty. Three wooden chairs sat around an oak table, and a small sofa leaned at an odd angle in the corner. Sandwiches and tea had been brought quickly. The bread was soft and still warm from the oven.

"Of course, my lady. The *Queen's Mystic* is a fine ship.

Captain Jade and his crew are excellent sailors," Captain Boorough replied with a smile and twist of his beard.

"That may be, but I will inspect it tomorrow before I agree to hire them," Caylee stated with authority and a stern look at Captain Adams, who had already voiced his disagreement at her being allowed to go down to the docks.

When the two captains had left, Caylee turned to study Svlain, who shook her head quickly.

"No, I do not know the name of the ship," the land nymph said to Caylee's unasked question. "However, Captain Boorough said the ship's name was the *Queen's Mystic*, which could also be a slender woman?"

"All ships are named after women," Brett explained as he stood and looked out the window of the small room.

"We will just have to be cautious," Erica stated as she studied Caylee. Then a small smile formed on her lips. "A disguise would help."

The disguise was a good one if Caylee said so herself. She traded her royal dress and dragon travel clothes for a modest yet slightly ugly pink dress. The dress had been supplied by one of the fort's corporals who was married. A large hat hid Caylee's long hair, and a stiff apron covered the whole ensemble.

"Try to walk differently," Erica grumbled as she studied Caylee in the private quarters they had slept in that night. She and Erica had shared one room, while Wizard Col had bunked with Brett. Svlain and Zain were in a third room. Captain Adams and the other dragon warriors were nearby, and as always, the posted night guards stood to watch. But to Caylee, just being out of the castle was exciting. And on top of that, the excitement of getting to travel to the market and down to the docks to inspect the ship was pure heaven.

"That's better," Erica said as she tilted her head, then

nodded. "Maybe if you carry something heavy, that can help hide your walk."

"What's wrong with my walk?" Caylee demanded, tying the ribbon on her hat again.

"Nothing, if you're going to a ball," Erica replied.

"Are you sure you don't want to come?" Caylee asked. She turned to study her friend.

"No, I think just you, Col, and Svlain should go. Of course, you will have three guards. Captain Boorough thought the smaller the group, the less attention you will get," Erica said with a smile. "Plus, Brett said he would have tea with me while you are gone."

Caylee's excitement lasted until the third block away from the barracks. Then her frustration took over. Col didn't allow the group anywhere near the center of the market. They had skirted the entire area by four blocks and only the smells of cooked sweets and meats drifted her way.

She tried not to pout, but their path took twice as long as it should have to reach the docks. Even then, she was only permitted to stay within the safety of the large warriors that surrounded her.

The docks were still exciting to her. Even here, there were carts set up to sell items. She saw everything from fresh fish to odd-looking clams, all nestled inside buckets of ice. On one cart she saw jars of honey and jams and tried to talk Col into letting her purchase some. But after a firm shake of the wizard's head, she turned her attention instead to the boats.

Over fifteen ships lined the wooden dock that jutted out to the small harbor. The ocean lay beyond, and the smell of salt water, fish, and sand filled her nostrils. Some of the boats were small, just big enough for four or five men to fit in. She knew they were fishing boats because they had nets and buckets tied around their sides.

The larger ships had many men moving about their decks. Large sails were tied to huge wooden poles and when a man dropped quickly down a rope on the nearest one, she gaped at the height and the speed at which he had moved.

"Here, I believe this nearest one is the *Queen's Mystic*," Col stated as he moved to study the dark painted words along the front of the boat.

Caylee didn't see the ship Col was pointing to because she was focused on the farthest ship on the pier. The vessel she studied was made of golden wood. Its wrapped sails were white, and a bright blue flag flew above the back cabin on the ship's stern. The ship faced inwards, and it was the carved figure of a mermaid on the bow that had caught Caylee's attention.

"What is the name of that one?" she asked, pointing at the golden ship.

"It is this one we are here to inspect," Col said sternly as he pointed at the first ship again.

"But it is *that* one we must use," Svlain said quietly, and she too pointed to the carved mermaid.

"That, ladies, is the *Fair Maiden*," came a deep and jolly voice to their right.

Turning quickly, Caylee had a chance to see two intense tan eyes studying her before the dragon warriors blocked her vision of the man. Col stepped quickly forward, a deep frown on his face.

"Ah, the *Fair Maiden*, was it?" Col asked quickly, waving the guards back a step.

"She's the finest ship in Byways," the deep voice said. Caylee moved to get a better look at the speaker.

The man was tall. His long dark hair reached down to

the tip of his high collar. He already had a day's growth of beard on his face, which gave him a rugged look. His nose was bent slightly to the left, as if it had been broken once. Studying him, she thought the man quite handsome and continued to openly observe him.

His tan eyes flashed in her direction once before settling on the wizard. This allowed her to continue her survey. He wore tall tan boots and dark pants with a bold blue shirt that had brass buttons. A white sash hung over his chest, and a bright red bird sat on his shoulder, gazing at her. Caylee had never seen a bird so bright. Its beak was yellow, and its eyes were clear blue like the sea.

"Do you know the captain?" Col asked. Caylee was dazzled when the man smiled and bowed his head quickly.

"That I do. Captain Rouen at your service," the man said. To Caylee's delight, the bird repeated the last words, "*At your service.*"

"Oh, you talk!" Caylee exclaimed as she stepped forward.

The bird and man studied her, and the man's smile widened slightly. "That he does. This here is Chaos, the smartest bird in all of Genoa."

"I wonder," Col said, drawing the man's attention back to him and away from Caylee, "is the *Fair Maiden* available for chartering?"

"She is, and her crew is the best that sails the whole Alluvion, if I do say so myself." Captain Rouen gave another bow of his head.

"*Say so myself.*" Chaos echoed the captain's words.

9

____

THE FAIR MAIDEN

Captain Bryce Rouen watched the odd group depart from the docks. Bryce did not doubt that the man named Col was a dragon warrior. Col's bald head showed off the traditional tattoo that confirmed he was from one of the southern tribes.

Col traveled with a land nymph, a beautiful brunette, and three very large warriors. They had just commissioned him and his crew to take them to Pescara. Col wanted to return with his full company later that night for an early departure the next day.

Col didn't speak of their final destination, only of Pescara, but to Bryce, the destination never mattered. It was the pay and the safety of his boat that drove him. As he watched the group disappear, he knew something felt off with this commission, but he couldn't quite figure it out yet.

He continued to study them as the group walked down the docks. If his eyes stayed a little longer on the brunette, he told himself it was because of curiosity and that was all. Although he did appreciate a fine figure, and the woman did have a nice one.

"Tell Eno we have a job," Bryce stated. Chaos immediately lifted off from the perch on his shoulder and flew off towards the ship.

Bryce had work to do before his ship was ready for another journey. Work that a ship's captain was required to do. Dreading the pending duty, Bryce took his time as he walked to the headquarters of the pier boss.

B.R. Glorb was one of the most unpleasant men Bryce had ever had the privilege of meeting. Unfortunately, Mr. Glorb had full authority in Byways when it came to ships and their jobs. If Bryce were to take this new job, he first had to acquire a permit from Glorb, and the last time the *Fair Maiden* had been in Byways, there had been trouble.

Scratching at an ich on the side of his neck, Bryce stopped and studied the pier boss's shack and thought about his life. Bryce had been a ship's captain for over five years now, which made him one of the oldest captains who ran a free hauler ship.

Most ships were part of a private fleet, paid for and employed by the shore towns up and down the coast. These ships were well stocked, well employed, and mostly overrun by brigands. Other ships were small fishing vessels or pirate ships masquerading as legal ships.

Captain Bryce L. Rouen was a free hauler. This meant a lot to him. It meant he called the shots. He made the decisions, and he alone could cause his ship to fail or succeed. Failure was something he constantly worried about.

Bryce thought of himself first as a boss. He employed twenty-four men, who depended on him to find good jobs. That mostly meant hauling cargo, but sometimes it also meant taking on passengers like the job the pretty green-eyed brunette needed.

Shaking his head, he turned his thoughts back to his

current task, talking Glorb into a permit. Shaking the pouch of coins hidden in his pocket, he took a deep breath and opened the thin wooden door leading into Glorb's domain, fully prepared to grovel and even bribe if he had to.

Twenty minutes and fifteen coins later, Bryce left with his permit, hoping the job with the green-eyed beauty would reimburse him. His freshly printed permit would allow him to take on passengers and haul cargo to wherever the odd group needed to go after Pescara.

"Captain," Eno, his second in command, said as Bryce climbed the gangway up and set foot on his ship. "Chaos says we have a job."

"The bird is correct," Bryce stated as he waved the permit in the air. "And we can take on cargo heading to Pescara."

"You did collect the down payment first, right?" Eno asked. He was a tanned bald man of thirty who had speculation on his face along with two full days' worth of stubble.

Cracking a smile, Bryce winked at his friend and lifted an arm for Chaos. After the bird landed softly on his shoulder, he pulled out the pouch of coins. "I got more than our usual fee, and seeing as the leader was well connected, I charged them double what we usually get."

He received a hearty chuckle and a solid slap on his back from Eno. Then the large man started shouting orders to the crew.

"Eno, make sure the guest quarters get a good cleaning," Bryce requested as he returned the coin pouch to his pocket. "And tell the crew we will run dry this trip."

His words were met with a nod of understanding, then a shake. "The men won't like hearing there won't be liquor allowed," Eno grumbled, but he turned to complete his duties as Bryce went to his cabin.

The *Fair Maiden* was Bryce's pride and joy. She was also his only means of income, and he treated her as if she were the most precious thing on Genoa. The captain's cabin was at the stern of the ship and was quite large. There were four levels behind the mizzenmast. His quarters consisted of two rooms, one he used as an office and the other his sleeping room.

His officer's lodgings were directly below him, along with some of the crew's sleeping quarters. The rudder equipment ran behind the crew's quarters back wall, so that if repairs were needed, they could gain access without having to go over the rails.

Before the mainmast, there were storage compartments where the cargo was kept, along with several lifeboats. Supply rooms and the galley were found between the foremast and the mainmast. His cook was a small man who appeared to enjoy much of his cooking. Cen Spa had three chins and spoke of numerous wives whenever he was away from the port, but he could make a delicious meal out of water and bread.

Bryce locked his door and walked over to a safe hidden in the side wall behind a painting of a rather thinly clothed siren. Chaos flew to his perch near the back windows as Bryce flipped the lock's dial. He heard the locks release and pulled the money pouch out from his pockets.

"Did you check?" Chaos' question had Bryce glancing the bird's way.

"Twice," he replied, throwing the bag into the safe. It landed on several papers and hit the other three-coin pouches towards the safe's back wall. "Before this trip is through, we should have enough to buy another boat, if I want to expand." He closed the safe's door then spun the lock.

"Something off with that bunch," Chaos said, his words echoing Bryce's thoughts.

Chaos was a Scaridae bird from the long island. His bright red plumage and orange beak hid an intelligent brain. Not only could Chaos talk, but the bird was quite apt at business decisions.

"I agree," Bryce replied as he sat behind his large wooden desk. His maps and charts lay before him. Ignoring them, he pulled his logbook closer. He glanced at the figures he had spent most of last night studying. "We need to replace the shrouds on the mizzen before we set sail."

"The one with green eyes." Chaos's words caused Bryce to turn and look at the bird, but the bird was quiet for a moment. Then he continued. "She has magic."

"Magic?" Bryce asked. He stood and drew closer to the bird as he thought of the pretty brunette.

"Magic in her words," Chaos explained as he tilted his head and studied Bryce with his yellow eyes. "I liked it."

"Magical words," Bryce said thoughtfully. He turned to look out his high window at the harbor beyond the port.

"Pretty magic," Chaos stated. "Pretty woman."

Bryce was lost in his thoughts of magic and deep green eyes for several minutes. Work above deck continued outside and an occasional laugh or curse word could be heard while he stood there pondering. Finally, frustrated at all he didn't know, he shrugged his shoulders and turned from the window, dismissing what was out of his control for now and focusing on what he could control.

"Well, until we know more, we best keep our toes out of the water." He sat once again at his desk and got down to work.

Caylee didn't like the conversation going on around her, so she wrinkled her nose and took a steady breath. The words *unknown, record,* and *questionable reputation* kept being thrown around. Svlain stood up from the seat next to her and raised her hands.

"Enough!" the land nymph said in a slightly raised voice. "My head hurts from all this, and what have you all accomplished by shouting?" The pretty green face was set in a scowl, and Caylee nodded her head in silent agreement.

"Nothing," Erica stated from her seat on the other side of Caylee.

"Exactly," Svlain said as she returned to her seat. "I have already told you, to succeed we need the *Fair Maiden,* we need Captain Rouen."

"I thought you did not know the name of the ship, or its captain," Captain Adams said accusingly.

"That was before I went to the pier," Svlain retorted. "I know it now."

"What time did you say we would be there?" Captain Adams asked Col, who stood by the door to the room, packing his travel pipe with tobacco.

"The time remains the same as the last time you asked, just after three," Col said, giving the captain of the guard his scowl. "We have just over an hour to prepare. I suggest you get your men ready."

Caylee smiled at the wizard, who kept packing his pipe as he watched the disgruntled captain leave the room.

"Are you ready?" Caylee turned to Erica who nodded

once and stood to leave. "Col, Svlain, and I are both sure of the ship, but hearing some doubts about Captain Rouen…"

"Fear not. What is written on paper is not always the whole story," Col said. He set his pipe to his lips once, then seeing a frown upon her face, immediately took it out again. Col knew Caylee disapproved of smoking as much as she disapproved of eating meat. "I did some asking around after we got back. It seems the captain is well-liked amongst the Byways guards stationed here."

"His man Eno is known as far south as Rigel City," Svlain added. "His people are from the city of Druson in Malic, at least Eno's mother was. I am not sure about his father; I think he was from one of the islands out east."

"We will know more once we inspect his ship," Col advised. "I want you and Erica to remain behind."

"No, we all leave," Caylee said calmly as she looked over at Brett. "Brett had another vision, one that showed us sailing before the sun sank tonight."

"What did it show?" Col demanded. He turned to where Brett stood near the small stove in the corner of the room.

"It was dark. There were sharp teeth and blood." The man shook his head and turned his green eyes towards Col. "But then water came, and the moon's calm light reflected on its surface."

Col studied him for a minute, then nodded and once again placed his pipe in his mouth. He quickly put it out again when Caylee coughed softly.

"Very well. I will tell the others and smoke my pipe in peace outside," Col added with a grumble. He turned to leave.

After a small meal of cool salad with water cherries and a delicious slice of pink fruit cake, Caylee and her odd band of protectors picked up their belongings and made the journey to the piers. The military presence was there, but Col wanted them disguised so they would draw less attention.

Caylee could hardly contain her excitement. She had traveled by smaller ship years ago, but never on such a large vessel as the *Fair Maiden,* and not as far as Col's little green book indicated they needed to go.

As they moved through the back streets of Byways, she thought back to the odd book Col had found in Valorna. "The Brown Gull's logbook" was the title and the date carved into the cover was a long word that Col advised her indicated the locations of the moons. Since he was not an astronomer, and Genoa had only recently started using the Midzark years, the words held no meaning to her, but Col guessed it was well over eight hundred years old.

"The Trillium is said to be on an island far out to the east," Col had told them before they had started their journey. *"It speaks of a large island cut in half by water. Where the water starts, the writer told of a mirror that they claim showed the lost."*

"Lost what?" Shiarra had asked.

"The book is not clear. It only says the mirror can peer through time and even the barriers to other worlds," Col replied.

"So, could it find Zander too?" Caylee quickly asked. *"And what of Charlotte?"*

"One thing at a time," Col replied. He waved his large hands to calm her, then picked up the book once again and opened the pages to a rough drawing of a vast mountain. Its peak rose high above the clouds and disappeared into a sharp point covered in white. A slash of water dropped from the

peak, and mist surrounded the bottom where a rough X was drawn.

"The Trillium?" she had whispered. Col nodded his head.

Caylee was pulled from remembering this discussion about the book when her feet hit the first pier plank. Looking up, she saw the large ship before her and a very tall bald man standing near the head of the gangplank. The smile on his dark face was warm, but his large muscles spoke of much power.

"Ah, you must be Col," he said as the wizard stepped from the bridge to the deck of the ship. If Caylee tilted her head and squinted her eyes, she could see that the two men looked similar. Both were relatively bald. Col still had his mohawk, but it was very short now and peppered with grey. Both men had large muscles and were covered with many tattoos. The men spent a lot of their time out of doors, and the sun had tanned their skin to a dark brown. Col was two inches taller than the other, and Caylee wondered who would win in a battle if they were ever to fight.

"I am Eno," the man explained with a nod. "Captain Rouen is waiting for you in his quarters." With this, he turned and walked down the length of the ship.

Col nodded once and followed, along with Captain Adams. The others brought their supplies and bags aboard and waited. It didn't take long, no more than five minutes, before Col and Captain Adams returned. Col had a smile on his face, but Captain Adams was frowning slightly.

"Come along," Col instructed with a wave. "Our fare has been secured and our cabins await."

"When do we depart?" Svlain asked as she gripped her husband's hand.

"As soon as our bags are settled." Col nodded to Pren

and his warriors. "Secure the cabins first, then we will meet."

"This way," Eno stated, waving his large hand towards an open hatch.

The hatch led down one deck to a long wooden hallway. Oil lamps lit the interior, and wooden doors were set in the walls every ten feet. At the end of the corridor, Caylee could see a vast room with tables and benches.

"Here are the cabins. There are three cabins for the women and three for the men. Extra hammocks are in the cupboards," Eno advised. "The crew sleep one deck down, so you have this whole deck to yourselves at night except for the cook, who sleeps in the galley."

It was decided that Caylee, Erica, and Svlain would share the middle cabin, and the six dragon warriors would split the two surrounding rooms. The men were another subject. Grant insisted he have his own cabin.

In the end, Grant was given the smallest cabin while the remaining men split two cabins between the ten of them. This worked well because the dragon warriors insisted on keeping their guard duty both day and night while on board.

Caylee's disappointment in her fiancé grew when she saw his selfishness. But as the deck hands moved to launch the ship, her disappointment vanished as excitement took over.

The clear water, the fresh air, and the possibility of adventure blew all other thoughts from her mind. Standing on the deck of the ship, she watched the land melt away behind them.

10

BLUE TO GREEN

Long before the sun and Grenata, the green moon, had set, they were beyond the shores of Byways.

Bryce stood with his long legs spread wide on the quarterdeck, watching the day surrender to the night. The feel of his ship was comforting to him, its movements and sounds familiar.

Col wasn't telling him their full destination, but for now, Pescara would do. Col had provided an extra incentive, in the form of two more bags of money, to launch that day and take on no more passengers or cargo. In one day, Bryce had managed to earn more than twice the fee of a normal trip. True, he hadn't had time to replace some of the boards on the decking. But luckily, his cook had already stocked the galley, and they could always get more supplies at their first port, the dragon tribes islands.

As the night crept in like a thief, he watched some of his guests mill about the main deck as his men went about lowering the sails. Night on the open ocean was long and treacherous if you didn't know where you were. Bryce Rouen always knew where he was.

His eyes narrowed when the woman with green eyes climbed up from the lower deck. Her long dark hair was tied back away from her face. She wore dragon warrior clothing, a sexy little red top and black leather pants with various weapons strapped across her body. He hadn't pegged her as a warrior, but there were several others in her group he had.

Col was one. Then there were six rather large warriors, all with the dragon insignia on their leather sashes. Of course, the dragon tattoo was a dead giveaway, even for the women. He had counted six women warriors in the group, each as impressive as the men. In Bryce's mind, the women warriors were far more dangerous. Women usually were.

He moved down to the main deck and pretended to inspect the roping, but his eyes were on the green-eyed beauty. She was with the small wind nymph, a pretty little thing who waved her tiny hands when she spoke. As he drew closer, their words drifted to him, causing him to smile.

"Sick as a slug," the little nymph was saying, but a smile was on her lips. "Zain is with him now, but Grant is insisting we turn the boat around."

"I'll make sure to check on him before bed," the brunette said as she leaned forward and looked at the dark water below. "Do you think we'll see any merpeople?" she asked with excitement in her voice.

"Caylee, don't lean so far over," the other said, tugging on the woman's sleeve.

Ah, so the pretty maiden was named Caylee. Bryce thought the name suited the woman and smiled again as Caylee leaned even further over the railing.

"Erica don't be such an old woman. This is exciting!"

Caylee exclaimed. Bryce saw a splash of water spray up and mist her face as she laughed.

"See! You'll catch your death," Erica exclaimed as she tried once more to tug on Caylee's tunic.

"Your highness." A deep voice sounded from the other side of the main mast. Bryce's eyes narrowed at the formal words. "Sparring is about to begin if you wish to join us and attempt to gain another level."

Staying where he was, Bryce watched Caylee turn with a pout on her face. She nodded once to a large dragon warrior and then turned back to Erica.

"You can watch if you want, or I believe Brett was going to see about some tea below deck," Caylee said.

"I think I will join him for tea," Erica replied. She turned to the warrior. "Pren, make sure you wear her out. It has been far too long since she exercised."

As the three turned, they spotted him; and he realized he had long forgotten to pretend to be busy. He stood there with his hands empty and his mouth hanging open, which was a dead giveaway he had been eavesdropping. He had been so shocked at realizing that the woman was a royal that he forgot to hide his intentions. Erica smiled once and then hurried back down to the lower decks while the man, Pren, stood his ground until Caylee laid a hand on his arm.

"It was bound to happen," she stated. She stepped forward, only to have Pren's arm shoot out and stop her.

"Still," he growled, and Bryce was shocked, then amazed, when one of the man's hands moved over to his short sword. This caused Bryce to laugh, and he placed his own hands on his hips.

"My friend, there is no need for that. The *Fair Maiden* sails under the royal flag. She's never carried an actual royal before, but still, she and her crew are loyal. There will be no harm done to Princess Caylee aboard my ship," he said with a nod.

"There are other things we fear than you, Captain," Caylee said with a smile on her face. "However, until we are further from the mainland, I think my true identity should remain between us."

"As you wish," Bryce said with a deep bow of his head. "However, if your men continue to address you as such, the secret will be out before breakfast is served." He smiled and studied the large warrior. "Did I hear you say you were sparring?"

"Her... I mean Caylee here has only gained a warrior level of two." Pren pulled his hand away from his sword. "She has asked that we train her for the next test since we will be on board for several days."

"Very well. Would it be possible for some of my men to train as well?" Bryce turned to Caylee. "The night shift might like to join in the training, if permitted."

"I will leave that decision up to Col," Caylee replied, then she followed Pren to the main deck, where there was enough space for training.

"Did you have to call me that?" He heard Caylee's whispered words before he turned to head back to his duties as captain. As he walked away, he heard Pren's reply. *"I don't like the way he was watching you."*

The training went on for two hours after the sun had fully set. Lamps swung from poles as both the men and women warriors paced through their extensive warm-up routines.

When the sparring exercises started, Bryce was shocked to see it was full contact. There were no pulled punches or hits. Instead of sharp knives, however, short wooden pulls were used, and a quick *whack* could be heard each time they made contact with their target.

It was hard not to watch the group, and even his men, who hadn't joined tonight's exercise, paused in their duties to watch some of the impressive flips and duels. Col joined the training, and Bryce narrowed his eyes when a flicker of magic came from the man's fingers.

"Of course, she would have a wizard with her," he murmured, berating himself for being such a fool.

The royal princess of Genoa would never travel without guards and a wizard or two. He thought back to the land nymph and shook his head. She wasn't a wizard, but maybe her husband was? The man had looked like one, but he hadn't pegged Col as a wizard either.

Hadn't he heard that Princess Caylee was recently engaged? His knowledge of the royals was limited. He knew the queen was married to a Materan and that they had three children. The oldest were twins, Caylee and her brother, Zaner. No, Zander, that was it.

The youngest was a girl. He knew she had been named after one of the giants from the other place, Midzark. He had never met a giant, nor a royal for that matter, and wondered momentarily about protocol.

"Find Eno and ask him to meet me in my chambers," he told Chaos. When the bird flew off, he glanced once more at the fighting princess, then with a frown on his face, turned and headed to his chambers.

"A royal!" Eno exclaimed after Bryce had told him the secret identity of their travelers.

"You should have asked for more money," Chaos chimed in from his perch.

"I should have denied them the use of my boat," Bryce mumbled. "Trouble, the whole lot of them."

"Trouble?" Eno asked as he sat his large frame in the chair across from Bryce's desk.

"You think the royal princess is just on a nice cruise? Maybe she wants to see the world before she gets hitched?" he asked with a sneer. "Maybe have one last adventure before settling down?" He shook his head and got up from his chair to pace to the window. "No, there's trouble about."

"We know Pescara. We have traveled there plenty of times. What trouble are you talking about?" Eno asked as he leaned forward and scratched at his bald head.

"Mark my words, there is trouble. Why do you think we left port so quickly?" Bryce asked, his eyes glancing out the dark windows at the unseen waters.

"Do you think she is a runaway? Maybe she got cold feet and is now fleeing her fiancé?" Eno asked.

"I doubt it. I think the sick pale one is her beloved. No, I think the princess is on a mission. And there is one thing I know about the royal family—there is always a quest," Bryce said soberly as new worry for his ship and crew filled his mind.

Two days after departing Byways, Caylee's muscles ached from sparring. Pren and Tonkee, along with the other dragon warriors, kept her busy with exercise. The third level of dragon training was intense and very demanding. Col helped with the mental training while Zain supplied her with salves for her sore joints and muscles.

Grant, who was suffering from severe sea sickness,

remained belowdecks, sequestered in his room. He was pale and could only keep down liquids at the moment. Zain was hopeful his herbs would aid him, but Grant still turned a pale shade of green when food was mentioned. Caylee had tried to spend the early mornings with him in his room, but after the first hour, she would excuse herself and go above deck for some fresh air.

Caylee loved the open sea. This was something she had always known about herself, but she had never had time to indulge it. Even while visiting the Draydon tribe, who lived along the cliffs of Faro, she hadn't had much time for sailing. And the small boats the tribe used were nothing compared to the *Fair Maiden*.

She loved the feel of the larger ship. Its gentle sway allowed her to sleep peacefully. The subtle sounds of the wood creaking as it moved through the deep waters spoke to her of comfort. Even now, as she stood looking out at the sun's bright reflection off the water, she felt at peace, despite her deep yearning for her missing family.

"There will be rain before the night comes," Captain Rouen said from behind her.

She had gotten used to the man's sudden appearances when she was above deck. The first two times he had appeared like this had startled her, but now she had come to expect him. Part of her liked talking to the captain, yet another part of her felt hesitant, almost guilty. She couldn't explain the second feeling and had spent several hours each night pondering this unexplained response until she realized that it had to do with Grant. Maybe she felt guilty because her fiancé was below deck, sick and miserable, while she was above enjoying the trip.

"Rain?" She lifted a hand to shield her eyes from the bright sun.

"Look," Bryce said. He pointed over the ship's banister on the port side. "Weather here always comes from the ocean's horizon."

Caylee turned and saw fat clouds far out at sea, resting on the horizon. They looked harmless, almost friendly.

"Will it be a storm?" she asked, her hands resting on the railing as the ship cut through the water.

"No, just a gentle rain I think," Bryce replied as he leaned against the railing and studied her for a minute. "By midday, we should reach Typhon Island."

"The dragon islands?" she asked hopefully.

"The same," he replied with a smile. "It will be our last port before Eras."

She turned her eyes from the vast ocean to study the captain. Today, his black hair waved in the faint wind. His blue shirt had a missing button near his neck, and it drew her eyes to the faint scar at the bottom of his tanned throat. As she studied the scar, she watched his heartbeat from a vein, and her thoughts made her face warm. Her heart rate increased as her eyes remained on his neck.

"We should be back on track tomorrow morning," Bryce continued, his words interrupting Caylee's thoughts. She quickly averted her eyes back to the ocean.

"Have you ever gone to a tribe's celebration dinner?" Caylee asked as she gripped the railing hard while trying to calm her heart.

"Celebration?" Bryce asked. He turned to study her, his back to the sea.

"No doubt my arrival will prompt the elders to have a celebration," Caylee stated as he frowned. "The tribes will find any excuse to throw a party."

"No doubt your royal highness's appearance will cause

quite a stir," he said. She thought she heard a ridiculing tone in his voice.

"No doubt." She turned to look into his tan eyes. "My family is of the Draydon tribe," she explained. "We rarely get to visit our tribe family. Isn't going home a good excuse for a party?"

A flicker of sadness passed behind his eyes before it was shielded from her. Then a cocky smile passed on his full lips, and he nodded once.

"We should be fully stocked before night. If allowed, my men and I would enjoy a good party." He tilted his head. "Do you know where we could get an invitation?" he teased.

"I just might." She returned his smile.

In her mother's time, the islands off the cliffs of Faro were only used for escape from attackers. Now, the islands had been turned into extra living villages for the tribe. The largest was big enough to house a shipping port with over a thousand residents who lived there yearlong.

Caylee had visited the tribal island twice in her life, and both times had resulted in a grand celebration from the leaders. She had fond memories of those parties and the warriors who lived there.

By mid-afternoon, the *Fair Maiden* had gained the port. The captain and his men busied themselves loading supplies for the next leg of their journey. Before they were finished loading the ship, Caylee's troop traveled inland to the main hall of the tribe. When they arrived at the tribal buildings, they were well received.

The village was smaller than the tribal village on the mainland. Most of the buildings here were made of stones and wood. The normal leather tents would not stand up to the strong winds the island received. There were several fire pits with wooden stumps surrounding them, and two guard buildings sat on the outskirts. The village was surrounded by tall trees and a stone mountain sat on the southern side of the island, away from the port.

Caylee knew most of the trading ships stopped here on Typhon Island to restock or drop off goods. Near the port, there had been a few inns and cafés, along with three vast warehouses the traders used to store supplies. But the tribal homes were separate from these and appeared smaller, almost rustic compared to the other buildings on the island.

"The last time I saw you, you had braids and freckles," the elder by the name of Braunch said to her. He smiled, showing her that he was missing two front teeth. His dark eyes winked at her.

"Last time I saw you," she replied with a smile, "you had more teeth." She remembered Braunch. He was a friendly elder who had always kept candied Bim berries in his pockets for little kids, and himself.

"Ah, grew up like your mother," Braunch said with a wider smile. He reached in his pocket. The bag of candy was given a shake before he held it out for her.

"I see your candy bag is like your smile, open wide," she replied with a wink at the old elder. She grabbed a handful of the sugar-coated berries.

Laughter surrounded her, but she suddenly had to fight back tears when she realized that the last time she had been here, her family had been standing beside her. The loneliness hit her hard, and she had a hard time swallowing the candy while fighting her tears.

"There, there," Svlain said from beside her. She gently took Caylee into her arms. After a long hug, Svlain led her towards some chairs near an open fire pit.

"Svlain, I miss them so much," Caylee murmured.

"I know, I miss them too." She patted Caylee's back as Erica sat next to her and held her hand.

"Are we staying here tonight?" Grant's question had Caylee glancing up at him.

She was shocked to see annoyance in his green eyes, not concern for her. She wondered about his reaction until a dragon warrior walked past their group, and Grant wrinkled his nose at the passing man. Surprise overshadowed her sadness when she discovered he was disgusted by the tribal village and its warriors.

How had she not known this about Grant? For almost eight months she and Grant had been an item. He had arrived in Castle Pines as a student of law who had studied in Valorna for two years. He had traveled to Castle Pines to be an apprentice under the royal council.

Their entire relationship had been centered around Castle Pines. She realized now that she hadn't traveled anywhere since she and Grant had started dating. She had gone into Pinewoods, but usually for shopping or her royal duties with the village women. She had never seen Grant outside of the castle. As far as she knew, he never went to the forest or village.

Thinking about it now, she realized Grant was not fond of the other races in Genoa. She knew he didn't like Erica. He often called her the 'nymph,' saying the word like being one was bad.

Squinting her eyes up at Grant, she realized now that there was quite a bit that she didn't know or like about him. He appeared to dislike the dragon village, a place she felt very much at home in. He didn't like Erica. No, that wasn't correct—he hated Erica. She knew this, and had known it for a while, but had chosen to ignore it until now. She disliked how he treated the other servants at the castle and had seen how harshly he ordered others around, including herself.

"No," she finally replied, her voice rather stern as she shook her head at him. "We will sleep on the ship; the tribe has no spare space for all of us."

"Fine," Grant replied as he continued to glance around.

Shedding her despair of her missing family from a minute ago, Caylee stood and squared her shoulders. She felt her anger towards Grant flowing from her and decided now wasn't the time to deal with it.

Instead, she looked at Svlain and Erica. "Let's see if we can help get ready for the party." Then she turned her back on Grant and walked away.

11

THE SEE IN CELEBRATION

Bryce left nine of his men on duty to watch the ship. The other fifteen he took to the dragon tribe's celebration with strict orders—behave and no drinking. He'd fully intended to follow his instructions until he arrived and saw Princess Caylee.

She was in her sparring outfit—bright red leather pants with a black tank shirt—which caused a buzzing sound to fill his ears the moment he laid eyes on her. She had her hair braided in intricate coils and when he saw a wink of silver, he realized she had twisted beads into the braids.

"Welcome," Caylee said with a wide smile. "The food is on the veranda and drinks are over there." She pointed towards a shaded tree where large barrels and crates of ice stood.

"We thank you for the invitation," Eno said with a bow of his bald head.

"No thanks are necessary," Caylee replied, her dark brows lifted in amusement as she moved closer to Bryce. "I see you brought your bird." She studied Chaos as his men moved towards the food.

"He enjoys a good party like the rest of us," Bryce responded. He studied Caylee as her green eyes continued to look at the bird. "If you like, you can pet him. He does not bite."

"Are you sure?" she asked but her hand was already halfway up to the bird's red chest. "Oh, he's so soft."

"He preens himself enough, he should be," Bryce said with a chuckle as he felt Chaos' claws dig into his shoulder at his snide statement. "He doesn't like to admit it, but he has a mirror above his perch in my quarters."

"Oh, if I were this pretty, I would too," Caylee said as she continued to run her hand along the bird's long feathers.

"You haven't looked in the mirror then," Bryce murmured. Caylee stopped petting the bird and looked at him. He thought he saw speculation in her eyes, but it quickly turned to humor.

"I believe you just paid me a compliment," she said with a smile.

He was quiet for a minute, then Chaos decided the tension needed to be cleared and croaked quite loudly, "Compliment." Caylee's smile widened and she turned her attention back to the bird as Bryce tried to steady his heartbeat.

"Oh, pretty and smart. Aren't you?" Caylee said. She reached up to pet the bird again, but as she drew near, Chaos did something that surprised her, and Bryce. The bird spread its wings and hopped over to sit on Caylee's left shoulder.

"Oh," she exclaimed, freezing her movements at the unexpected visitor.

"Chaos," Bryce scolded and moved to retrieve him, but Caylee waved her hands.

"Oh no, he's fine. I was just startled." She reached up to pet the red feathers once again.

"He usually doesn't do that," Bryce explained. "I guess I forgot to remind him to behave."

"That is quite all right." She turned very slowly towards the tables. "What does Chaos eat?" she asked, her hand still stroking the bird.

"Mostly seeds," Bryce replied as he studied the camp. He saw small wooden structures all with stone bases. There were glass windows set in most of the buildings that were thrown open to let in the afternoon breeze. There were outdoor tables and several fire rings. They were unlit, but piles of wood sat next to them for when the evening turned cold.

He had been told there were over six hundred tribespeople who lived together, while another six hundred villagers lived in the surrounding town. He didn't think the tiny island could support that many but knew that ship trade kept the town well supplied. He had been visiting this island for over five years, yet he had never set foot inside the dragon tribe's area, until now.

"How do you find it?" Caylee's question brought his attention back to her, and he realized she had turned and was studying him while he inspected the community.

"It's amazing," he replied. He turned to continue his inspection. "There, is that a smithy? And what are those buildings for?" He pointed at two odd cone-shaped structures.

"The beads are packed there and cooked," Caylee replied.

"And that? Oh, look at that carving." Forgetting his manners, Bryce quickly walked over to a large log that was in the process of being carved. A tribal man stood on either side, each with plates of food in their hands as they studied the carving.

"Are you the workmen?" Bryce asked as he drew closer. The carving was of a giant octopus. Its curved legs twisted and turned about in the grain of the wood. The head was still hidden inside the massive beam of wood, not yet carved.

"We are," one man replied.

"Captain Rouen, this is Bren Tif and Coren," Caylee stated. "If you don't recognize their work, they happen to be the same men who carved your ship's mermaid."

"I thought so!" Bryce exclaimed, moving closer to the wood carving. "Excellent work. Tell me, how do you carve the small details?"

As the carvers started their explanation and described the tools they used, Bryce completely forgot the food and celebration. He watched as Bren used a small metal knife, one that was sharpened down to a fine point, to add details to the creature's suckers. Then Coren explained about the sealant used when the carving was finished.

"So, I should be using this on the wood twice a year?" he asked, appalled that he didn't know how to properly preserve his own ship's figurehead.

"Your carving is only two years, so the salty water should not have done too much damage. But you will need to strip and clean it first," Coren advised as Caylee thrust a plate of food into Bryce's hands.

"What is this?" he asked, looking down at the plate.

"It's food," she replied with a stern look. "A man can't stand about talking and miss his supper."

When she walked off, leaving him perplexed, he shrugged his shoulders and started eating as the two brothers continued to advise him on how best to maintain his ship's carving.

Three hours, two plates, and a quick glass of ale with the carvers later, Bryce left the party just as the rain started to gently fall, just as he had predicted earlier. He had two pails with him. One held the liquid stripper needed to ensure his wooden mermaid was clean, while the other was a sealant that was guaranteed to keep her looking like freshly carved wood.

"There you are," Cen Spa, the ship's cook, stated as Bryce walked on board and moved to stand under the over-hand railing of the main deck. "You missed all the excitement."

"Excitement?" Bryce asked, quickly scanning his ship for any damage. All he could see was the rain making the deck slippery.

"Not here," Cen Spa said with a shake of his scruffy head. His cook was a simple man with little education. What he lacked in learning he made up for in the kitchen. "Well, mostly not here."

"What excitement?" Bryce asked with a frown as he set his supplies down.

"The fight. Well, more like an argument. Though the guy deserved it, if you ask me," Cen Spa said with another shake of his head as he scratched at his jaw.

"What are you talking about?" Bryce asked, feeling frustrated and confused at the same time.

"Let's just say the wedding's off," Cen Spa stated with a crooked smile. "The little princess gave her man the heave-ho."

"You missed!" The shout came through the red ball of Io Maltesea's magic. "Your creature never showed up."

"You were already gone," Io Maltesea replied with her thoughts on other problems.

"I tried to delay us," the voice rising from the red mists declared. "This captain is taking us past the long island. Could your creature wait for us there?"

"No," Io Maltesea barked. "I require it here to hunt the queen and king."

"Hunt them?" The voice grew louder. "They escaped?"

"They had help," the sorceress said as her fingers flexed in anger. "No need to worry, my Lanart is tracking them now. I do not know how the entangled crystal's magic did not hold, but my creatures will find them."

"What are your orders now?" the voice asked.

"Once the queen is captured again, I make my way to the heart. I intend to suck all the life out of Genoa with my bare hands," Io Maltesea said with a sick smile.

Caylee trained hard the next day to distract herself from the previous night's argument. Sweat trickled down her face as she lifted her fists at her opponent, who circled her as they sparred on the ship's top deck.

"Lift your left fist higher." Col barked the order as he stood by watching the training. "He is going to jab you in the ribs if you do not move your elbows closer together."

Before the wizard was done with this order, Dovic, her sparring partner, had done just that.

As Caylee landed hard on the deck, her right rib already aching from the quick blow, she had a second to rethink her life. Here she was, a princess of Genoa, sailing on a ship that was stuck out in the middle of the Alluvion Ocean, halfway between the dragon island and the long island, which Captain Bryce said they would reach before tomorrow evening if the weather remained good. Her left hip hurt, her right rib now ached, and she was drenched in sweat. On the plus side, for the first time in a year, she felt refreshed.

She was active again. She hadn't exercised much in the past year. She hadn't done much in the past year except go to council meetings. But she was also not engaged anymore. This thought passed through her mind, and she frowned as Col moved to stand over her.

"Did he hurt you?" Col demanded, a frown on his face and concern in his brown eyes.

"No," she replied, giving her rib a quick rub.

"Then get up and do it again, this time correctly," Col grumbled. He moved off to watch.

Standing, she faced the warrior Dovic, a warrior with the level of seven. She was training with him today because he was more her size, thin and wiry. He was a man of mixed race with dark skin and long black hair, which was braided back much like her own, but Dovic had a thin mustache and a broad smile.

"Don't let me at those ribs again," he taunted, raising his fists.

Caylee mirrored his movements and took a small step to her right, which Dovic immediately copied.

"Keep your weight on the back leg," Col advised, and Caylee shifted.

She ducked underneath the left jab that was aimed at her and then returned with a swift kick to the back of her opponent's leg. Instead of falling, Dovic rolled over and ended up back on his feet. Before he could turn to face her again though, she moved quickly and hooked her arm around his throat.

"Good!" Col shouted.

"Damn, the girl can move," Caylee heard one of the warriors lining the training circle say.

"Ten coppers on Caylee," another goaded. Before Caylee had her legs wrapped around Dovic's midriff, the betting had proceeded. She heard the wagering get as high as two Tooms before she launched herself at her opponent again.

Her right hook grazed past Dovic's left ear as he bent backward, limber as a willow branch. He sprung his upper body back towards her and had her off guard as he lunged with his left hand. Luckily, Caylee had all her weight on her back leg, which allowed her to repeat his prior moves. Unluckily, Dovic was ready for the action and did a leg sweep. Caylee landed hard on the wooden decking of the ship, again.

"Umph," she exclaimed before quickly rolling to her right. She tried to scramble up, but Dovic's left knee landed in the middle of her back, and she felt him lightly tap her on the side of her head.

"How the mighty have fallen," Dovic said as he stood over Caylee. She rolled over and looked up at him as she tried to catch her breath.

"I demand a rematch!" Caylee finally said as she climbed up and stood on wobbly legs. She had been sparring over an hour and still hadn't managed to knock Dovic down once.

"No, no more for today," Col stated as he squinted at the bright sun above them. "Go get cleaned up. We will turn our lessons to archery after lunch."

"But..." Caylee started to argue, but after the last copper had passed between the warriors behind the wizard, she realized the training had taken a lot out of her. She felt exhausted. "Fine." Turning, she saw Captain Rouen and Eno standing on the ship's higher deck, watching.

Taking a defeated breath, Caylee nodded at the two men. She felt embarrassed as the captain's smile widened, and heat crept into her cheeks. Trying to straighten her spine, she marched towards the stairs.

"Great," she hissed once safely below. "What a fierce warrior I make."

Her embarrassment had made her temporarily forget her troubles of the night before. That is until she moved past the closed door to Grant's room. Then embarrassment turned to anger, and it was this feeling that followed her into her rooms.

As she cleaned up and put on a fresh dress, she thought back to the night before. The trouble with Grant had started after she'd delivered the plate of food to the captain. She'd only delivered it because she didn't want the man to go hungry. How was she to know that Grant would be infuriated by her simple act?

"Why did you do that?" Grant demanded as she returned to the wooden table he was currently sitting alone at. She didn't like that he had sat at a table far from everyone else during the celebration. Even here Grant kept distant from those whom she thought of as friends. She knew he had been distancing himself and her while at the castle, and on board

the ship, and now at the dragon tribe's village. It bothered her, as she loved to surround herself with family and friends. However, since the table was under a large tree, she didn't complain too much because the evening shade felt nice.

"He's distracted and probably wouldn't get any food until it was too late," Caylee replied as she sat down next to Grant.

"He can get his own food," Grant growled, causing Caylee to study him in confusion. "You are not a servant."

"I know that. I was just being nice." She started to eat the rice meal she had gotten for herself.

"I know what you were doing," Grant said as he pushed his plate of uneaten food away. "And I know why you were doing it," he sneered.

"Excuse me?" she asked. She lifted her cup of cold ale.

"I see the way you look at him," Grant commented, softly pounding his fist on the table. "And I see the way he looks at you."

Taking a deep drink, Caylee understood that Grant must be in one of his moods. She hoped his sour mood wouldn't spoil the celebration.

"It is creepy how he stares at you all the time," Grant continued.

"How do you know?" Caylee asked, realizing too late that her question would just feed Grant's anger even more.

"I have eyes," he growled. "You do not pay me that much attention. I have been deathly ill in my cabin since we left that sea town and have only seen you twice. I could have been dead for all the attention you gave me. But the captain needs food, and you jump right up and fetch it for him like you were a servant."

"I did not." Caylee squared her shoulders in defense.

"We should have never come on this pointless trip,"

Grant continued. "We should head back to the castle tonight. We can take the dragons and be home in three days."

He pulled on her hand as if he intended to march over to the dragons, which sat on the northern side of the village, and procure one for the trip. When she remained in her seat, he turned and glared at her.

"This trip isn't pointless," she said calmly. "I'm searching for my family." She looked up at him as he stood above her.

"It was always them before me," he exclaimed, leaning down towards her. "You never want to hear what I have to say. You are always ignoring me. But now, it seems your family is more important than me," he continued, much to her horror. "I hope they are never found!" He growled the last words. "They never liked me anyway."

"Caylee?" Erica asked, interrupting Grant as she and Brett walked over to the table. "Is everything all right?"

"Butt out of our business, nymph!" Grant jeered at Erica, pounding his fist on the table once more. "You are always sticking your nasty little nose in our business. I am sick of it," Grant continued as Caylee quickly stood and faced him. Her anger grew while Grant's face reddened even more with anger.

"Don't talk to her that way," Caylee hissed.

"I will talk to her any way I want; she is only the help," Grant mocked.

"We are done here," Caylee stated, making a chopping motion with her hand, then she turned to Erica and Brett. "I'm sorry."

"Do not apologize to them," Grant growled. He grabbed her arm and pulled her, so she was facing him again.

"Do not touch her!" Brett barked as Caylee's guards rushed forward.

"Back off," Grant hissed.

"I'm leaving," Caylee stated quickly. She yanked her arm away from Grant's grasp, then waved at the guards who were now surrounding her. Turning, she marched off with Erica, still surrounded by her three guards.

Sitting on her bed in the ship's cabin, she shook her head at the memory. Grant had, of course, followed her to the ship. The argument had continued aboard, and the battle of words that followed had resulted in her ending their engagement.

Just thinking of the harsh words Grant had said had her now fisting her hand in the bed's linen coverlet. Her teeth clenched when she remembered the hurt and pain his words had caused, but she also remembered the feeling of relief she had felt afterward, when he had walked away from her.

Lying on the bed, she took a moment to analyze everything she knew about Grant. When she was done, she was shocked to discover her parents had been right all along. Grant was not a nice person.

12

WHERE THERE IS SMOKE

Caylee's appetite evaded her during lunch. Even the rice cakes didn't distract her from her mood. Her thoughts disturbed her and left her with a deep brooding attitude. She realized that Grant wasn't the man she thought he was, and that her relationship with him had been an illusion.

Her mind kept pondering the incidents that should have been clues for her. Times where Grant mistreated the staff of the castle or dismissed them sternly in front of her. She remembered Grant's dislike of Erica, of each time he had called her friend by her race and not her name, as if it were an insult. Stirring her food around on her plate, she remembered her mother's words about Grant the night before her parents had disappeared.

"He doesn't put a smile on your face, little dove," Tresstéanna *had said. Then she pushed a strand of Caylee's hair back and looked deep into her eyes. "I don't see the spark."*

Caylee frowned now as she thought back to that

moment and pushed more food around on her plate. What spark? What was her mom talking about?

"Are you looking for life's answers in your bowl?" The deep voice of Captain Rouen jerked Caylee out of her funk. Glancing up, she studied the man and her frown deepened when she felt her heartbeat quicken.

"Oh," he said, holding up his hands as if in surrender. "Sorry."

"Sorry for what?" she asked as he proceeded to sit across from her at the table in the galley.

"Sorry for whatever put that frown on your pretty face."

"I'm just deep in thought." She studied her plate again with no real interest in eating. "Captain—"

"Please, call me Bryce," he said, continuing to study her over his plate of food.

"Bryce," she said with a nod of her head. She liked the name and so said it again, this time with a slight smile on her face. "Bryce, have you ever been engaged?"

"Oh, so the rumor is true," he said with a nod. He took a large bite of fish.

"Rumor?" she asked with another frown. She turned to study the other tables around the long galley.

Three ship crewmen were eating together at one table. Four dragon warriors were sitting at another while the cook, a short fat man named Cen Spa, was behind a low counter serving the food.

"Well, you can't have a huge argument with your betrothed on a small ship and not expect everyone else to know about it," Bryce stated with a smile. "Word travels fast on the *Fair Maiden*."

"I see," Caylee said. She pushed her plate away so she could cross her arms on the table in front of her. "And what is the word?"

"Well, my lady," Bryce said with another wide smile, "word is you have freed yourself of the ill-tempered bloke quite nicely."

Her eyes narrowed as she studied him quietly for a time. Then she slowly nodded once. Her eyes narrowed even more when his smile increased to dazzling.

"Let's just say the wedding is off," she finally said as Bryce nodded once and took another bite of his lunch. "I can't stand a chauvinistic bigot, and I fear Grant fits that bill." She smiled when Bryce's head tilted a little in confusion, but when a rolling laugh came from him, her smile increased.

"Oh!" he said, his right hand moving quickly to his side as if trying to hold in his laughter. "Oh, can I use those fancy words of yours some time? I know a merchant trader in Pescara who 'fits that bill.'"

"Sure, if you answer my original question," Caylee relented finally after Bryce's laughter had died down. "Have you?" When his tan eyes looked at her with confusion, she asked again. "Have you ever been engaged?"

"Ah, I fear the thralls of love have yet to ensnare me." His smile was genuine, but there was a teasing in his eyes that had her feeling uncomfortable.

"Well, I'm sure it's not for a lack of trying," she said primly. She moved to stand but stopped when his hand shot out and landed on the table inches from hers.

"Please." The smile quickly fell from his face. "I didn't mean to offend you. I only meant that, as captain, I don't get much time for the joys of life."

Caylee studied him for a minute. After seeing the honesty in his eyes, she nodded and settled back in her seat.

"Aren't you a bit young to be a captain of your ship?" she asked. His eyes turned hazy with thought.

"Let's just say I inherited the Maiden," he replied. It was Caylee's turn to tilt her head in confusion.

"So you come from a sailing family?" She watched in fascination as his dark brows moved together in concentration.

"My mom ran a store in Druson," he replied, shrugging his broad shoulders. "She never set foot on a ship as far as I know."

"I'm sorry," she said quietly.

"Sorry? Sorry for what?" His eyes moved from her face back down to his plate. "Oh, she's not dead. At least I don't think she is." He took a large bite of his food.

"You don't know?" she asked, astonished.

"It is kind of hard to travel down the River Mazel in a ship so large," Bryce said with another shrug.

"Oh," Caylee said, unsure how to respond as her thoughts turned to her mother.

"My dad was a captain in Rigel City. He fell head over heels for Mom, and I was the result. Dad ran the barge that traveled up and down the river, so he was away most of the time." Another shrug was followed by a quick smile. "I traded the barge for a ship as soon as I could." Now he leaned closer and pointed his fork at her. "How do you like ocean travel?"

His quick change of subject and his question caught her off guard for a moment. "I love it," she replied with a broad smile, allowing the subject to change, but wondering more about his past. "I had done some traveling on the tribe's boats, but nothing like this." She looked about the galley again. "I would love to learn more about the ship."

"Ah, I can help you with that," Bryce replied. "I heard you have more training after lunch, but what about after? I could show you some of the functions of running a ship."

"Neat," Caylee said with a smile. "After archery then."

"After," Bryce said with a return smile.

Bryce studied the chart with his eyes, but his mind was on something else. Or more to the point, his mind was on someone else. Caylee.

She was an enigma to him. She was a soft woman who could wear royal dresses but also dressed as a fierce warrior at other times. He thought about how she had struggled in her sparring and training. She always got back up after she had been thrown down on the ship's hard decking.

"Not such a fierce warrior then," he said out loud to himself.

"Who?" came Chaos' question, startling Bryce and reminding him that the bird was sitting on the wooden perch by the window.

"The little princess," Bryce answered, turning to study the bird. "I think she has bewitched you too."

Chaos tilted his head as his eyes focused on him. "She holds magic but has not used it."

"Yes," Bryce murmured as he scratched at the day's growth of beard on his chin. "I wonder about that too."

In truth, Bryce had completely forgotten the woman held magic. He had been so enthralled by her green eyes and full lips that all else had slipped his mind.

"The men like her," Chaos said, interrupting Bryce's thoughts.

This was the truth; Bryce had seen as much each day

they traveled. Even now as they drew near the island Eras, which was nestled near the long island, the crew went out of their way to help the little princess. Just this morning he had seen Cen Spa bring Caylee a bag of apples that she favored.

"Do we stop on the long island?" Chaos asked, interrupting Bryce's thoughts.

"No. I think our supplies will last until Pescara." Bryce turned back to his charts, dismissing Caylee from his mind, or at least trying to for a time. "Besides, it might be dangerous with our unique guests."

"You fear the inhabitants might be as rough on nymphs as they were on talking birds?" Chaos asked.

Turning from his charts, Bryce studied his friend. His bright red feathers and odd eyes were only a shell. Inside the odd bird sat an intelligent mind and kind heart. Chaos's start to his life had been hard, and the long islanders had caused it.

"Yes, so we will sail far north of the harbor and ensure all are safe," Bryce replied as he walked over and petted the soft feathers that ran along the top of the bird's head. "Far north."

It was the sound of running feet that caught Bryce's attention first, then the shouting.

"Water!" he heard a second before the dreaded word, "Fire!"

Sprinting from his cabin, he saw smoke coming from the starboard side hatch, where the cook kept the food supplies.

"Grab the buckets!" Bryce shouted and aimed a look upward towards the sails. "Drop the sails! All stop!"

His shouts had the crew responding fast. His men set about following orders while he ran forward towards the smoke. The warriors, and Caylee, were already there passing buckets down the hatch steps. Each fighter was wearing their leather fighting gear, but they also had long leather sleeves on their arms for their archery practice.

"Make room for the captain!" Eno shouted, and the warriors stepped aside as black smoke continued to billow up and out.

"Who is down there?" Bryce demanded.

"Cook and Bran and Ebod," Eno stated.

"Keep the buckets coming," he ordered. He grabbed the next full bucket and marched down into the hold.

The smoke filled his eyes and lungs as he ripped his handkerchief off his neck and dunked it in the bucket. After it was soaked, he covered his mouth. He passed two more men on his way to the red flames.

Cen Spa was there at the head of the bucket line, throwing the water onto the fire. Bryce was glad to see the flames were limited to the piles of crates. So far, the fire had not reached the decking or support beams.

"More water!" He threw his bucket on the blaze, then passed it back to be refilled from the barrels above deck. "Cen Spa, cover your face!" he shouted. He shoved the fat man out of his way so he could take over.

Two hours and four shifts at the head of the line later, all the hot spots had been doused by water. Unfortunately, the main food stores had been burned to a crisp. The hold now smelled like water, burnt meat, and the nasty smell of sweat.

"All gone," Cen Spa muttered as he rummaged around in the ashes.

"Eno, see who was on duty near the hatch. I want them in my cabin in fifteen," Bryce ordered. He turned back to face the cook. "Cen Spa, I need a report within the hour.

We will anchor until I have all the answers." Turning, Bryce came face to face with the wizard Col.

"Captain, may I have a minute of your time?" Col asked, his face dark with soot and grime, much like Bryce imagined his face was.

Nodding, he led the way up out of the blackened hold. He took a deep breath of fresh air when he got to the deck. When Caylee handed him a water skin, he looked down at it with confusion.

"Drink. Your throat must be hurting you." She pointed at the pouch. "Drink."

He nodded, and as he led Col towards his cabin, he drank the cold water. It felt like heaven on his parched throat. He drained the whole skin before he reached his quarters. Once the door was closed, he walked over to his cabinets and poured a large glass of ale. "Do you want some?" he asked and, without waiting for an answer, poured a second.

"Captain, I fear we are the reason your ship has been put in danger," Col said with a nod as Bryce handed him the cup of ale.

"The reason?" Bryce repeated as he took a large drink of ale. It stung on his raw throat, but it put a fire in his belly. Anger started to build as he studied the wizard. Anger not at the man, nor the fire, but the unknown.

"We have had some, issues," Col replied, the cup of ale still in his hands as he looked back at Bryce.

Dark eyes studied Bryce, eyes that held many secrets. Secrets that Bryce feared had put him and his ship in danger.

"Issues?" Bryce asked. He walked over to sit behind his desk.

"How much do you know about the royal family?" Col asked.

He ripped the handkerchief from around his neck and used it to wipe his face off as he thought of the question and his response. When he was done, he threw it down and answered.

"I know the queen and king rule in Castle Pines. I know there are three children and that all creatures are now seen as equals, at least on the mainland," Bryce answered with a shrug.

Col nodded and, after glancing at his cup of ale, downed the contents in one gulp. He then walked forward and set the glass on the desk and sat opposite Bryce, leaning forward with his hands on his knees.

"Captain. I fear we are in dire times," Col said. "The king and queen have disappeared, along with Prince Zander and Princess Charlotte."

Fear was a buzzing sound in Bryce's ears as he listened to Col's tale of red mists, magical dangers, and a mirror that would show them where the royal family had disappeared to. When Col mentioned a spy, Bryce's anger lit up again.

"On my ship!" he shouted and stood quickly.

"I do not know," Col replied with a shake of his head. "But Princess Caylee has already been attacked."

"Then why bring her?" Bryce demanded.

"According to my research, she is the only one who can look into the mirror," Col replied calmly.

"And the warriors?" Bryce asked, returning to his seat.

"Guards," Col answered. "But I fear we were relaxed on your ship, thinking she was safe."

Saying no words, Bryce nodded, and they sat silently until a knock came on the door.

"Enter," Bryce demanded.

Eno and Adler, a skinny lad of nineteen who was the ship's lookout, came in. The boy spent most of his time in the crow's nest far above the ship's decks, watching for dangers ahead and around the *Fair Maiden*. Bryce knew the kid but since he rarely spoke, didn't know much about him.

"Adler was in the nest and saw everything," Eno advised.

"Report," Bryce ordered, already wishing for another cup of ale.

"Sir, he says he saw a figure sneak down into the hold minutes before he saw smoke," Eno replied as he rested a hand on Adler's skinny shoulder in a protective manner. "The figure then came out and went back down the main stairs."

"Did he recognize the person?" Col asked.

"He did not," Eno replied again for the young lad. "But he thought it was a man."

Bryce nodded and dismissed them, then turned to study Col.

"Who in your group do you suspect?" Bryce asked.

"Captain?" Col asked.

"Do not toy with me. I know you already have a suspect." Bryce leaned forward to study the wizard. "Tell me."

He saw defeat in the man's dark eyes before Col nodded once. "It can no longer hurt her, but I have always suspected Grant Worthington," Col replied.

"The fiancé?" Bryce asked.

"No longer engaged, but yes. Grant has been surrounded by suspicions since the queen and king first disappeared. I had eyes on him in the castle. Guards kept him away from Caylee after the disappearances, but here on the ship..."

"He has been sequestered to his cabin," Bryce said thoughtfully. "Ill?"

"So he said, but since he was confined, I fear I let my guard down," Col replied.

"Eno!" Bryce shouted, and his man entered seconds later. "Bring Mr. Worthington here, under guard." Eno nodded once and immediately left again.

"I do not...." Col started to speak, but Bryce held his hand up to stop the wizard.

"Sir, this is my ship, my rules," Bryce said, giving the man a hard stare. Once Col nodded, Bryce stood and filled the empty cups with ale in a friendly gesture. "I would, however, like your opinion."

When he received a nod from Col, Bryce returned to his seat and thought for a minute before continuing.

"Does he hold magic?" Bryce asked.

"Unknown. I do not think he has magic, but I fear he holds magical items," Col replied.

"So, confining him to his rooms might prove more dangerous?" Bryce asked, when he received a nod. He then continued. "Can you inspect his cabin?"

"The magic that was used on the royals is still unknown to me. It might be better to lock the room, for now," Col advised.

"Understood," Bryce said as the door opened and Eno, along with two dragon warriors, entered. The large men were dragging the angry, pale man between them.

"What is the meaning of this?" Grant demanded. His green eyes filled with anger when they landed on the captain. "I insist your men release me."

"Did you start the fire?" Bryce asked. His voice was calm but his anger was inches from escaping. Had this man started the fire that could have burned his ship down and killed them all?

"I do not know what you mean. I have been in my cabin the entire time," Grant replied, but Bryce saw the lie in the man's eyes.

"You, sir, do not lie very well," Bryce growled as he stood. His hands balled in fists.

"Captain." Col quickly stood and then faced Grant. "Grant, you are suspected of high treason against the royal family. Of causing the disappearance of the queen and king, of Prince Zander and Princess Charlotte. You are also suspected of instigating the attack on Princess Caylee and starting the fire in the cargo hold of the *Fair Maiden*," Col explained as he walked around Grant. His dark eyes narrowed each time he came face to face with him. "What do you say to these charges?"

13

THE LONG ISLAND

Caylee was in the middle of her target practice when the fire started. As the shouts of alarm began, she was confused at first. She looked quickly out to sea for the danger until Col ran towards the front of the ship. Then her confusion quickly turned to fear.

Worry filled her as smoke billowed up from the storage hole, but it quickly turned to panic when she saw Bryce march past her and disappear into the smoke. He had looked so handsome, his face full of anger and determination, that her heart had skipped several beats. But they increased when he didn't return immediately.

As she helped with the water buckets, she only saw him walk out of the dark smoke-filled corridor twice, the last time with Col close behind. They were in his chambers for a long time while she and the others attempted to clean the messy, wet deck. When Eno came out and called for two guards. Her friends Pren and Lolli quickly stepped forward and followed the man down the main stairs.

They returned, marching Grant between them, each holding one of his arms as they went into the captain's chambers. Her heart sank into her stomach, and she suddenly felt ill. Worry that Grant had lashed out because of their argument the night before grew in her. Shaking her head, she stood in disbelief as her mind raced through the possibility that Grant could have started the fire.

Thoughts and past images came to her, images of Grant beyond normal rationalization, his angry face beet red. Images of him standing in her chambers, demanding she fire Erica. Then of him in the castle's hallway, angry at her because she wouldn't make time for him. Even of him trying to tell her not to worry about her missing family, that it wasn't her concern.

Fear and disbelief turned to anger, and she quickly made her way across the wet deck towards the captain's cabin. Her fists clenched and her right hand reached for her short knife as she rushed into the room.

"Where are they!" she demanded as she launched herself at Grant. She hit him hard, and they tumbled down onto the floor. She landed on top of his body, startling him, his green eyes going wide with shock as she drew the knife close to his throat.

"Where is my family!" she hissed inches from his face.

"Stand!" she heard Col shout out at the guards in the room.

"No one move!" she warned. "This is between me and Grant."

"What has gotten into you?" Grant's words squeaked out, and she slowly laid the sharp edge of the knife against his skin.

"I will ask you one more time, where is my family?" she demanded between her bared teeth.

"Caylee?" he squeaked.

"Tell me!" She purposely nicked his neck and took satisfaction when a small trickle of blood leaked out.

"They are gone!" he replied quickly. "Gone and out of your way."

His words shocked her, and she let the knife lift an inch from his skin.

"Out of my way?"

"Yes, now you can be queen, and we can rule together!" Grant hissed in satisfaction. "I can be king!"

"What did you do?" Col demanded.

"I got them out of my way. I knew you would never do anything, never think of getting rid of them as I did. I did it for you, for me. For us." Grant leaned up off the floor towards her. "For us."

Caylee scrambled away; her fingers numb as the realization struck her. When the knife clattered to the floor, Grant scrambled towards it, but Pren and Lolli had him pinned long before his fingers got close to the weapon.

"How, how did you get rid of them?" Bryce's question had everyone's eyes turning towards him.

"I had help. But it was my idea," Grant spat out, his green eyes swiveling back to Caylee. "The sorceress gave me the magic, but I am the one who completed the task."

"Are they dead?" Caylee asked, already feeling her strength leave her body.

"No, but they will be soon." Grant's words had Caylee's eyes narrowing. "The sorceress has your parents; your brother has been banished to Earth, and Charlotte, the little witch, is missing. Lost. She never fell into my trap, so we do not know where she ended up, but she is gone too," he said with satisfaction.

"The sorceress?" Col asked.

"Io Maltesea. She is from Pon Hellz, a world apart from

Genoa. She governs there so I can rule here," Grant spat. "She is more powerful than you and has chosen me to control Genoa."

"What have you done?" Caylee asked, appalled by Grant's words.

"Now that our supplies are gone, we can head back to the mainland," Grant stated as he sat between the two large warriors who once again held his arms. "I heard the cook say that there were enough supplies, and we did not need to stop again for a while. Now that they are gone, we will have to turn around," Grant said calmly as his eyes turned to the captain. "Captain, I order you to turn the ship around. We head back to the mainland. Once there, Caylee and I will get a dragon back to Castle Pines where she will be crowned queen. Then we can finally get married now that her family is not here to stop us. Then I can be king!"

"You're mad," Caylee whispered.

"Take him to the brig," Bryce ordered. He took a step towards Caylee as Grant was forced out of the room still shouting demands.

"Caylee," Bryce said softly, but she shook her head at him and turned to leave.

"I need time." She stopped when she felt Col's hand rest on her arms. "Col, did you know?"

"Did I know he was mad? No," Col said with a shake of his head. "No, but I suspected the rest. I should have told you."

"No," she said as she shook her head at him. "I wouldn't have believed you, not then." Then she walked out of the room.

She found Erica and Svlain already sitting in their room. She took comfort in their presence and tried to smile when she entered, but as Erica rushed towards her for a hug, the tears started down Caylee's cheeks.

"Oh, little bird," Svlain said. She embraced her after Erica had finished hugging her. "Is it true?"

"Oh, Aunt Svlain, it's all true!" Caylee said. She sat on the corner cot in their little room. "All of it. Grant did all those things to get rid of my family. He set the trap at the pass for Zander. He's the one who…" She sobbed and couldn't say anymore as tears overtook her.

"Shh," Svlain said gently, pushing some of Caylee's dark hair behind her ear. "It will all be fine."

"But my family," Caylee wailed. "He sent them to another world."

"Your mother has been out of Genoa before," Svlain said sternly. "And with your father there this time, I am sure they will be just fine. Your brother, well, we all know Zander is probably having a blast on Earth." Caylee looked up at the nymph who studied her with her green eyes. "Remember the car?"

A flash of large dying cats came to Caylee's mind before she remembered Zander's and Corbin's stories of the red sports car.

"I have no doubt he and Corbin are playing with a car while there, and we will get them all back soon," Svlain said, giving Caylee a side hug.

"But what of Charlotte?" Caylee asked.

"Charlotte, she's the one I worry about the least," Svlain said sternly. "Do you not remember that it was she who sent your mother a message years before she was even born. While we were stuck in Midzark."

"The vision," Caylee asked.

"Vision, ha," Svlain said with a bark. "That was no vision. She brought your mother forward in time. Snatched her out of the tub, of all things, and plunked her down into her future self. All so she could take a peek at you three children playing with a ball."

"It was a kite," Caylee said thoughtfully, and suddenly she felt a little better as she remembered the story her mom had told her.

"See!" Svlain said with a smile. "And here we are, on our way to discover their exact location so we can get them back."

"But Svlain, how could I have been so stupid to trust Grant. I almost married him," Caylee said as a shiver ran through her body.

"Posh!" Erica scolded. "You would have seen the light long before the wedding day."

"My little bird is smarter than that, and I never want to hear you call yourself stupid again," Svlain said with a stern look on her face.

"Oh, but I was," Caylee insisted.

"Maybe, but now you are no longer making poor choices, are you?" Erica spoke up.

"And your eyes are seeing the light now, right?" Svlain said.

Smiling at Svlain's misinterpretation of the Earth phrase Erica had used, one which Tresstéanna had taught her long ago, she nodded once.

"There, now do you feel better?" Erica asked as she set a glass of water in Caylee's hands and wiped one of her tears with her handkerchief.

"No and yes," Caylee replied. She took a sip of water. "He set the fire. Oh, the damage he caused," she said miserably.

"Why did he set fire to the food?" Svlain asked quickly.

"He said he wanted us to go back to the mainland now

that we don't have any supplies," Caylee replied, shaking her head.

"Will we? Will we have to turn around?" Erica asked.

"I don't think so. Cen Spa said something about a long island," Caylee replied. "Have either of you heard about it?" Both women shook their heads no. Caylee wondered about the island, part of her yearning for the excitement of the unknown.

The *Fair Maiden* lifted her sails before dinner that night. Bryce and his men kept busy with repairs to the front hold where the fire had been. When he was satisfied with the work, he returned to the aft to check on his other duties.

Bryce wasn't happy that they were headed to the long island. But he had talked with the cook about their supplies and a stop was needed if they were going to continue their journey east. Col had insisted they couldn't delay their travels by turning around, so the stop was agreed upon.

Bryce had hesitated to tell the wizard about the rumors he had heard lately about the island. He figured the warriors would keep a close eye on the princess, so he let the matter drop without speaking any warnings. Caylee would probably spend her time on the ship and never set foot on the island after the events of today.

A smile crossed his face when he once again envisioned Caylee straddling the traitor on the floor, a knife to the man's throat. Her pretty face had been fierce and her green eyes ablaze with her anger. Shaking his head, he watched the sun dip below the water's horizon far behind them. The waves turned a soft pink, reflecting the sky's colors.

"It sure is a pretty sunset," Caylee said from behind him.

"We will have fair weather tomorrow," Bryce replied, keeping his eyes on the sunset.

Caylee came up and rested her arms on the banister to his left. They sat in silence for several minutes as the crew continued to light the lamps that hung about the ship.

"I want to apologize," Caylee finally said, and he turned to study her profile.

"For?" he prompted, no longer watching the sky and water turn pretty colors when he had a more beautiful scene to study, one which was much closer.

"For the fire. For Grant, and all he did," Caylee explained.

Her shoulders slumped. She wore a dark blue dress tonight that had silver threads coiled in the neckline and small buttons set along the sleeves. Her hair was wrapped in a tight bun at the nape of her neck. A single ribbon was tied around her small throat with a round pendant hanging from it.

"Why are you apologizing for him?" Bryce asked as he leaned closer to get a look at the image on the pendant.

Caylee turned towards him and caught him looking, so she held it up with a smile on her lips. He saw the outline of a mermaid and returned her smile.

"This was made by my mother's sorcerer. Belent carved it after they returned home from their trip to Midzark," Caylee advised him. "It's my mother."

Bryce leaned closer and his eyes grew wide with shock. "That's my mermaid!" he exclaimed. He reached out to touch the broach with his index finger as Caylee laughed.

"Your mermaid is my mother too," Caylee said with another smile. "That's why I chose this ship."

Bryce tilted his head in confusion as the light around them grew dim.

"The *Fair Maiden* carries an image of my mother in mermaid form." When this explanation didn't clear things up for him, he pulled his finger away from the broach to look up at her.

"When my parents traveled down into the Kylix to return the goddess, they found themselves in another land called Midzark," Caylee said as she dropped the broach back in place. "Mom had a magical flower that allowed her to turn into a mermaid. Dad quickly followed, though I don't see many images of Dad sporting a tail." She laughed, then continued. "Mom returned the goddess to her cradle, which was under water, and then they returned home."

"Where the story of their adventures and success was told to the world," Bryce said with a smile.

"You knew the story," Caylee said bashfully.

"Yes, but I like hearing you tell it to me," Bryce teased. "Is that when your parents fell in love?"

"Oh no, they fell in love long before that," Caylee replied. "I think for Mom it was when Dad kidnapped her, then rode them both off of a cliff, but for Dad it was before that," she said with a smirk. "He said he fell in love when she gave him a granola bar." She quickly described what a granola bar was, but left out the details of what form her dad had been in.

"Bryce, the long island..." Caylee asked, turning to look out at the dark sea beyond the banister. "Can you tell me about it?"

"There is not much on the island," Bryce explained as he stood close to her. "But Pescara, that island holds more wonder." He spent several minutes describing the vast island of Pescara. "The Tower of Della Val is something to see," he continued. "Its white petals open during the day, leaving all around to marvel at its height."

"And it glows?" she asked, bumping him with her shoulder. "Or are you just teasing me?"

"Yes, it glows," he said with a smile. "Brighter than the moons."

"Will we see it from the ship?"

"Yes." He was deep in thought for several minutes until Eno interrupted.

Bryce spent the rest of the night making preparations for the following day's supply stop. When his mind would go back to his talk with Caylee, he would find himself sitting still with a stupid grin on his face.

Long before breakfast the next day, they docked in the small port on the island's northern side. Bryce's men knew to keep close to the ship, but their duties kept them busy. Cargo was ordered according to the cook's request and payment was made to the port master. Since Eno was in charge of this, Bryce went over the logs and was in the middle of copying their recent loss into his records when Eno came in with a frown on his face.

"Sir, the warrior wizard is asking if the lady Erica has been seen on board recently," Eno asked, his face dark with worry.

"Is she not in her chambers?" Bryce asked, not even glancing up from his books.

"Sir, it appears the wizard and a few others went ashore," Eno replied. "The little wind nymph was one of them, along with the princess."

"What?" Bryce asked, finally looking up from his desk. "How many went ashore?"

"Nine total. But when they returned, Erica and her man Brett were not with them," Eno stated. "But now Tonkee said they have gone past the time allotted for return."

"When were they to be back?" Bryce asked as he stood and moved towards the door.

"Two hours ago," Eno said with a shake of his head. "Col asked me to speak with you."

"Chaos," Bryce states as he raised his hand for the bird to fly onto it. "Come." He walked out into the bright afternoon sunlight as Chaos' claws dug into his shoulder.

"Sir," Col said quickly as he drew near. "Tonkee and I need—"

"I know what you need, I did not authorize shore leave," Bryce said sternly. "Chaos, find them." The bird quickly lifted and soared into the sky. "Now, tell me," He demanded as Caylee came rushing up to them.

"Oh, Bryce, she's missing," Caylee said quickly, her eyes wide with fear.

"We will find her." Col patted her slender shoulder with his large hand.

"We were shopping along the pier when she and Brett saw a shop they wanted to enter. The rest of us continued down the street, and I told them we would meet at the far end in a half hour. But when we finally got there, they weren't there. We waited for a whole hour before going back and searching the store." Caylee twisted a purple ribbon at her dress's waistline with her hands.

"And has the man Brett been found?" Bryce asked, already concerned.

"No, at least not in the shop," Col provided.

"Did you go behind the shop?" Bryce asked. He quickly

turned to Eno. "Never mind. Eno, gather the men." He turned back to his cabin to collect his weapons.

"What are you doing?" Caylee demanded as she and Col followed him into his cabin.

"I am going to search the village." He picked up his broad sword, which hung on the wall near his desk.

When he turned, he was shocked to find Caylee bending down and lifting the front of her skirt. Since she wore leather pants and long boots under the skirt, he only paused a minute.

"You are staying here," he demanded. He heard Col snicker once. He turned his attention to the wizard and saw a frown on the man's face.

"Good luck," Col said, and quickly walked out of the room.

"What?" was all Bryce got out before Caylee was checking the straps of a short sword.

"I'm going." She reached up to tie her long hair back into a single braid.

"No," he replied as he pointed in her direction. He fell silent when she turned her green eyes on him.

"I outrank you, Captain," she said quickly. "That is my best friend, and if you think she's in trouble, I am going."

Shaking his head, he marched past her and turned to see Eno had gathered not only five of his men but all the dragon warriors, one who quickly handed Caylee her bow and quiver.

"You all cannot go." He turned to Col. "We will draw too much attention."

"If we split up, we won't," Caylee replied sweetly.

"Eno, take that half along the northern roads. I will take the others south." Bryce stomped off down the plank towards town.

14

TRAVELERS BEWARE

Caylee wasn't going to panic yet. After all, maybe Erica and Brett were still shopping. Maybe the two were having fun exploring the outlying village and had lost track of time?

And maybe pigs could fly.

Her thoughts turned darker the longer they searched the village. Panic started to rise with each step. They had retraced their way through the village, this time with Bryce in tow.

"Are you sure this is the store?" Bryce demanded as they stood outside the little storefront that sported the name "Auntie Willies." There were a few ceramics in the window along with two wooden chairs.

"Yes. She saw a blue kettle she was interested in," Caylee replied, her hands on her hips. "But we checked..." She stopped talking when Bryce ignored her and entered the store, leaving her standing there. She quickly followed with a frown on her face. The little white-haired lady behind the counter looked up with a smile.

"Back so soon?" she asked when she saw Caylee.

"Yes, Ms. Mizi, I'm still looking for my friends," Caylee explained. She stood back when Bryce moved forward.

"How much?" he demanded as he quickly rounded the small counter and stood over the older woman.

"Bryce!" Caylee scoffed only to be quickly shushed by him.

"Tell me!" he hissed back at the woman. "The price!"

"Oh, dear," Ms. Mizi said with a sweet smile. "I'm afraid she has already been sold."

"Sold?" Caylee asked.

"When? No, where?" Bryce demanded.

"I believe a gentleman who lives along the southern shores was the successful bidder." Ms. Mizi tilted her head back to Caylee. "Are you still interested in the little pot?"

"What of the man?" Bryce demanded.

"Oh, he was a fighter. No use selling them when they can fight like that." The sweet smile came again to Caylee's shock.

"Caylee!" Bryce barked once and then grabbed her arm and quickly marched her out of the store.

"She has been sold?" Caylee asked as their group hurried down the road leading south out of town.

"Yes, but first let's find Brett," Bryce stated as he let out a loud whistle.

Unsure what he was doing, Caylee glanced quickly to the sky and almost squealed when a dark shadow flew over them. Chaos landed on Bryce's shoulder, and her shock deepened when the bird started speaking in perfect sentences.

"I found the man," Chaos informed them. "The group with the woman went into the forest south of town. I cannot follow."

"He speaks?" Col asked, speaking Caylee's own astonishment.

"Yes," Bryce barked, turning to the group. "You two, go back to the ship and make sure no one else leaves, including the other nymph. Tell Kent to lock it up. Chaos, show us," he demanded. The bird quickly lifted into the air.

They followed the bright red bird out of town along a dirt road. Before they passed the last house, the other party, led by Eno, joined them.

"I hope to catch up with them before the forest. If not, it might be better if you return to the ship and catch up with us further south," Bryce explained to Eno as they continued their fast pace down the dirt road.

There were few travelers along the road. Most had wooden carts filled with odd purchases. Caylee saw that each person carried weapons, but since they all left the large group alone, she ignored them and kept looking for her missing friends.

"There!" she shouted when she saw a dark figure lying along the side of the road.

Brett lay in a dirty pile in a small ditch near a large rock. His clothing was torn, and blood leaked from his lip and his left temple. Col quickly used his healing magic on the man, who then awoke with a start.

"Where is she?" Brett demanded as he tried to get up from the ground. It took three of them to hold him down until they could check him for more wounds.

"Calm down," Bryce ordered.

"They took her!" Brett said bewildered. "Sold her right in front of me. Sold us both, but then they left me when I attacked them."

"We know," Caylee said. She wiped the dried blood off her friend's face. "We have the bird tracking her."

"We have to find her," Brett demanded.

After Col confirmed he didn't find any more injuries, they helped Brett stand. They tracked their missing friend to the edge of a vast forest before Bryce called a halt to their travels.

"Look, we have two or three hours before it starts getting dark. We have to be smart about this." He turned to Col. "Can your magic be used to track her?"

"No," Col replied.

"Mine can," Caylee stated after she spotted movement high up in the nearest tree. Without another word, she stepped forward and did something she rarely did. She used her magic.

Her magic was one of her heart, much like her mother's magic. She could talk to animals. But unlike her mother, Caylee had not spent years perfecting her powers. Since the disaster years ago north of Tharian, with the large cats, she refrained from using it. However, with thoughts of her small friend Erica being sold, Caylee set aside her fears and reached out to her inborn magic.

"Hello," she said, her power floating through each syllable of her word.

"More humans," came the response only Caylee could understand.

"Hello, can you please come down here?" She smiled when a small brown creature scampered down the limbs of the nearest tree. It looked like a type of monkey. It was tiny and had a long bushy tail and big round eyes.

"It looks like a lemur," Bryce stated, and Caylee heard wonder in his voice as the creature came close to where she stood.

"Hello, I'm Caylee." She smiled at the creature. *"I'm looking for my friend."*

"I'm Stemp," the creature replied in its chirping sounds. *"Humans came in my forest. Are you going to enter too?"*

"Do you know which way they went?" Caylee asked as her friends drew closer to her.

"South," Stemp replied.

"Can you show me?" Caylee asked.

When Stemp nodded, Caylee turned to her friends. "He says they took her south. He will show us."

"Eno, return to the ship, set sail for the southern tip of the island. Go quickly and keep an eye out for our signal," Bryce instructed. Eno and two of his men took off back down the road. Then Bryce turned to Caylee and nodded once. "Lead the way."

Bryce knew the road went from the northern tip of the long island to its southern tip. There were two main towns on the island. The northern one was called Norrish, while the southern one was simply named End. The forest wasn't deep, but it was long and thick with underbrush. No trails could be seen, and the light disappeared under the branches of the tall trees.

The little creature led them into the dense forest that ran on the eastern side of the road. If the group they tracked was hiding in the forest, Caylee's little animal friend would aid them in finding them. However, if the band had just used the forest to escape being tracked, then their main destination would be the southern town of End.

Either way, Bryce didn't want to have to retrace their

steps all the way back north if, or when, they were successful in rescuing Erica from the slave trade. He hoped Eno would get the ship south in time to pick them up.

As they fought their way through the thick underbrush and branches, Bryce's thoughts turned dark when he envisioned the little nymph and her situation. For too long, the island had been used to hold the scum of Genoa. Most who resided here had never set foot off the island, which meant most had never seen any of the vast creatures the mainland held.

Nymphs, whisps, and trolls were not found here. So when an exotic person came to the island, they were either attacked and killed or quickly snatched up and sold to the elite, who then displayed them as an oddity. In Erica's case, Bryce was sure it was the latter.

"What will they do to her?" Caylee asked from beside him.

"They will not harm her," he quickly replied.

"But they bought her?" Caylee asked.

"Yes," he said with a shake of his head. "Most who live here have never seen a nymph. My guess is she has been sold to a wealthy landowner on the southern tip of the island."

A high squeal came from the lemur and Caylee smiled. "He says we move close to the group."

"Draw your swords," Bryce instructed, and he watched with fascination as Caylee drew an arrow and notched in her bow.

They moved forward in silence, vines and branches barring their way. A thin trail that snaked ahead into the darkness kept them walking in a single line.

"Is it sure they went this way?" Col asked from in front of Caylee.

"Yes, he is sure." She looked up at the little furry creature.

"How close?" Bryce asked. He was a step ahead of Caylee now.

"Twenty, maybe thirty yards," Caylee responded. "The forest ends to our left."

"I think there should be cliffs here, if I remember correctly," Bryce supplied. His eyes scanned to his left, but he couldn't detect any end to the dark trees.

"Stemp says there are cliffs. He says the water is deepest there too," she provided.

Bryce remembered the form of the island and thought there was a portion of land that might stick out into the ocean. If he remembered right, the land then turned back west towards where the southern town lay. "We must be near the end of the forest."

"There!" Col shouted. Bryce felt the air sizzle with magic as the wizard reached the small clearing first.

"Don't hit her!" Bryce heard Caylee shout as they rushed forward towards the opening.

The sky was a dark blue where the trees to their left gave way to a high rocky cliff. Col was standing to the right of the small trail, his hands glowing orange as he sent small balls of magic out towards two large men who were holding onto Erica's arms. Bryce had a second to register how small the woman looked between the men before six more, each with their weapons raised, rushed at them.

He raised his sword and dispatched the first man with a quick jab. He turned to his left and saw Caylee shoot a skinny man in the arm. The arrow barely slowed the attacker. Bryce rushed forward towards him, his sword already slashing out at the man. His weapon clashed with the man's sword as Caylee quickly swept at the attacker's feet with her bow.

"He's down!" she shouted. She turned with a new arrow already notched. All the kidnappers were engaged in battle with the dragon warriors. She struggled to shoot without hitting her friends. "Erica!" she shouted, and Bryce spun in time to see a man race back into the forest with the nymph slung over his shoulders.

When Caylee raced after him, Bryce's heart almost stopped. "Wait!" he shouted at Caylee's back. He quickly took chase when she didn't slow down. He reached the trail seconds behind Caylee, and the forest quickly swallowed them up. The sound of fighting died behind them as they raced down the trail.

"Faster!" Caylee shouted.

"Let me pass!" Bryce ordered but the trail was so narrow that he couldn't push his way past her.

"There he is!" she shouted, and he heard her drop her bow as she took a running leap at the man's legs. She did a full tackle and the man, along with Erica, tumbled to the ground in a heap. Bryce raced up and pointed his sword at the man's throat while the two women tried to get untangled.

"Stay down!" Bryce growled at the man who lay there with his eyes wide.

"Hey!" They heard a shout.

Bryce looked up in time to see ten large men running toward them from another trail. Turning, he grabbed the neck of Caylee's dress and pulled her up, and then propelled her back down the trail, away from the oncoming attackers. Then he reached down and hoisted Erica over his shoulders and took off after Caylee, who had quickly stooped and picked up her fallen bow.

"Run!" He all but pushed Caylee forward, away from the danger that was pursuing them.

They ran back towards the little clearing and their friends as he shouted a warning at the others. He turned to let Erica down from his shoulders, and Brett rushed forward.

With weapons raised, the small band of fighters faced the trail and watched in horror as over twenty enemies emerged from the forest. They were outnumbered, but Bryce knew the dragon warriors were fierce fighters and hoped for the best.

Before the fighting even started, he saw ten more islanders emerge from the northern trail behind them. He stood in front of the women, trying to block them. Caylee now stood with her bow ready. Brett too stood next to Bryce, trying to safeguard the women.

As he watched the dragon warriors rush forward towards their attackers, Caylee's story of her parents' meeting came back to him. Spinning around, he looked down the cliff at the water far below. The cliff they stood on was over a hundred yards high. He didn't see any rocks on the shore below nor any jutting out of the water.

"Caylee," he shouted. He raised his sword when an attacker came near. "I think we should jump." He blocked the attacker's sword and pushed the man back as Pren rushed forward to engage the enemy.

"You and Erica jump," he shouted again. When he turned, Caylee already had her bow strapped about her body and Erica's hand in hers. She was coaxing her friend towards the edge of the cliff. "Brett, get the women over the edge," he shouted. With his free hand, he pointed out to sea where the *Fair Maiden* had just sailed into view.

Brett nodded once, then raced at the women. He lifted

them, one under each of his arms, and quickly jumped over the side of the cliff. Bryce watched them disappear, then spun back towards the battle in time to see the sharp edge of a sword come slashing down at him.

Caylee swallowed a bucket of water before her head finally lifted above the salty water of the ocean. Brett still had ahold of her, and she saw with relief that Erica was tucked under his other arm. Brett's grip was almost too tight, and she could feel his long legs bumping into hers while he kicked to keep them afloat.

"We can swim!" she shouted, and he quickly released them both. Her heavy skirt wrapped about her legs, and she had to use her arms to keep her head above the water.

"Swim towards the boat," he shouted, and quickly glanced up as another person jumped into the water next to them. Concerned it was an attacker, Caylee felt relief when she saw Pren's head rise above the water.

"My lady!" he shouted and moved towards her. "Move away from the edge so you do not get squished."

With the aid of Pren, she swam away from the cliff. Before they had gone too far, they had been joined by Eyelan, Bre, and Subree. The three women were of the lowest rank in the dragon protectors and Caylee knew the rest would follow based on their ranks.

Honi, West, Dovic, and Parsa came crashing down into the water all at once, each with their weapons sheathed. When Kayla and Reg joined them, both at level seven,

Caylee knew most of her friends were already in the water. However, she hadn't seen Bryce yet, and worry for the captain filled her.

"Where are the others?" she asked, her eyes on the top of the cliff. From this distance, she couldn't hear any of the fighting, and the waves kept trying to push them all back toward the shore.

"There!" Pren shouted.

Caylee looked where she pointed. Tonkee's and Lolli's heads could be seen high up on the cliff. When she saw a dark-haired Bryce between them, she breathed a sigh of relief. Until she saw he was slumped forward.

"No!" She watched in horror as Lolli wrapped his thick arms around Bryce's middle and then spun on the spot, throwing the still form of the captain over the cliff and into the water. Tonkee landed seconds behind the still form and when Caylee didn't see her bright red curls break the surface right away, she panicked.

"Look out for Lolli!" Pren shouted as several wet heads swam towards the last warriors to hit the water.

"Where is he?" Tonkee shouted when she finally surfaced above the water. Her freckles stood out on her pale face as she searched the water.

"Over here!" Lolli shouted, and Caylee saw the warrior once again had his thick arm wrapped around Bryce's shoulders.

"Everyone, swim for the ship!" Col shouted, and Caylee realized she hadn't even seen the wizard jump off the cliff, she had been so focused on Bryce.

"Is he..." she started to ask Lolli, but Pren was there beside her before she could continue.

"Swim, Your Highness. We will check on him once we get to safety." He lifted her arm.

"I need to lose my skirts," she shouted. She tried to untie them from around her waist.

"Here," Pren said and lifted his small knife. "I'll cut them off."

Once the skirts were gone, she quickly swam with the others to where two smaller boats had been lowered down from the *Fair Maiden*. By the time Caylee made it on deck, her arms and legs felt like stone. She had swallowed more water than she should have, and the taste of salt made her stomach turn.

As she lay on the deck, she lifted her head to watch them hoist Bryce onto the ship. Col rushed over to see if he could help and a second later, she saw the soft glow of his healing magic.

"Where is Zain?" she heard him shout.

"He got hurt saving me," Erica said weakly next to her.

"No, he got hurt saving both of us," Caylee replied. She smiled at her friend. "But he's strong and Zain and Col are good at healing."

"Don't worry, Erica," Brett said as he tried rubbing Erica's hands so they would be warm. "Here, here is a blanket." He placed a soft brown cover around Erica's shoulders, then went to find another one for Caylee.

"He was worried sick about you," Caylee told her friend.

"He fought so hard when they tried to take me," Eric stated as tears welled up in her eyes. "I tried to use the wind to save him, but they had me tied up." Tears spilled down her cheek, and she quickly wiped them away with the blanket.

"You're safe now," Caylee said and moved to hug her friend while looking over at where Bryce still lay unconscious.

15

THE WATCH DUTY

Caylee sat and watched the rise and fall of Bryce's chest in the faint light of his cabin. Col and Zain stood close by and talked in hushed tones, while Svlain moved about making a pot of tea. The small stove in the cabin had been lit and its warmth seeped slowing into Caylee's frozen limbs.

She had changed into a dry, warm dress minutes ago, then had rushed back up to find they had already stripped Bryce from the waist up and had his wounds wrapped. The bandages covered most of his chest, and she felt a sickness settle in her stomach.

New thoughts and feelings confused Caylee as she settled into a nearby chair. Memories of Bryce flashed through her head, and she let them take over as she watched him breathe. She remembered the first time she had seen him, standing on the pier, his legs spread wide while Chaos sat on his shoulder. The wide smile had flashed, and his tan eyes had almost laughed at her.

She then had an image of him standing with her at the ship's railing, the sun's light turning a pretty hue of pinks and oranges. His dark hair waved in the breeze while he told her about places he had seen or been to. Then the image of him marching past her into the billowing smoke of the fire caused her heart to skip a beat. He had been so brave, so bold walking straight into the blaze. Then she thought about him standing before her and Erica, protecting them both from the attackers on the island. He had protected her and her friend with such courage and fierceness.

Her feelings intensified, but then she started to doubt herself. She had once had romantic feelings about another man, Grant. But even now, sitting in the dark cabin onboard a ship, she realized those feelings had been different.

Grant had been a comfortable companion to her. She thought he had been almost easy, like slipping on a favorite pair of shoes. He had just shown up at the castle and immediately stepped into the role of a suitor. Grant had not filled her with romance. Her relationship with him had been more like a strong pull of newness.

She tried to analyze the feelings she had towards Grant and found she only held anger towards him now. Forgotten were all the spouts of love she had claimed to feel when defending him to her parents. The demands of romantic justice now seemed frivolous to her, and her cheeks pinkened when she thought of how harsh she had been to her family and friends when they had told her of their dislike towards Grant.

How had she been so blind? And more importantly, how could she ever trust herself or her heart when it came to men now? She had been fooled once by a handsome face. Sitting and watching Bryce fighting for his life, she was filled with a feeling of dread.

Was she romanticizing her feelings towards the captain

because he had shown her kindness? Maybe because he was brave and had helped save her and Erica? Maybe he only felt friendship towards her? After all, she was a princess, and he was a sea captain. A man who lived an exciting life on the ocean, a life full of adventures. Maybe she should set aside romance. Maybe her heart was destined to be broken.

"He's alive," Zain said, his face sober as he ran a hand through his disheveled hair.

"I was able to close the smaller wounds, but the one on his shoulder is too deep. I will need three more tries before it closes completely," Caylee heard Col say.

"Here." Svlain set a warm cup of tea in Caylee's hands. "Drink this."

The cup helped warm her cold hands, and she smiled at Svlain. The smile fell away again when she looked back at Bryce.

"How is he?" she quietly asked the nymph.

"I have seen worse," Svlain replied, tucking the sheet around Bryce's chest. "Down in the Kylix, our friend Kip got badly hurt."

"From the roots!" Caylee said with a nod.

"Yes. The burns were deep, and it took a while for him to heal," Svlain said, her green eyes studying the sleeping captain. "But like Kip, Captain Rouen is young, and he will heal."

"You should go lie down," Zain said as he squatted next to her chair. "The water was cold, and you all are suffering from hypothermia."

"I'm fine here," Caylee replied with a smile. She lifted the cup to her lips for a sip. The warm liquid seemed to flow down her core and settle somewhere in the middle of her aching stomach. She took two more deep sips before she felt her eyes grow heavy with sleep.

"Leave her here," Svlain said softly. She lifted the cup from Caylee's hands as the medicine took effect. Caylee nodded off to sleep.

"I do not care! I am the captain on this ship, not you." Bryce's voice woke Caylee, and she frowned at the curse words that followed.

"Lad, I do not care if you are the king himself, I am your healer, and you will stay put until I tell you," Zain said calmly, and she watched him lean down over the dark form lying on the bed.

"Where is Eno?" Bryce demanded. Caylee heard his voice crack a little and knew it was the pain that caused it.

"He is doing his duties for your ship," Zain replied. "Hold still."

"Ouch!" Bryce responded, and Caylee smiled as she leaned forward.

"If you are a nice patient, Zain will give you candy afterward," she said sweetly.

"What are you doing here?" Bryce demanded. He turned to Zain. "What is she doing here?"

"*She*," Caylee said as she stood and walked closer, "was concerned for you and then fell asleep next to your warm stove."

"I need to..." Bryce started to say but he was interrupted when Svlain walked into the room. Bryce saw her and tried to pull the bed covers higher on his exposed chest. "Ugh, another woman."

"Don't be so shy," Caylee said with a smile.

"Out! All women out of my cabin," Bryce tried to shout.

"Now, that is no way to speak to us," Svlain said with a smile as she set the new bandages down next to the bed. "After all we did for you."

"He's just grouchy because we saw his manly chest," Caylee said with a smirk. "Svlain, remind me to thank you for the tea." The teasing wasn't lost on Svlain, who darkened a little and dipped her eyes downward.

"Sorry, but you needed your rest," Svlain muttered before moving to help change Bryce's bandages.

"Ouch!" Bryce said again. He frowned at Caylee. "Do you have to be here?"

She gave him a goofy grin and then crossed her eyes at him and stuck her tongue out. "I like it here."

"Well, at least turn your back or something," he growled.

"I saw it all last night." She smiled when he stuck his tongue out at her. "Zain, I think your patient is having a fit of modesty."

"Children," Zain said with a sigh. "Behave."

"Oh, this has healed nicely," Svlain said, but Caylee wrinkled her nose at the dark red opening on Bryce's left shoulder.

"I think I will wait outside." She felt her head go a little light.

"Sit down before you pass out!" Svlain ordered, and Caylee felt her butt hit the floor a second later.

"I forgot you faint around blood," Svlain stated as she helped Caylee to the chair. When the buzzing in Caylee's ears stopped, she heard Bryce shouting from the bed.

"What happened! Is she alright?"

"Our little bird is just squeamish around the red stuff,"

Zain said with a chuckle. "Now lie back down before you rip your wound open again.

"I'm fine," Caylee said but her voice sounded far off.

"Here, drink this." Svlain passed a cup to her.

"It's not tea, is it?" Caylee asked, leaning her head back.

"Just water," Svlain replied with a smile.

"Thank you," Caylee said as Svlain moved back towards the bed.

"Stay there until I get these wounds repacked," Svlain scolded, and Caylee sat in silence for a time, feeling embarrassed. She had always felt faint around blood, ever since the cat attack when she had been small. But having Bryce see her weakness had her cheeks going pink.

After Svlain was finished with the bandages, Caylee quickly made her escape and headed down to her room to get ready for the day.

Bryce's frustration grew that day as he lay in bed. He was being watched by either the healer, Zain, or the man's watchdogs. It seemed that the male dragon warriors had nothing better to do than sit by his bed and force him to rest. He started thinking of it as the watch duty of the invalid, which caused him to frown. Not that they needed to force him to sleep, which was another thing that Bryce was frustrated by. He felt that every time he blinked, hours had passed because he had nodded off to sleep.

Once, when he woke, Caylee was there to check on him. He wanted to talk to her, but before he could speak, she made a quick escape out the door. Her fast retreat only caused him more frustration.

"Here, go ahead and try this soup," Svlain urged him the next time he awoke.

"I just ate," he grumbled as he tried to open his eyes fully.

"That was lunch, this is dinner." She frowned down at him until he opened his mouth for the spoon.

The soup tasted great. He recognized the cook's stew filled with spices and tomatoes. There was a thin slice of bread next to his bowl, but Svlain kept spooning the soup towards him until he grumbled that he could feed himself.

"If you think you can..." the nymph said with a smile. "Let us help you sit up; I do not want to reopen that wound now that Col and Zain just got it closed."

It took help from the dragon warrior Lolli, who was currently on watch duty. But once he was settled back against the pillows, Bryce was able to hold the bowl himself. When the bowl was empty, he reached for the bread and felt a tight pull along his chest from his wound. Glancing down, he saw the bandage was smaller than previously, but there were two new angry red slashes on his left forearm and bicep.

"How bad was I?" he asked. He glanced up when the room remained quiet. Lolli and Svlain gave each other looks, then the dragon warrior scooted off back to the corner where he had been sitting.

"Let us just say another inch to the right and a hair deeper, and we would not be having this conversation." Svlain picked up the plate and handed him the slice of bread. "Do you want more soup?"

Her answer had his stomach rolling around for a second, then it growled, and he nodded.

"Yes. And I need to speak with Eno." He took a big bite of the bread.

After a while, Eno came in along with the wizard Col. Both had stern expressions on their faces when Bryce asked if he could get out of bed.

"Not until Zain says you can," Col scolded. He placed his hands on his hips as he studied Bryce. "But your color is better."

"Yes, you are no longer pale," Eno replied. "The ship is sailing fine. We should make Pescara the day after tomorrow."

"Any problems?" he asked. He smiled when Chaos flew into the room using the open window.

"None to speak of," Eno replied. "No more troubles from the long island and the weather is clear for now."

"And where have you been?" Bryce asked the bird, who had settled on the foot of his bed. With his question, Chaos started to preen his feathers.

"Him? He's been with his girlfriend," Eno said with a smile. He turned to leave the room as Col laughed and then explained the other man's statement.

"Your bird there and Caylee have had quite a time together," Col explained, then he too turned and left. Svlain returned with another bowl of soup. This time she had a plate of fruit with it and left it on his side table for him.

"Caylee?" Bryce asked the bird after the nymph had left again. He saw Chaos pause in his grooming before he reached for the soup.

"Why not?" the bird asked before attacking his feathers again.

"What have you two been discussing?" Bryce asked as he started on the second bowl.

"Why, you, of course." Chaos settled on the bed, quite

satisfied with his appearance. "The princess had never met a fully talking bird before and asked many questions about my origins."

"I bet she did," Bryce mumbled in between bites of bread.

"She also has not traveled out this far and wanted to learn more about Pescara," Chaos continued, his odd eyes glancing Bryce's way without blinking. "She also was under the impression you knew your father and that your mother runs a shop." At Chaos' words, Bryce spilled a steaming drop of soup on his bare chest and cursed as it burned.

"You did not tell her the truth, did you?" Bryce hissed as he tried to mop up the spill.

"It is not my place to correct a lady," Chaos scolded. He resettled his feathers quickly. "If you feel you need to lie to her, then that is your business."

Bryce glanced around and was thankful that Lolli still sat in the corner of the room, his dark eyes closed, and his thick arms crossed over his chest. Bryce hoped the man was asleep but couldn't take any chances.

"Look, we agreed this was better, for all involved." Bryce nudged the bird with his foot from under the covers.

"Yes, but if you feel for her, she deserves the truth," Chaos scolded. "She might appreciate that you two have more in common than a love of the sea." With this, the bird hopped off the bed and flew over to his perch near the window.

Bryce studied the black night sky outside the windows. He marveled that today was the first day in years that he had spent doing nothing. He had been so busy the last few years that he hadn't had time to think much about his past.

A past that wasn't filled with a loving mother who ran a shop, nor a father who was a barge captain. In reality, Bryce hated the bastard that had sired him. Bryce's mother was another story. She wasn't the nice patron of a family shop as he had told Caylee. The reality was much harsher. She ran a shop, but her wares were usually illegal, and her transactions often took place in dark rooms that stank of ale and smoke. Bryce had escaped his mother's clutches long before she could think to sell him.

One thing was true—his childhood had been filled with ships. After all, Parros was a city on the edge of the ocean. Its coastal location allowed Bryce to explore and escape his childhood.

Before he was old enough to be on his own, he had obtained a job as a cabin boy on his first ship. Within two years he had moved up the ranks, and he was second in command before he could grow a beard. He had obtained the *Fair Maiden* with hard work and a sharp mind, which was something he valued more than any hard lesson he had learned in Parros.

His eyes turned back to the sleeping form of the dragon warrior. After confirming the man was asleep, he lifted his right hand in the pale light of the room. When the flare of magic glowed from his fingers, he frowned at it as thoughts of his father filled his mind.

"Curse the gift and the man," he hissed, then he let the magic die away from his fingertips.

Grant Worthington paced the dirty cell once again and snarled as he walked. The brig he was in was only six by ten feet long. His captors provided him with a cot, a pot, and three meals a day.

Every day the large ship guards would come to clean his cell or provide food and water. The men kept a close eye on him and had their swords held at the ready if he made any wrong move. But he had a plan. Well, the sorceress had one.

The day before, while the ship was moving to rescue the landing party, his guards had been called away. Finally left alone, he had been able to use the amulet to call his mistress.

"Why do you bother me?" Io Maltesea had hissed.

"I have been discovered," Grant said into the glowing red pendant.

"What has happened?" she demanded.

"We reached the long island, but they have locked me up. All attempts to return to the mainland have failed," Grant explained. *"She knows it was I who set the trap for her parents."*

"Fool!" Io Maltesea hissed, and the pendant grew deep red in Grant's hands. *"Have you not wed the woman yet?"*

"No, she broke off our engagement."

"Come to me and bring the little princess." Io Maltesea's words excited Grant as the light in the pendant faded.

He had time to ponder and plan. But escaping from his cell would be difficult. He had to ensure his attempt would work, as he knew he might only get one chance at Caylee. He didn't intend to waste it.

16
____

THE OPEN SEA

Caylee watched the warriors sparring on the deck below and sighed deeply. She stood on the cathead of the ship inches above the figure of the mermaid. Her hands wrapped around the banister while her thoughts were elsewhere.

She had briefly checked on Bryce that morning and discovered him asleep with Lolli once again standing guard. The large warrior had been vigilant in his watch. Caylee thought it was because he felt responsible for the captain, since he was the one who had thrown Bryce over the cliff's edge two days earlier.

Caylee had eaten breakfast with Erica and Brett, who were now talking about getting married when they returned to the mainland. Brett's parents were excited about the union, and Svlain and Erica had spent most of the previous day talking about Erica joining them down in Rigel City to live. Caylee had been saddened to think about her friend leaving her but realized it was bound to happen eventually. She wanted Erica to be happy so said nothing.

But this would mean that Caylee would be left alone

again. If she didn't find her family, what would happen to her then? She did not doubt that the council would crown her queen, but Caylee didn't want that. She didn't mind the chores of the seat, the council meetings, and day-to-day jobs. But when she thought of a lifetime with these duties, Caylee became depressed.

It was these thoughts that kept her from seeing the beautiful vision ahead of her. The sparkle of the sun's rays off the water, the blue of the sky, and four of Genoa's moons shimmering above were unseen by her. Another sigh escaped her lips when she felt movement behind her.

"What a pretty sight," Svlain said as she came to stand behind Caylee.

"What?" Caylee asked and turned to study her mom's friend. "Oh, yeah, I guess."

"Little bird," Svlain said, placing a hand on Caylee's cheek. "What bothers you today?"

"I don't know. Everything. Nothing." Caylee placed her hand over Svlain's, which still rested on her cheek.

"Restless?" Svlain replied with a nod. "Love will do that."

"Love?" Caylee asked quickly and would have moved back a step except the railing was there.

"Oh, child. I see it in your eyes. I never saw it there with Grant, but I see it now with your captain." Svlain smiled and grabbed Caylee's hands. She held them in her own. "Do you question that?"

"Oh, Svlain, I don't know what I feel. I thought I loved Grant, but how could I have loved such an evil man and not known his true intentions?" Caylee squeezed her friend's hands.

"You doubt your choices then, not your love?" Svlain

tilted her head. Her long green hair fell to the side before the wind blew it back around to rest behind her.

"I do. How do you know? How do you know if a person is good and how do you know if you love them? Or maybe you just, I don't know, have indigestion?"

Svlain laughed and dropped Caylee's hands, then moved to the banister to look out at the water.

"When I met Zain, I admired him. I was awed by his healing abilities and intimidated by his fighting skills. However, I was impressed by his overwhelming care for the injured. He was so gentle and kind to me in my time of need. But I fell in love with the man, not his actions. Those only helped ease the fall," Svlain said with a smile as her green eyes looked out at the water.

"Bryce is kind," Caylee said. She leaned against the railing and watched the fighters down below them. "I see now that Grant was not very kind. Not really. He would do nice things for me, but never for others. But I have seen Bryce do kind things for others without hesitation."

Svlain nodded and leaned against the banister. They watched in silence as Zain came out of the captain's cabin and joined the exercise below them. When Zain stripped off his tunic and started to spar with Col, Caylee heard Svlain sigh from next to her.

"And being infatuated with the person you love doesn't hurt either." Svlain's words caused Caylee to laugh out loud.

"Bryce is handsome," Caylee said with a smile that faded quickly. "But I doubt my ability to understand a person. Grant is still too recent and the harm he has done is too great for me to overlook."

"Yes, but do not measure others against him. He is a rock in a flower garden. Enjoy the flowers and throw the rock away." Svlain nodded and then walked down the steps towards where her husband stood laughing over the prostrate form of Wizard Col.

Caylee smiled as she watched Svlain pull her husband's hands and lead him down towards the stairs leading to their cabin. She wondered if Svlain was right. Was Captain Bryce Rouen a flower? Was she comparing him to Grant? Just the thought had her frowning and turning back to study the sea.

Two hours later it was she who was lying on the deck. Sweat rolled down her back and face as she scrambled up to face Eyelan. The dragon warrior was level six and had promised to take it easy, but so far Caylee didn't feel the woman was keeping her promise.

"Hold your sword tighter!" Col shouted at her. "You keep losing it."

Caylee wanted to roll her eyes at this but shifted her sword to her right hand again. Eyelan faked going left but Caylee caught the movement in the woman's dark eyes. She quickly shifted her weight to her back leg just in time. Eyelan's left leg swept out and she tried to trip Caylee. Using her opponent's shifted balance, Caylee thrust the top part of her body forward and landed with a woosh on top of the woman.

"Good, now what?" Col shouted, and Caylee realized that was as far as her plan had been thought out.

The moment of her indecisiveness allowed her opponent to shift and then Caylee found herself once again lying on her back. This time Eyelan was grinning down at her with the wooden practice sword held at her neck.

"It appears third time is not a charm," Eyelan said, throwing Caylee's previous words back at her.

"Yeah, well, that's my mom's saying," Caylee grumbled, stretching her back as she stood.

"Go again," Col shouted, and Caylee moaned as she rubbed her butt.

"Can't I just aim an arrow at her?" She gritted her teeth when she heard the whine in her voice.

"You will not always have your bow," Col stated with a frown.

"I have a meeting to talk with Cousin Aiden over the trans rock in a few minutes," Caylee said. She gave her backside another rub.

"You have time for one more. This time think two steps ahead. Give yourself an escape move too," Col urged. Before she was ready, Eyelan was pouncing on her.

"Give yourself an escape move." Caylee mocked Col's words a few minutes later as she rubbed her sore bottom again. "Escape move, my butt," she hissed as she walked down to her chambers for her meeting.

She had been talking with her cousin every day since their departure from Castle Pines almost a full month before. Each month on Genoa was sixty-seven days except Agnia and Lilthia, which held sixty-eight. Since mid-summer's day had just passed, they were still in the first month of the year, Agnia. Which meant she had ten more days before they would move into the following month. Time was moving too fast and yet her family was still missing.

Shaking her head, she found the box that held the trans rocks. She had brought three. One allowed her to talk to her cousin, whom she had left in charge of Castle Pines. The second went to Wizard Shiarra, and the third was for the royal council, to be used in emergencies only. She opened the box to the stone for her cousin and warmed it in her hands. Unwilling to sit because of her injuries, she stood in her chambers and waited.

"Hello, Caylee?" She heard Aiden's voice and smiled.

"Hello, cousin."

"Where are you today?"

"The chart shows us a day away from Pescara. After that, we have a long stretch of ocean. Col thinks there are a few islands, but he's not sure if they are inhabited or not."

"And this Trillium?" he asked.

"I think we should reach it before the month is up, but it's north. So far the winds have been taking us due east."

"Listen to you. You sound like a regular sea-faring maiden," he teased.

"That I am," she joked back. "How is the council?" she asked, and when Aiden went into a long speech about Counselor Blake and the others, she held in her sigh. Suddenly, her sore bottom didn't seem like a hardship.

"Sorry I stuck you with the job," she said after he had explained about the counselor's recent attempts to undermine Aiden's authority.

"Oh, not to worry. My pop says hardship builds character."

"Well, he would know." She laughed, then turned sober again. "Col hasn't had any luck getting the traitor to tell him about the mists yet, but I will keep you posted." She hadn't told Aiden that it was Grant who had betrayed the family. She didn't want to admit it out loud yet, so she had kept Grant's name from her reports, for now. After saying her farewells, she placed the rock back in its box. She knew she had stalled long enough.

"Time to go back and learn some more fighting moves. Are you ready, butt?" She gave her rump a soft pat as she opened the door.

Bryce stood just outside in the hallway, speculation and anger on his face. His eyes narrowed and focused past her into the dark room.

"What are you doing out of bed?" Caylee asked as Bryce tried to see into the room.

"Who were you talking to?" he demanded. He tried again to glance into the room behind Caylee.

"What?" Caylee asked.

"Not what," he growled. "Who?" This time he jutted his head past her and saw that the room was empty, to his relief and disappointment. At the moment, he couldn't tell which emotion he was more pleased with, as the anger was still too overwhelming.

"Talking to, who were you talking to?" He glanced around the room one more time.

"No one." She took a step back. "Oh, myself, I guess."

"No, I heard a man's voice," Bryce growled. The beast of jealousy was too well fed for him to tame it by the time Caylee had opened the door.

"You were listening at my door?" Caylee asked, and he missed the speculation in her tone because he was still trying to see into the corner of the small cabin.

"I heard a man's voice," he insisted.

"And what if you did?" she asked. This time he caught the speculation and glanced down at her.

She had her hands on her hips. The soft leathers and tunic she was wearing showed him her full figure. Her hair was tied up and a faint line of dirt was smeared on her face. To him, she looked beautiful, and he had a hard time formulating words or remembering what they were currently talking about.

"Um." His mind went completely blank.

"What if I had a man in there, what would you do?" She raised a hand to poke him in his stomach. "What if I had a whole battalion of men in there. What would it be to you?"

"Um." He realized he was well over his head in the error now. "Nothing, I guess." He took a step back.

"Nothing!"

He realized too late that that was the wrong word. Maybe he should have said sorry?

"I don't think you understand, Captain," she said with a deep emphasis on the last word. "Your duty is to steer this ship, not babysit me."

He took another step back as she closed in on him. Her anger had flames of fury sparking in her green eyes and two red points high on her cheeks. She continued to berate him and poked his stomach once again for good measure. Her words no longer registered to him because he was lost in her beauty.

He thought Caylee furious was a beautiful thing to witness.

"Well?" she demanded, and he realized she was now standing out in the hallway and his back was to a wall. Her hands were once again on her hips and her green eyes were narrowed to slits.

"Um," he repeated, realizing too late that he hadn't been listening at all. "Sorry?"

"Sorry?" She sucked in a big breath.

"Look!" He held his hands up. "I am sorry. I do not know what I was thinking when I heard the man's voice. I was just coming down to let you know I was feeling better, and to say thank you for, well, you know." He suddenly he felt too big, too clumsy and awkward. "Well, thank you." He tried to walk away but her next words stopped him.

"It was my cousin," she whispered.

"Excuse me?" He turned to see her looking guilty suddenly.

"My cousin, Aiden. I was using a trans rock to check up on things."

"Trans rock?" he asked, confused by the word.

"You know, the magical rocks that let people speak from great distances." She tilted her head when he remained silent. "Have you never heard of them?"

"I have not lived around magic much," he said with a shrug of his shoulders. Too late he realized his mistake and the pain in his hurt shoulder caused him to wince.

"Oh, did that hurt?" she asked as she rushed forward.

"Just a little." He smiled at her. "You are not going to faint again, are you?" he teased.

"No," she said, narrowing her eyes again at him.

"Good," he replied with a sigh. "Look, the warden said I could take a short walk, but I think this is all the energy I have. I think I need to head back. But I was promised another walk at sunset. Would you, if you want, would you like to take a walk with me?" Suddenly the hallway felt too hot. She stared at him for a second, then smiled, to his relief.

"I would love to," she replied.

He nodded once then turned to walk back up the hallway and out to the fresh air. Once there, he headed right to his cabin, where he ignored the bed and sat behind his desk.

Sweat that had nothing to do with the heat covered his back, and he had to wipe his palms on his pants before he picked up his chart. He sat there for several minutes with a stupid grin on his face, not even looking at the maps

Fog settled around the boat late that afternoon, causing the ship to slow in its travels. There was no way to navigate when you couldn't see three yards off the bow. Eno had ordered the sails to be lowered, and the ship hung in the water, suspended between the mists and the depths of the ocean.

Caylee knocked on his cabin door right after dinner. Since the fog left the sky dark, they walked up on deck where the lamps had already been ignited. The eerie light shone down upon the empty deck, giving the night and ship an odd look.

Caylee wore a lightweight blue cloak over her silver dress. Her hair had been curled in ringlets around her soft face, and Bryce was once again awed by her beauty.

"You might catch a cold, Your Highness," Bryce said teasingly.

"Thank you, Captain Rouen." She smiled.

"We cannot have you catching a cold." He reached behind her towards her hood. But first he trailed a finger along one of her dark locks. It was soft to his touch and had a hint of the mist clinging to it. Then he pulled her hood up and gently placed it on her head. "We should pass the Straight of Nereis tomorrow."

Caylee glanced over his shoulder, then asked, "You said you've seen Pescara before?"

He nodded; his eyes still intently focused on her. He stood less than a foot from her and the soap she had washed with filled his senses. It had a floral hint to it.

"Did you, I mean, have you seen the Tower of Della Val?" Her hesitation caused him to smile a little as he remembered his awkwardness a few hours before.

"The blossom of Pescara is quite a vision to behold," he whispered. "The white tower shines in the day's light and its petals gently open at the sun's apex." Again, he brushed a finger along her hair. "Beyond Pescara is unknown to many, but Eno has traveled beyond its shores many times."

"Has he ever seen the Trillium?" Caylee whispered.

"No." Bryce lowered his head and thought for a second about kissing her. His lips were only inches away and already he could taste her. But then something sparked in him. He didn't realize it was his magic. He only realized he suddenly felt they were in danger.

"No!" he growled. He twisted quickly and pulled his broad sword out of its sheath. He aimed it at a phantom shape that hung in the air two feet behind him.

17

THE FLOWER OF THE SEA

It took forever for Caylee's heart to settle back down after Bryce called out to his men. The broad sword was sheathed quickly, and the search had started for the dark phantom.

"You did not see it?" Col demanded of her as she sat next to the warm fire in Bryce's cabin. This time she was surrounded by Col, Svlain, and Erica while Bryce and his men did a complete search of the ship.

"I only saw a faint outline," she stated as Erica wrapped a blanket tighter around her shoulders. "Col, I thought..." She hesitated then looked up into her wizard's eyes. "I thought it was Zander."

"The prince?" Col asked thoughtfully, scratching at his facial hair.

"It felt like him," she explained as she tried to remember back to when she had seen the shape. "But he felt angry." She said this more to herself than the others.

"What were you doing?" Col asked.

"Well..." She hesitated and a smile slipped out. "I think Bryce was going to kiss me."

"Ah," Col said as he leaned back on his heels and thought a moment. "I think I will go join in the search." He left quickly as Svlain clucked her tongue at him.

"I think you embarrassed the wizard," Svlain said with a smile. "But I am glad you are well."

"So?" Erica demanded as she brought a platter of biscuits with tea over and set it on the table. Since Bryce had been injured, they had gotten used to taking tea in the larger quarters belonging to the captain. It was the only room that sported a good-sized table and chairs. Plus, the stove kept the room at a comfortable temperature.

Caylee gave her friend a questioning look, then took a small biscuit from the plate.

"Did the handsome captain kiss you?" Erica finally asked as she sat next to Caylee.

"Oh," Caylee said with a smile. "Well, no, we were interrupted."

"Ah, biscuits!" Captain Adams said as he strolled in and walked quickly over to the table. "Is there any ale? A foggy night just calls for some," he said with the sound of hope in his voice.

"I will fetch some," Svlain said with a sigh.

"Have they found anything?" Erica asked as she pushed the plate over towards the captain. Captain Adams sat in Svlain's vacated chair, his bristling mustache dripping with small raindrops from the fog.

"Nothing so far, but Captain Rouen and his men are doing a fine job searching the ship." Captain Adams took a large bite of the biscuit. "Needs butter," he mumbled a second later, his mouth full.

"Captain, is Grant still..." Caylee started then realized she had no idea where Grant was currently being kept on the ship.

"Locked away?" the captain finished for her. "Yes, my dear, he is quite secure."

"Good," Erica said with a nod of her head. "We should have left him on the long island, if you ask me."

"Now, now," Captain Adams said with a shake of his head. "Then how can he answer for his crimes against the royal family?"

"Has he given you any indication where they are, I mean other than the name of the place?" Caylee asked.

"Pon Hellz is what he called it," Captain Adams provided. "Never heard of it, but then up until a few years ago, I had never heard of Midzark either."

"So, you think this place rests beyond the ice fields that surround Genoa?" Erica asked, her eyes wide with wonder.

"Might be." The captain took another biscuit from the plate.

"Here, wash it down with this," Svlain urged as she handed the man a small bottle of ale. "But make sure that Captain Rouen does not see it."

"Never saw a ship captain so against spirits," the captain mumbled as he took a sip of his ale.

"Eno was telling me it had to do with Captain Rouen's father," Erica said with a shake of her head. "A drunk, from what Eno said."

"Drunk?" Caylee asked, studying her friend.

"I guess he died by the bottle, and Eno said the captain's mother wasn't much better either," Erica said with another shake of her head.

"I heard the captain's father was a military man who died in battle," Captain Adams stated, his mouth still full of food.

"But I thought—" Caylee was interrupted by Col and Bryce when they entered the room, followed by Eno.

The men shook the mist off their coats, and Col moved to stand next to the stove. Caylee could see fine water drops clinging to Bryce's dark hair as she studied him.

Had he lied to her about his parents? Or maybe what he had told her was the truth and he had lied to Eno? As she looked at him, she wondered why he had felt the need to lie at all. Maybe he had told his crew about drunken parents to keep the crew from the bottle?

"I felt no dark magic in the spot," Col said as he warmed his hands near the stove. "But from what you said, it felt like Prince Zander?" He aimed a questioning look over at her.

"Yes, but he has never appeared that way before," Caylee explained, her mind still on Bryce.

"But Charlotte has," Erica stated.

"Yes, but even then, it was different," Caylee told them.

"Different?" Bryce asked as he sat across from her at the table.

"Well, with Charlotte, she appeared to our mother in a vision. She had Mom appear, or more like transport." Caylee realized suddenly how hard it was to describe the vision her mother had had years ago while trapped in Midzark. "I know Charlotte knows things, some things even before they happen. But this didn't feel like Charlotte, it felt like Zander."

"Zander can manifest images," Col explained thoughtfully and moved to pick up a biscuit. "I have tutored him on his use of magic, but I never saw him throw an image from great distances."

"Usually because he lacks the focus," Captain Adams said with a frown on his face. "Lacks ambition, if you ask me."

"True." Col nodded and looked down at Caylee. "However, maybe he was trying to get you a message."

"Did he speak to you?" Erica asked hopefully.

"No," Bryce replied quickly. "But I felt anger aimed towards me."

"Yeah, well, I was distracted," Caylee said. She felt her cheeks heat up as she snuck a peek at Bryce, who smiled her way.

"Zander has always been protective of you," Captain Adams stated.

"Col, now that we are gathered, do you think it is time you tell me where your final destination is?" Bryce asked, his eyes focused on the wizard.

"We reach Pescara tomorrow?" Col asked as he scratched at the day's growth on his chin again.

"By sunset," Bryce informed them.

"Very well," Col said. He reached into his coat pocket and pulled out a tiny book no bigger than his palm. "The item we seek is described to reside on a far eastern island called Dua Sacro. From what I can ascertain, it is several days north of Pescara."

"I have never heard of any islands north," Eno said from his spot in the corner of the room. "There are many south, trading islands, and some of those islands are only rock."

"This island is said to be surrounded by ice most of the year," Col explained. He gently shook the closed book.

"May I see it?" Caylee asked, holding her hand out.

"Careful, it is quite old," Col stated as he handed it to her.

Bryce moved over to stand behind her as she opened the cover.

"The last words of Captain Gully" was written on the first page.

She turned to the next page and started to read a logbook for a ship called the *Brown Gull.* The log wasn't written by the captain, but apparently by a cabin boy named Jon. Jon explained that he was the only person aboard who could write and therefore assigned the job of transcribing the crew's adventures.

"It says their ship was stuck in the ice," Caylee said with a frown. "And then they walked towards a vast mountain. Once they reached an island, the air grew warm again."

"There, read that," Bryce said. He poked a finger at the bottom of the page.

"I'm getting to it," Caylee said, bent over the book. "They moved inland and followed the river, which flowed hot." Here she turned the page and continued reading. "The captain told some of his crew to remain behind while the others looked for supplies." Here she wrinkled her nose at the words. "Ugh, they had to eat one of their dead crewmen while they were stuck in the ice."

"How long were they stuck?" Svlain's question was ignored as Caylee continued reading.

"On the island, they went on a day's walk and found the fountain. Jon said the captain went mad two days later and refused to leave the falls."

"Falls?" Erica asked.

"The Trillium," Caylee said with a shake of her head. "The captain said he could see his dead wife in the fall's water. It says that each man claimed of visions deep within the falls and the boy, who was only ten, says he never saw anything."

"Fifteen of the men went mad," Col added with a shake of his head. "And only the boy survived the return trip to the ship."

"So why do you think the falls will show me my family?" Caylee asked.

"Because of what the next page says," Col replied.

Caylee continued to read, and her fears increased with each word.

"*Each man spoke of lost loved ones,*" Jon wrote on. "*But when I returned to the ship, I discovered that not all who had been seen inside the mirror were dead. Several of the crew spoke of family members in far-off islands who were later proven to be alive. It is my belief that those seen inside the mirror are lost to those who looked into the Trillium's waters.*"

"Is this why you insisted I come on the quest?" Caylee asked. She turned from the book to look up at her wizard.

"Yes," Col replied.

"And you believe this lad and what he wrote?" Bryce demanded.

"That lad was Jon Bezant, the first wizard who settled on the mainland well over three hundred seasons, I mean, years ago," Col told them.

Caylee awoke the next day excited to see the large island Pescara.

She had heard from Eno that there were many large cities on the island, cities said to be older than any found on the mainland. Folklore told that when the goddess created life, it had settled first on Pescara.

The fog from the prior night had lifted and the bright blue of the sky showed few clouds as she and Erica came up from breakfast. The weak sun reflected off the water and a cool sweet breeze blew her hair about. When they moved to the ship's banister to look out over the water, her excitement increased.

"Do you know if Col finish the list?" Caylee asked Erica as she took a deep breath of morning air.

"He and the captain were trying to finish it over breakfast. They asked me for a list of items and sizes before you joined me," Erica said with a smirk. "I told them we would be doing our shopping. Imagine men trying to order cold-weather gear for us."

Caylee shivered and smiled at her friend. "And it will give us a chance to shop." Her smile faltered as she studied her friend. "However, after the long island... Maybe we should let them?"

"No," Erica said firmly. "I'm not going to let one incident ruin shopping for me."

"Good," Caylee said, and her smile widened. "I was hoping you would say that."

The day was warm and bright despite the chill from the night before. Caylee spent her morning in fighting lessons and then went to clean up. She had ten new bruises from being thrown to the ground, most on her backside and one along her wrist. She had managed to duck one kick from Parsa and took comfort in the fact that she had actually seen it coming, unlike the other eight the warrior had sent her.

The afternoon passed slowly, so slowly that she asked each ship's crewman if they were sure they still were moving in the water.

"Relax, princess," Bryce said when he came to her as she drilled Eno about their location. "The island will soon be visible."

"But it's almost dusk now. Will I be able to see everything?" she demanded as she walked to the railing on the starboard side.

"You should have a whole hour to view the city before darkness sets in. Then you will marvel in the lights as we settle the *Fair Maiden* in the harbor," Bryce said with a smile as he too walked over to lean against the railing.

"But we can't go ashore until tomorrow?" Caylee asked with a sigh.

Turning, Bryce leaned against the railing and studied her for a minute, then nodded. "It is best if we keep the shopping for daylight."

"Is it true the homes are built of stone?" Caylee asked, still looking out at the water.

"Large stones, and they have clay roofs. But the greatest sight in the harbor beyond the tower is the high point lookouts," Bryce stated.

"The lookouts?"

"Stone castles, larger than any built on the mainland."

"Castles?" Caylee asked with a frown. "Who lives there?"

"Well, no one lives there," Bryce said with a frown. "They are lookouts."

"You mean there are vast buildings that are used only for looking out to sea?" She turned finally from the view of the water to study him. He wore brown today. His shirt and pants were the same dark color, but his belt was a lighter brown. His shirt's buttons were silver and were adorned with little anchors. She thought he looked very much like a ship's captain.

"Well, I suspect the guards use the buildings to live," he said as he tilted his head towards her. "But since there have not been many attacks of late, I would think only a few men reside inside their walls."

Caylee thought about this for a minute and then leaned back against the railing. Her dress was simple compared to the royal gowns she usually wore while at home. But the light blue material was soft and the thick lace on the arms kept it from being too plain. She, of course, had her riding leathers under the skirt, along with her comfortable boots.

"Do they know how old the lookouts are?" she asked.

"I heard once that the southern lookout dates back over a hundred generations. There are books that speak about the builders, but I have not seen the lookout myself," he said with a sigh. I have only been to Laguna Gulf on Pescara. That is where most of the towns are."

"And will I be able to see the tower from there?" Caylee asked hopefully.

"Well, see for yourself," Bryce said as the man high up in the crow's nest shouted, "Land ho!"

Excited, Caylee spun around and gasped in awe. Far out before them was a dark green blot against the ocean's water. Even from this distance, she could see the rising of stones on the crest of the island sticking out from the green.

As they drew slowly closer, she saw more. There was a spire of white jutting up from the left of the island. A bright glowing orb appeared to sit on the top and dark rocks sat at its base, separating it from the water.

"The Tower of Della Val," she whispered, placing a hand on Bryce's arm in her excitement.

"It closes at sunset, but the glow can still be seen," he said softly.

Forms and buildings grew more distinct the closer they got. She saw the red of the roof tiles, the dark grey of the stone walls, and even laundry that had been hung between the tall buildings blowing in the air.

The homes and buildings were built right against the shoreline and cliffs. The green of trees blotted between several buildings before the forest took over the hillside. Then, just when she thought the hill was too high for any structures, she saw the lookouts.

Massive stone structures imposed themselves on the top of the mountains. Many windows reflected the evening's light, more than she could count in the five-story castle-like building. The lookout was almost as long as the mountain's top. On the far left, however, the building disappeared, and a vast jut of rock was left. It stood there as if in defiance of the builders.

"It's beautiful." She studied the outline of the building as much as the forest and even the tower. "All of it."

"Pescara," Bryce said, and Caylee heard awe in his deep voice.

The day's light grew faint as they drew near, and Caylee was delighted to see the town light up as she watched. House windows weren't the only spark of light. Lanterns lined the roadways and twinkles of lights could even be seen far into the forest.

"Homes stretch far into the woods too," Bryce told her. "Sometimes you cannot even tell where one village ends, and another begins."

The tower took her breath away when the vast petals started to close. There were four, each pointing towards the cardinal directions, north, east, south, and west. It was the largest and most beautiful compass rose she had ever seen.

"Princess." Col's voice interrupted her thoughts. Turning, she saw the wizard's frown of disapproval as he cleared his voice. "It appears Mr. Worthington is willing to talk now."

"Grant?" Caylee asked as a coldness settled inside her chest and the beauty and excitement behind her were forgotten.

"Yes, but he says he will only speak to you," Col said gravely.

18

THE TRUTH

She refused to see Grant that night. Anger and a little fear welled up inside her after Col had explained his conversation with Grant. Once the wizard was finished, she turned her back on him and once again faced the island. No longer did she see the twinkling lights or the vast beautiful scenery before her. Instead, she saw Grant's angry face as he shouted that he had been behind the attack on her family.

"Talk to him later," Bryce urged as she felt his hand rest on her shoulder.

It took courage or cowardice, she wasn't sure which one it was, for her to shake his hand off her shoulder as she remained where she was. She felt the hand slip from her arm, and a new feeling filled her—loneliness.

"I will think about it," she told Col as she remained still.

"Caylee," Bryce said from behind her, and she thought she heard hurt in his voice.

"I'm tired," she said quickly. She turned from the view towards the stairs, wanting to escape from her feelings and him.

She paused at the top of the stairs and, without turning, sent a soft thank-you over her shoulder before she raced towards her room.

That night she didn't sleep. Instead, her heart and head waged a war. The battle raged on as her emotions ate away at her and tears threatened to fall. In the dark, with Erica and Tonkee sleeping in their bunks, Caylee, princess of Genoa, felt isolated.

Caylee's life lay before her, and she found herself lacking. She scrutinized her ability to make decisions that night in the darkness of her mind. Everything from the cat attack north of Tharian to deciding to marry Grant Worthington almost a year ago flashed through her mind. Embarrassments and wrongs weighed heavily on her, and all appeared to be solely her fault. Even the excitement of the next day's promised adventure didn't distract her from her deep despair that night.

By the time Erica awoke to get things ready for the day, Caylee's head hurt, and her stomach was sour. Instead of changing into her dress, she put on her exercise clothes and went up to the front deck, called the forecastle, to run through a warm-up.

Even here, with the sun slowly making its way up behind her, she felt her life's poor choices eat away at her. Taking a deep breath, she raised both arms over her head, closed her eyes, and tried to shake off the gloom of the night. On her exhale, she reached for her toes, feeling her muscles loosen just like her mind until she heard a small noise behind her.

"Glory be to the goddess," Bryce quietly said. Caylee spun around to face him. Her hands were still clasped together, and her heart raced inside her chest.

"What are you doing?" she quickly asked.

"The true question is what are you doing, and why have I not seen that move before?" He smiled. "I could get used to seeing that move again."

She knew he was teasing her, but the night's lack of sleep and her deep thoughts didn't leave her in the best of moods. "I'm stretching." She shrugged her shoulders and turned her back on him.

Not willing to expose her backside to him again, she instead worked on stretching her arms and shoulders. She didn't hear him move, but when he slowly walked into her vision, his face was set, and his eyes looked at her thoughtfully.

"You look like crap," he said with a frown as he placed his hands on his hips.

"Thanks, that's what every woman wants to hear." She continued her warm-up.

"I mean it. Did you sleep?" He reached out and brushed one of his fingers along her left cheekbone.

"Shove off." She batted his hand from her face.

"No," he said. He grabbed her chin to study her more with his tan eyes. "I mean it, what kept you up? Was it that stupid little man?" he demanded.

"No," she said, and then gave in when he continued to study her. "At least not entirely him," she finally added.

He nodded, then released her chin. "So, tell me, did you come to any conclusions?"

"Conclusions?" she asked in confusion.

"Yes, you know. Suppositions that you are the only one who messed up. That you were the only one fooled by the crazy, pale-faced fiancé of yours." He smiled at her when she narrowed her eyes.

"That is none of your business," she stated and, once again, she turned her back on him to continue her warm-up.

"Oh, I like when you go all princess on me," Bryce said as he spun her around and planted a solid kiss on her lips.

Before she had time to think or react, he released her and was holding her at his arm's length, smiling down at her.

"There, feel better now?" he asked, and she felt her anger rise to the surface.

"How dare you!" she spat only to find herself once again being kissed.

When she was finally able to catch her breath, her anger had doubled. But then she heard Bryce's laughter as he hugged her to his broad chest.

"Oh, don't be mad," he chided, using one of the odd contractions she had been raised with. "I promise, I did not just do that to tick you off."

She felt the rumble of laughter in his chest as he still held her close to him, and she felt her anger dissipate with each second. "You didn't?" She was shocked at how small her voice sounded.

"No, but it was a pleasant side effect," he replied with another laugh. "And I did not do it because I felt sorry for you either, if you have any doubt. I did it because I wanted to. I wanted to the other night, but we were interrupted."

"You did?" she asked and felt a smile cross her lips.

"Yeah. For some reason, I find I am attracted to you," he said as another laugh escaped. When the laughter stopped, he held her at arm's length again and a frown formed on his handsome face. "Why did you not sleep?"

She felt her shoulders slump, and she cast her eyes down before his hand brought her chin up again. Facing him, she took a deep sigh. "You were partly correct. I spent last night thinking about Grant. No, more about myself and all my poor choices."

"Ah, so all of the problems were because of you?" he asked with narrow eyes.

"Of course not!" she hissed. She stopped when he smiled.

"Good!" he said quickly. "Did staying up all night worrying about these 'choices' solve anything?"

"Well, no," she finally admitted to him.

"Of course not!" He repeated her own words back to her with a wide smile on his face. "So, stop moping. Go change into something pretty and then go shopping with your friends." He spun her towards the stairs and gave her butt a swat. "Go on, have fun," he said with another laugh when she spun on the spot and glared at him for his bold move. "Go on, before I have to kiss you again."

His laughter still rang in her ears all the way down the stairs. And as she changed for the day, she had a big smile on her lips and a new spring in her step.

Shopping seemed to be exactly what she needed.

The sun was bright above the stone shops and the townspeople were friendly. There were a variety of creatures that lived on Pescara, including sprites, gnomes, and trolls. Erica swore she saw a tree fairy, but it was from a great distance, and she wasn't sure if it was a fairy or a sprite.

They bought cold-weather gear—long coats lined with

fur from the local sheep and gloves made from the same material. Leather hats and boots sealed for rain or snow. Thick scarfs and long warm undergarments. Svlain found some long socks for them all.

Loaded down with their purchases, they returned to the ship with smiles on their faces. Since the dragon warrior women had also joined them, there were nine in their group, and the bags and boxes were quite numerous.

"Good lord, did you leave anything for the locals?" Brett asked as he helped carry the boxes up the plank.

"Nothing," Erica teased as she sent him a wink.

"My lady," Eno said as he joined them on the deck. The man's face was grim, and his eyes turned to watch Col slowly walk forward.

"Caylee," Col said, his face also set. She was immediately filled with fear.

"What is it?" she asked.

"We need to talk," Col said. He pointed to the captain's cabin.

"Here, I'll take these," Brett said, gently removing the bags from Caylee's hands.

"I think Tonkee and Pren should join us," Col said, nodding as the two warriors flanked Caylee.

"And me," Erica said with determination in her voice.

Bryce was waiting for them. There was tea set on the table, and the warmth from the fire filled the room. Caylee saw that Bryce no longer had a broad smile on his face. In fact, his eyes held worry.

"What is it? What has happened?" she demanded as she stood just inside the doorway.

"One of my men discovered the problem," Bryce stated and cleared his throat. "The cabin the traitor was using has..." Bryce paused then turned to look over at Col with uncertainty.

"The mist is here," Col said with a frown.

"What?" The word squeaked out of Caylee's throat, and she spun on the spot, half expecting to see a red haze fill the doorway.

"A crew member went in and was rummaging in Mr. Worthington's possessions when a vial broke. The man fled first, but he left the door to the room open. Luckily, I happened by and saw the mist as it started to fill the cabin. I quickly closed the door, but I fear that may not be enough to keep it at bay," Col said with a shake of his head.

"Have you spoken with Mr. Worthington?" Pren asked, his face going pale, which made the yellow dragon tattoo on his bald head stand out.

"Yes, he is refusing to speak to anyone but you, Caylee." Col turned his dark eyes towards her.

Seeing the worry in her wizard's eyes, and knowing Bryce feared for his crew and ship, she squared her shoulders and nodded. "Lead the way." Erica's hand grasped hers. Caylee took strength in her friend's presence.

Grant's cell was three decks down and towards the front of the ship where waves were known to disturb the ship the most. He had been placed in a large cell. Instead of wooden walls, there was a panel of steel rods that formed odd X's to bar his escape. A locked steel door sat dead center of the opening.

Looking past the bars, Caylee had a shock at Grant's appearance. It had been days since she had last seen him, when he had set fire to the ship and their food supply. Gone was the handsome blond man with light green eyes. Instead, the usually combed hair now was disheveled and dirty. His face was pale, and a scruffy beard covered his jaw. He wore clean clothes, but there was an unkempt appearance to them. His green eyes landed on Caylee, and she found it hard not to shiver as his gaze stayed on her.

"Caylee," Grant said with a smile. "Darling."

Standing stock-still, Caylee felt Erica's hand tighten in hers. They stayed feet away from the bars, while Col and the others moved closer.

"I brought her, now tell us what we need to know," Col demanded.

Grant's eyes moved briefly over to the wizard, then returned to Caylee as a sneer formed on his lips. "No, I will only speak with Caylee."

"No!" Bryce stood in front of her, blocking Grant's form from her vision.

"I do not answer to you, *Captain*," Grant hissed. He moved to the side so he could see her again. "Caylee, send them away." The request came out more like an order, in Caylee's opinion.

"Grant," Col said, drawing the man's attention back to him. "I will send the warriors, but the captain and I will stay."

"And the nymph!" Grant hissed, his eyes landing on Erica, who stood her ground.

"No!" Caylee said firmly and held tight to Erica's hand. "She stays."

"Darling, we do not need her," Grant crooned. Caylee tried to stop the shiver that ran down her back.

"Tell us!" Col demanded after the two warriors had left the hallway.

"The mist is the portal to Pon Hellz," Grant said quietly as they all drew nearer to the bars. "Io Maltesea provided me with all the tools needed to allow Caylee access to the throne of Genoa." The smile that covered

Grant's face was a little off, almost as if the man had gone mad while locked away. "The mist is what the sorcerers use to travel."

"Will the mist remain confined to the room?" Col asked.

Grant turned to study the wizard. His smile faltered a little at the question. "The mist goes where it pleases."

"So, it can get out of the room?" Bryce asked, drawing Grant's attention away from the wizard.

"You? I know you seek the throne too. Well, you cannot have it. Caylee is mine, and only I will sit on the throne when Io Maltesea comes," Grant hissed as he took a step closer to the bars. "She is mine, and through her, the throne will be mine also."

"I will never marry you," Caylee whispered, drawing Grant's attention once more.

"But, darling, that is why I banished your family, so you can sit on the throne," Grant said, and the odd smile covered his face again. "Your parents were holding you back. Your brother stood directly in your path to the throne, and the little witch saw too much."

"You're wrong," Caylee said, taking a step towards Grant. "My family never stood in my way. My brother is younger than me. I am the first heir to the throne and need have only asked and it would have been mine," she said as anger filled her. "I don't seek the throne of Genoa, only a comfortable place of service to Genoa's creatures."

"But you never asked!" Grant hissed. "I asked it of you several times. You denied me the throne just like my grandfather did!"

Confused, Caylee watched her former fiancé grasp the bars in his hands. His green eyes went wide and for the first time she saw hate fill them.

"Your grandfather?" she asked.

"Yes, the true king of Matera!" Grant replied with a smile. "King Gillard Haddock!"

Shaking her head, she turned to look at Col, who appeared to be as confused as she was.

"What do you mean?" Col demanded.

"My mother, Blaine Worthington, is the daughter of King Haddock. She was born months before the bastard son who now sits on the throne. It is she who should have ruled Matera all these years. She, not Calob and his stupid children, who should have sat in the riches of Matera's fortress."

"Your mother?" Caylee asked as the realization came to her. "Your mother is my father's niece?"

The laugh that came from Grant was high and long. When he was done, his green eyes turned to look at her with malice. "Yes, dear cousin, we are related, albeit distantly. How many times have I heard how similar I look to your brother? Both blond, both with green eyes and"—here he smiled and gave her a wink— "both handsome."

Caylee felt ill. Her stomach rolled as words came back to her, when people inside the court had compared Grant to Zander. Sure, there were big differences. For one, Grant was almost a whole foot shorter than Zander. Zander had their father's build, broad shoulders, and a wider jawline, while Grant was skinnier.

"So you attacked the royal family because you wanted the throne?" Bryce's question interrupted Caylee's thoughts.

"Well, that and revenge," Grant said with a smile as his fingers flexed on the bars in front of her. "But do not worry, all is not lost," Grant said as he quickly reached through the bars with his right hand and made a grab for Caylee's arm.

"No!" Erica shouted as Grant's fingers brushed across Caylee's sleeve.

Before Grant could get a solid clasp on her arm, he was thrown backward and flung through the air by Erica's wind magic.

"Foul nymph!" Grant shouted from his position in the cell's far corner.

Erica kept her magic blasting at him, and his body hovered against the ceiling and walls of the corner as he continued to spout curses at her.

"You can let him down," Col said gently to Erica, who stood with both her arms raised. Her pretty pale face filled with anger as she glared at Grant.

"He tried to touch her," Erica hissed.

Caylee smiled at her friend. "But you didn't let him, did you?" Caylee placed a hand on Erica's arm.

"Remind me to not anger you," Bryce said with a smile aimed at Erica, who finally lowered her arms. Grant came crashing down to the floor.

Grant continued his curses aimed at Erica, but the group was no longer listening as they made their way back up to the captain's cabin. This time Erica was tucked tightly against Caylee's side as they walked.

"I will secure the door to the room to prevent the mist from escaping," Col said soberly. "At least I will try."

When he disappeared, Caylee and Erica sat down together, their heads bent close together as they talked about Grant's admissions. When Svlain came in and poured them tea, Caylee finally looked up and realized that Bryce had left the room.

"He's not like Grant," Erica stated as she added sugar to her cup.

"What?" Caylee asked, turning to study her friend again.

"This captain of yours, he's not like Grant," Erica said

as she stirred her tea. "I like your Captain Rouen. Very much."

Caylee took a deep breath as she remembered the way Bryce had kissed her earlier on the ship's deck. When she felt her cheeks flush and grow warm, she looked down and added milk to her teacup.

"So do I."

19

INTO THE DEEP

The *Fair Maiden* stayed two whole days in the port along the eastern side of the Laguna Gulf. Supplies were stacked in the holds, including cold-weather gear for the crew and new ice-breaking equipment, which had been stored in the forward holds.

Bryce didn't mind the delay, as it gave him time to study the charts he had of the northeast seas. There weren't many maps, but with Eno's help, along with the wizard's book, they were able to estimate their course. He worried about the trip, but the extra payment Captain Adams had provided not only paid for the supplies but filled up the rest of the room in his hidden safe. Not that he was taking this trip for the money, at least not anymore.

When he wasn't pouring over the charts or doing his duties, Bryce spent his time with Caylee. He found it hard to be in her company and not kiss her again. But since they were rarely alone, his struggles continued even after they left the port on the third morning.

Standing behind his wheelman, Bryce watched the sun's rays hit the Tower of Della Val. Orange rays turned the tower a pretty color as the tower's massive petals started their movement. It started to look like a tall flower greeting the day.

"I've seen it for several days now, and it still takes my breath away," Caylee said from behind him.

"I've got it, Jap," Bryce stated after a moment, taking the wheel from his man. The short, stout man nodded in Caylee's direction, then hurried from the room, no doubt aiming for breakfast and a cup of hot tea.

"Can you do that?" Caylee's question had Bryce turning to study her. Her dress today was dark blue. A hint of brown lined the hem and the edge of its long sleeves. The garment lacked any of the soft lace she usually wore. Her long hair was clipped back from her face, and the soft, dark locks fell to her waist. As usual, when he saw its length, it took his breath away.

"Do what?" he finally asked when her cheeks turned a pretty pink under his steady gaze.

"Drive or steer or whatever it's called," she explained.

Laughing, he turned back to study the open water out the window. "Well, what kind of captain would I be if I didn't know how to steer it?"

"That's another thing," Caylee said as she slowly walked up to stand next to him. "You've seemed to pick up quickly on my mother's contractions."

"Con-what?" Bryce asked, studying her out of the corner of his eye.

"The abbreviations," she explained. "Don't, can't, didn't. You know, squishing two words together. Most of the castle crew have caught on and use them, even Erica, who grew up with me. But Col and my mother's other friends still don't use them."

"Ah, I've always been a quick study," Bryce said with a smile. "And I find the squishing very convenient."

"Now you're laughing at me." She leaned towards the window to watch the vision of the tower as they slipped past the point of land it sat upon.

"No," he said, subtly sniffing the air she stirred. Today's perfume reminded him of the small white flowers found in the high mountains.

"Oh, that's almost as pretty as the tower," Caylee said, pointing down towards the lower deck.

Tilting forward, his hands still on the wheel, Bryce watched Erica and Brett lock in an embrace several feet below them. The tall man was bent over, and his arms held the little nymph tightly, causing Bryce to smile.

"So, my ship holds a little romance," he said.

"They will be married before the year ends," Caylee said with a sigh.

"Ah, we have a romantic here," he teased.

"This match is long overdue," Caylee said seriously. "As children, they would dance around each other anytime they were near."

"And what will happen after?" Bryce asked as he returned his eyes to the open water before his ship.

"Once my family is found?" Caylee said with a shake of her head. "If they are found." He saw the smile drop from her face and felt sorry for her sadness.

"When," he said firmly. "When they are found."

"Yes, positive thinking." She nodded. "Then Erica and Brett will make a family, though I'm not sure where they will live." Again, worry crossed her pretty face.

"Missing her already?" he teased. A smile formed on her face.

"Desperately."

"Sir," Eno said from the doorway. "I have the duty roster for your approval."

"I'll just get out of your hair," Caylee said. She smiled when both men looked questioningly at her. "It means I'll leave now," she explained. She nodded at Eno and left.

"Here, look at these while I take over," Eno said as he handed Bryce the chart.

He walked over to the window so he could keep an eye on Caylee while he studied the chart. Or pretended to study it. He had a hard time keeping his eyes from the figures below. Erica and Brett had broken apart, though the man kept Erica's hands in his as Caylee joked and laughed with them. When they disappeared from his view, he realized he had been watching for almost half an hour. He still held the chart while Eno remained silently at the wheel. Finally giving his full attention to the roster, he made a few adjustments, signed it, then handed it back to his friend.

"Hard to focus with such pretty things aboard. Sir," Eno said with a quick smile. He left before Bryce could scowl at him.

Focus was something Bryce was lacking lately. And he knew whose fault that was. Caylee's. Three hours passed before Jap was back smelling of warm tea and sausage. Deciding breakfast had passed and lunch wouldn't be ready yet, Bryce made his way to his cabin for a cup of strong tea and whatever biscuits had been left behind. But when he got there, he was pleased to see a tea party already in full swing.

Caylee presided over the group much like the princess she was. Erica and Brett were there along with Brett's parents, Svlain and Zain. The wizard and Captain Adams were also present.

"Am I late to this party?" he joked. He smiled when Caylee stood to retrieve another cup for him.

"Not at all," Caylee replied as Captain Adams stood from the table.

"If you do not mind, I think I will get some fresh air," Captain Adams said as he left the room.

Sitting in the now vacant chair, Bryce smiled when Svlain pushed a plate of biscuits towards him. After taking two, he reached for the butter and was slathering one biscuit when Brett and Svlain both went stiff. The latter stood quickly while the other remained sitting.

Erica bolted from the table, and Caylee gasped loudly. Col grabbed the table and stood, knocking his chair over as he rushed towards the pale green nymph. Shocked by the response around the table, he quickly stood to his feet, confused.

"Don't touch her yet!" Zain shouted as he moved towards his wife. "Leave him!" he shouted to Erica who was reaching a hand towards her fiancé.

"Water, they will both need something cold after it's finished," Caylee said, casting a dark look at Bryce.

Still uncertain what was happening, he nodded and walked over to a pitcher to pour two tall glasses. By the time he returned to the table, Svlain was once again sitting, and her husband was speaking softly in her ear. Brett was nodding his head to Erica, and Bryce saw that his eyes were wide with shock.

"That was a bad one," Zain said quietly.

"Here.' Bryce shoved one glass towards each of them, still confused.

"Thanks," Svlain said. Bryce could see the woman was in pain. Glancing at her son, he saw the same look in his eyes.

"What has happened?" he asked as he moved to stand next to Col.

"They have had a vision," the wizard said with a grave voice. "A strong one from what I can tell."

"Very strong," Brett said. He reached out to grasp his mother's hand.

"You go first," Svlain said weakly as she drank the water.

"Very well," Brett said. After taking a sip, he turned his eyes towards Caylee. "You are in danger."

Caylee listened to Brett's vision with a growing sense of dread. The room turned cold and after his first few words, she found it difficult to remain seated.

She made her way over to the stove and placed another scoop of coal in it, then she turned back towards the table. Her eyes met with Bryce's and the room suddenly returned to a normal temperature. Bryce's eyes flashed towards her, and she feared his anger would lash out. She knew his anger wasn't directed at her, but she felt the heat of it as she returned to her seat.

"The vision was similar to my last one. I saw you, Caylee, jump overboard. I saw you throw yourself over the bow of the ship and land deep in the cold water," Brett stated, drawing Caylee's eyes away from Bryce's and toward her friends.

"There is more," Svlain said weakly.

"Yes." Brett nodded, then continued. "There was, something..." He looked at his mother.

"Something alive," Svlain provided suddenly. "It was there under the water."

"A monster?" Col asked as he leaned forward. "Sea monster?"

"I don't think so," Brett continued. "But I could not see it. I only felt it."

"It did not feel like a monster," Svlain provided. "Then I saw..." Here she placed her hands over her face as a sob escaped from her.

"We saw you," Brett explained, pointing to Caylee. "Lying on sharp rocks, dead."

"It won't happen," Caylee stated. She dropped back into her chair. "I won't jump. There is no way I will ever jump off the ship."

"Avoiding the possibilities of the future is very difficult," Brett said with a shake of his head.

"Your mother had similar issues," Col said gravely. "However, as useful as visions are, somehow they always omit all the details."

"You saw her dead. Do you mean she was not breathing?" Bryce demanded and all eyes turned to the captain.

"What do you mean?" Brett asked in confusion.

"What you saw? Did you see her pale in death, or dying?" Bryce demanded. "Tell me exactly what the vision showed."

"She was lying on the rocks." Svlain sobbed.

"Was there blood?" Bryce's question drew another sob from the nymph and a gasp from Erica, but he waved a large hand at Erica and stared at the two seers.

"No, she was just..." Brett started to explain then

changed what he was going to say and shook his head. After a moment he continued. "She lay there without moving."

"So she could have been asleep," Bryce demanded.

"I felt—"

"That's the problem. I think both of you let your emotions rule during the vision," Bryce stated with a frown. He turned to study Caylee. "If you jump, I am sure you will have a good reason. But if that happens, there will be a response from me and my men."

Caylee watched him as he spoke. "Response?" she asked, a loud buzzing sound in her ears.

"We have safety protocols," Bryce replied. He spent the next hour going over the ship's safety rules. He then took them all out to the deck and showed them the ropes, pullies, and flotation pads that were used when someone fell overboard. He finished walking them through these about lunchtime and joined Caylee for the meal. He continued instructing her on how to respond if you found yourself swimming in the ocean.

By the time she went to bed that night, her head was full of rules for what to do, and what not to do, if she were to find herself in the water. Some of the guidelines she knew and understood, but some of the instructions she had never heard of before.

Dreams of drowning and multi-legged creatures with sharp teeth haunted her in her sleep. When she awoke, she found it took several deep breaths to steady her heart. Even then, she felt sick to her stomach all day, and it was well after dinner before she could eat anything.

Another night of bad dreams resulted in a foul mood the third day after leaving port. No longer did she stand along the railing, looking out at the vast ocean, and dream. Instead, when she looked out, a fear of drowning would take over. Rough weather settled in after breakfast and most of the crew spent the day belowdecks. Rain and strong winds blew outside, and the ship rocked sharply back and forth. The air grew cold, and the sky turned dark, despite the time of day.

Since walking up to the captain's cabin was dangerous on the slick decking, she and the others spent their time in the galley playing cards. The hanging lights in the room swayed and every once in a while, a chair would slide along the floor. But the card game was lively, and the company was cheerful.

The morning passed quickly and, without realizing it was happening, Caylee had forgotten her fears by the time Bryce joined the group around lunchtime. The dragon warriors, Svlain's family, and Erica were all settled around one of the large tables.

"You cheated!" Kayla teased Reg, one of the male warriors, and the two started to wrestle over Reg's hand of cards.

"Now, now. There is no cheating," Pren scolded as three more started to argue. "Do I need to separate you all?" he warned as Caylee laughed from her chair near the head of the table.

"How much ale have they had?" Bryce asked as he pulled a chair up next to hers.

Laughing, she turned to study him. He was soaked from head to toe. His dark hair was slicked back from his face, and water dripped down his raised collar. The dark shirt he wore clung to his broad chest, and his sleeves were rolled up past his elbows. She found the wet look very sexy and was momentarily distracted as she watched a drop of water roll down his tanned throat and disappear into the shirt. It took a second for her mind to register his question and then she had to clear her throat before she answered.

"No ale, just good old-fashioned fun." She cleared her throat again.

"And cheating," Tonkee added from next to her.

"The storms letting up a bit," Bryce stated as he studied the mess of cards and coins on the table before them. "Everyone should be able to walk above deck after lunch."

"That might be for the best. If they stay here and play cards any longer, there may be blood spilled," she replied with a laugh.

"Cook is making stew," Bryce replied as he leaned closer to her. He smelled like rain mixed with a deep alluring musk. "He made you a special pot, I guess."

"Cen Spa has a soft heart," she said. She turned back to face the table, but her mind was still on the man next to her.

They ate lunch while the arguments about cheating at cards continued around the room. The laughter and joviality increased when they were told they were allowed above deck. She and Erica decided to take a quick walk while Bryce and Col were in deep discussion.

"I see that," Erica said as they stepped into the hall leading up towards the stairs.

"What?" Caylee asked as she looked back one last time at Bryce.

"That," Erica teased with a smile. "The captain looks great all wet and manly."

"I'm not going to reply to that," Caylee said, tilting her chin up. But then she smiled and looked sideways at her friend. "But yes, yes, he does."

They were laughing when they neared the stairs. Erica went up first and both women had to use the rope tied next to the wooden steps to keep their footing on the slippery wood.

"I think the rain stopped," Erica said as she neared the door leading out into the open air. "I don't hear it anymore."

Erica had just stepped out when the door was slammed shut behind her. The quick action pushed Caylee back a full step down the stairs. She would have fallen, but luckily her hand was still around the rope, and she caught herself quickly with a laugh.

"Oh, did the wind do that?" She stared up at the closed door until she heard a muffled cry from the other side. Then she raced out the door and saw Grant standing on the deck. He was soaking wet, his feet spread wide as he held Erica high over his head. His beard had grown another inch, and his green eyes were alive with hate. His lips were peeled back, and his teeth were bared as he lunged towards the railing. Erica kicked at him and started to scream.

"Grant!" Caylee shouted, standing stock-still in the open doorway, paralyzed by fear and confusion.

"Once this creature is gone, then you will return to me," Grant growled loudly as he rushed to the railing.

"No!" Caylee shouted. She was finally able to move as her best friend's body was thrown over the railing.

She ran quicker than she had ever run towards the wooden railing of the ship. She heard shouting behind her and saw a dark form slam into Grant as she hurtled past him. Headfirst, she dove over the railing and towards the dark water far below. As her body fell towards the surface, she saw a small hand disappear below the dark waves. She sucked in a deep breath only seconds before she hit the cold water.

20

PROMISE KEPT

Bryce saw Caylee leave with Erica and a second later made an excuse to Col and followed her. He told himself he wasn't stalking Caylee; he did have to return to the wheelhouse after all. And if he took his time, he'd have a few more minutes with her. He was entitled to that, wasn't he?

He had reached the hallway when he saw the women walk up the stairs using the rope guides. Thankfully, he had dried off a little while eating. He grabbed his wet coat from the side peg and had just reached the stairs when he heard the shout. Confused, he rushed up the steps and out the door in time to see Caylee dive over the ship's banister.

"Man overboard!" he shouted. He raced towards the banister as Eno wrestled with a figure near the railing. Concerned, he moved closer and hauled the man off his first in command. He was shocked when he realized it was the prisoner, Grant.

"What in the hell?" he said, still gripping the man by his collar.

"Hold him!" Eno shouted as two crewmen came running forward.

"All stop!" Bryce shouted. He pushed Grant at the crewmen and turned to look down into the water, fully intending on jumping in himself until Eno grabbed his arms tightly. The muscular man's hold was strong like iron.

"No sir!" Eno shouted. "Get the pads!" he ordered as more men rushed up. Some had the floating pads and another had ropes. They were quickly flung over the railing.

"Do you see them?" one man shouted as Bryce leaned over, trying to spot Caylee.

"Them? Who else went in?" Bryce asked, but then he remembered that Erica had been with Caylee. "Cats." He once again tried to jump overboard.

"No!" Again, Eno stopped him. "She knows the safety instructions," he shouted, holding onto Bryce's collar and refusing to let him get near the railing.

"I have to!" Bryce shouted.

"Use the boats," Eno ordered as he pointed to the small lifeboat the men were currently lowering towards the water.

Nodding once, Bryce raced over and jumped six feet down into the already full boat. "Faster!" he shouted. He leaned over to look at the water. Fear filled him when he realized he hadn't seen Caylee or Erica raise their heads above the surface since he had first looked.

When the boat was finally in the water, two men manned the oars while Bryce moved to the front to look for the women. His heart raced and his mind grew numb. His only thought was saving Caylee.

The *Fair Maiden* had stopped dead in the water. The rain had subsided, but the waves were still quite strong. Each time the small lifeboat crested a wave, he expected to see the two women in front of them. But with each wave, nothing was seen of either.

"Caylee!" he shouted, leaning further overboard.

He yelled until his throat was raw and hoarse. They searched until dark, and he did not give up hope, not even when Caylee's skirts were found floating near the front of the ship.

His men had to drag him back on board. They threatened to tie him up if he didn't call off the search for the night. Reluctantly, he agreed to return to the ship. But it was only the hope that the wizard or the seers could locate Caylee that made him agree.

But when he stood once more on deck and saw the wizard's pale face, hope left him, and he collapsed.

The water swallowed Caylee up after she slammed into the surface.

She didn't have time to think, time to wonder why she had just jumped headfirst from the ship. Her only thoughts were of her friend, Erica. Even now, as the darkness of the ocean surrounded her, she strained her eyes to find her friend.

She saw a pale blob a few feet below her and kicked downward to swim towards it. When her skirts hindered her, she unclasped the restricting folds, leaving her only in her undergarments. Once free, she swam with both her arms and legs towards the pale figure.

Erica's dress was tangled, and it took both of them

seconds to release the underskirt. By then, Caylee's fingers were numb from the cold water and her lungs burned, yearning for air. She pointed towards the surface and thought she saw Erica nod, but when she tried to kick them towards the water's horizon, she found her legs wouldn't move. Panic set in as all of Bryce's instructions about swimming in the ocean fled from her mind.

"Do not fear," came a deep voice so close that Caylee turned her head quickly to her left. Darkness surrounded them but inside that darkness swam two figures.

"We will save you, child of air," came a softer voice.

Erica tried to kick out as Caylee's hold on her friend loosened. Fearing they were under attack from sea monsters, Caylee swung out her arm before she felt warm hands reach for her.

"Here, you can use our gift," came the second voice.

Caylee's breath exploded from her lungs, and she was sure she was going to drown. She was shocked to realize her body took the water in as if it were air. Turning, she looked down and saw an arm was clamped on her left forearm. She panicked when she saw long webbed fingers covered with scales holding her tightly.

"Our gift allows you to live," came the first, deeper voice, "but we must go deeper to sustain it."

The light shifted and she saw a figure swimming next to Erica. Her friend's eyes were wide with fear. She and her friend were alive thanks to two merpeople.

The mermaid next to Caylee was a dark turquoise in color. Her long dark braids swirled around a pretty face. The hair matched the mermaid's tail, while her skin was several shades lighter. Big round eyes the color of the sky blinked at Caylee in curiosity. The torso was human above the waist. A pretty swatch of shells and seaweed covered her chest, and a small satchel was tied around her shoulders. Below the waist, the tail started, and it swirled in an odd movement as the mermaid swam.

The merman who was helping Erica had a dark red tail. His long hair matched the tail, but his skin was closer to pink than red. His chest was bare, and he too had a bag tied around his body. Both had tails about six feet long and hair that had never seen scissors. They were beautiful creatures, and they smiled at her while she surveyed them.

"I am Clausen," the merman said as he continued to grasp Erica's arm. "This is my sister Claretha."

Unsure how to respond, Caylee continued to study them in silence.

"Our gift should allow you to speak," Clausen said as he smiled. "But we really must move deeper."

"Deeper?" Caylee said. She felt the cold water pour down her throat.

Before either Clausen or Claretha answered, they started to drag the women further down into the darkness of the ocean.

"Please," Caylee said as Claretha's hand tightened on her arm. The powerful tails made fast work of their descent, but she needed to tell them they were heading in the wrong direction. "We have to go up, not down."

"No, it was foretold we would save you," Claretha said, looking back at Caylee with a smile. Caylee marveled that even the mermaid's teeth were a soft shade of turquoise.

"Foretold?" Caylee asked, finding it weird to speak underwater. It felt much like blowing bubbles instead of speaking.

"Grandfather and Mother spoke of this day," Clausen said from beside her. Erica was still clasped in his grip. "No harm will come to you, but we must deliver you to them as instructed."

Caylee turned to look back up towards the surface and discovered they were already too deep in the water to even see the outline of the ship. As the light grew fainter, their new friends' tails and hair started to glow faintly. The deeper they traveled, the brighter the lights got. When they stopped moving downwards, large rocks and a sandy ocean bottom could be seen in the colorful lights cast from their forms.

Caylee and Erica were dragged along as the brother and sister swam at great speed past boulders and outcrops on the ocean's bottom. Small shoals of fish swam by each a bright blur as they passed. She saw more colorful lights from tails and realized there were hundreds of merpeople. She guessed they must be nearing a village and wondered quickly if that was the word the merpeople used.

"This is our pod," Clausen told them. "Here we are safe in the rocks, free to grow and live safely."

"Safe from what?" Erica asked, having found her underwater voice.

"There are larger things in this ocean than ships," Claretha said as she slowed her swimming. "Here, see how the rocks have been made into homes?"

Caylee and Erica saw bright glowing grasses near a high rocky formation. Doorways had been carved in the rock's face, and several mermaids and mermen were going about their business, swimming in and out of the homes. All who caught sight of the two women stopped and gawked. A beautiful orange mermaid swam close, her red eyes wide with awe.

"Is this them?" she asked in a high voice.

"It is. The time has come," Clausen answered. "Ask the others to join us in the dome."

"I will fetch the firsts," one yellow merman said. He was more of a boy than a man. His hair was only down to his shoulders, and his tail was half the size of the others.

"Thank you, Flike," Claretha said. She started swimming again, this time heading along the rocks. They moved upwards a little along the pod's homes. "Come, the dome is this way."

"Is it true they come from above water?" another mermaid asked. This one was young too. Her pale green eyes studied Caylee and Erica with wonder.

"Yes, we do," Caylee answered. She smiled as the mermaid squealed and quickly swam away, either in fear or embarrassment.

"And do you know the designers?" one asked.

"Hush, there will be time for all this when the firsts are gathered," Claretha scolded. The other creatures swam in silence the rest of the way.

They moved around the large cliff face and swam out past a field of the glowing grasses. Caylee saw some mermaids using sharp rocks to cut the grass. She guessed it was a food of some type but didn't feel now was the time to ask.

Past the fields were more homes arranged in circles and clumps, some with six doors and others with only four or three. Each time they passed a home, several merpeople would exit and join the procession behind them. She could hear whispers behind, but each time she looked back, the talking would cease.

"There," Clausen said. Caylee looked forward and saw a vast mound of rocks ahead. The rock formation wasn't natural. Large piles of stones had been layered one on top of the other. There was a massive dark hole at the base and fear suddenly filled her.

"What is in there?" she asked Claretha, but the mermaid either didn't hear her or wasn't inclined to answer.

When they reached the dark hole, bright lights flashed on, illuminating a long wide tunnel. The lights came from odd shells that opened when they passed. Since the procession of sea creatures followed them, Caylee dampened down her fears.

"Here we are," Clausen stated as they reached the end of the tunnel. He spread his free arm outwards, and the shells that lined the interior flashed with light.

The dome was a massive room. It had a high rocky ceiling, and the floor was flattened and smooth like marble. Seats lined the walls, and, on one end, two pillars of marble held up two massive chairs.

As the remaining merpeople filed into the dome, Caylee and Erica were guided to the two chairs, which remained empty. The colorful merpeople filled the empty chairs around the walls. Caylee found it hard to not stare at the beauty.

"Welcome," came a booming voice that drew Caylee's attention from her surroundings.

While she had been distracted, the two chairs had been occupied. In the first sat a large dark purple mermaid. Her long hair flowed about behind her, and lavender eyes smiled down at Caylee. The second held a dark green merman. His hair was as long as the first.

Both were beautiful creatures of unknown age. Their face scales were smooth and neither had grey hair, so she assumed they were still young. The two creatures smiled down at them.

"Are you Bettina and Cargnet?" Caylee asked as Claretha swam them closer to the chairs.

"You know of us?" Bettina asked, her lavender eyes going wide.

"My father was there at your birth," Caylee said with a smile.

"Kriston," Cargnet said, his deep voice booming out around the dome. "Are you his daughter?"

"I am," Caylee replied, studying the two. She was in awe that she was meeting the two whom her father had witnessed being born years before. The Protector, Dreail, had been both mother and father to the first merpeople, a birth made possible by the goddess herself in honor of Caylee's parents. The wonderful gift of life had been given to these creatures because Tresstéanna and Kriston had risked their lives to save the goddess. They had returned her corporeal body back to the cradle by changing into a mermaid and merman by way of a magical flower. This story had been one of Caylee's favorites as a child and, now that she was faced with the two creatures, she couldn't contain her excitement.

"We owe much to your parents," Bettina said with a slow nod of her head. "And are quite pleased to aid in the rescue of their daughter, as was foretold at our birth."

"I do thank you for that," Caylee said. She tried a graceful curtsy but ended up flopping about next to Claretha, who tightened her hold on Caylee's arm. "But my parents are in danger. They have been banished to another world. I need to get back to my mission so I can locate them and return them home."

The dome erupted in chaos as Caylee's news was heard. When Cargnet raised his hands, the noise quickly subsided.

"Tell us what has happened," he pleaded.

Caylee told them of her family's disappearance, of the quest to find the Trillium, and Grant's betrayal. The arena was quiet while she spoke and only once did Bettina interrupt and ask a question.

"Poor child," Bettina stated as she left her chair and swam down towards her. "This mirror, I have not heard of it, but we know of the island. We call it Rime Gaunt. Our people do not swim there as the water is too cold for our bodies."

"The cold comes from the island itself," Cargnet explained as he swam close to Bettina. The last time we were near it, we lost half of our children due to the cold."

"I need to go there, but first, I need to join my friends back on the ship," Caylee stated.

"Your ship is no longer in the same place. The waves no doubt caused it to move. However, there is a place we can take you that is closer and where your friends might pass on the way to Rime Gaunt," Cargnet provided.

Svlain was making another pot of tea in the captain's quarters when she felt the shooting pain of a vision, seconds before her eyes dimmed. She saw Caylee lying on sharp rocks, but this time she saw past her emotions. Details she had missed in the first vision came to her. The rock was two hundred feet tall, a massive pillar of stone that jutted up into the afternoon sky and split the clouds that dared to pass it. Large birds of prey swooped around the peak of dark stone. They dipped and circled about the rock, which housed their nests far above the crashing waves.

The vision showed Caylee, clothed only in white under-garments, lying amongst the broken rocks along the northern side of the island. Erica was a few yards away, still wearing her torn and soaked dress. As the vision continued, Svlain saw ice crystals race towards the two unconscious women. Before the speeding frost reached them, Svlain's vision ended, and she awoke to her friends and family surrounding her.

"Mom!" Brett said as Zain laid a cold cloth over her forehead.

"I am all right," she said weakly.

"Here, drink this," her husband urged. She drank the cold liquid and smiled at those gathered around her.

"I know where they are," she said.

Captain Rouen rushed forward.

21

ROCKY GROUND

Bryce paced back and forth in the small space behind his desk as the new day arrived outside the windows. The long night was behind him, yet the worry and fear for Caylee were still there.

Sometime during the night, he had finally admitted to himself that he was in love with the woman. It was an emotion he had never felt towards another in his life, but now he felt it so strongly that it took his breath away.

He hadn't slept the whole night. After he had collapsed, his men had carried him into his cabin, where he had regained consciousness. After a cup of strong tea, he had brushed off any concerns and proceeded to take control, shouting orders to continue the search.

After Svlain's vision, he gave new orders to aim for the island known to Eno as the Rock. The island was only minutes away, but he worried it was minutes Caylee and Erica didn't have. What if they were too late? What if the seer's vision was wrong?

"Captain," Eno said as he joined the group that had settled inside the cabin.

"Well?" Bryce demanded as he stopped his pacing.

"The wizard still has not found them," Eno supplied, speaking of the trans rocks Col had discovered were missing sometime in the night. It appeared the prisoner had done more than throw helpless women overboard during his free time. He had also pilfered and hidden the rocks that allowed communication with the castle back on the mainland, along with the book that described the Dua Sacro island.

"What a mess," Captain Adams exclaimed as Bryce started his pacing again.

"We will worry about that later. Right now, we need to hurry and find Caylee and Erica," Svlain urged.

To Bryce, it felt like hours before they heard the shout come from the crow's nest. He was the first to reach the deck, and he shouted orders as he ran forward. The first sight of the small island filled him with fear.

A dark, foreboding black rock thrust up into the morning sky. Even the sun's rays didn't brighten the stone's surface. Large dark birds flew about the pointed top of the island hundreds of feet above the water. Waves crashed against the shore as the ship grew closer, and they could all see how sharp the rocks that lined the shore really were.

"Bring us to that point and anchor," he shouted, his eyes already on the northernmost tip of the odd island. "Make ready the boat!"

He silently urged his men and boat to move faster and felt his frustration grow as time seemed to slow. He silently wondered if Caylee would be alive.

The ship couldn't get too close to the shore. The rocks were too sharp and shallow around the northern side. The small boat was lowered and once again Bryce joined the crew, this time accompanied by Brett, the wizard Col, and the healer Zain.

"There!" he shouted as his men rowed them past rocks as dark as the pillar that sat in the middle of the island. "Over there!"

It was the white of her clothing that he first spotted. He didn't know if it was Caylee or Erica, but his heart raced as they drew closer to the figure lying on the dark shore. Before the boat landed, Bryce threw himself into the cold water and waded quickly towards the figure. He felt the rocks bite into his leather boots and ignored the pain as he quickened his pace.

"Caylee!" he shouted. He felt his heart pound wildly in his chest.

She was so pale. Her hair lay around her head, wet and dark as the rocks. She wore only her undergarments, short white britches with a little lace around the end and a short-sleeved top with the same pattern around the neck. Her face was turned towards him, but her eyes were closed. When he saw her chest rise and fall, he quickly cried out.

"Caylee!" He skidded on the sharp rocks and landed next to her. He lifted her off the rocks and into his arms as he said her name again.

"Bryce?" she moaned, and he squeezed her harder.

"Caylee, are you alright?" he demanded, his arms shaking.

"You're squishing me," she complained, and a laugh escaped him.

"Thank the goddess." He held her at arm's length before bringing her in for a swift kiss.

"Bryce," she hissed, and her eyes grew wide when she saw the men standing behind him.

"Erica," Brett shouted and raced past them.

Bryce turned to see Brett picking Erica up from the rocks as his men surrounded them.

"Where are the blankets?" Bryce demanded. Then he gave in and gave Caylee another kiss.

Sitting in Bryce's cabin with the fire blazing and blankets wrapped around her and Erica, Caylee drank more of her hot tea while they told their friends of their adventure under the sea.

"There were small children. They had the most colorful tails and hair," Erica exclaimed as Brett continued to run his hands up and down her arms as if trying to use his body to warm her.

"We weren't cold while we were with them," Caylee explained. "And the water felt warm."

"You could breathe it?" Col asked as he leaned closer.

"While they touched us," Caylee explained. "They know of the island but called it something else."

"Rime Gaunt," Erica provided.

"Bettina and Cargnet said we should reach the ice in two days if we head due north," Caylee explained, taking another sip of her tea. Bryce hovered around her.

She had enjoyed waking up in his arms, and the kisses he had given her had almost stolen her breath. She hadn't been able to ignore the worry she saw in his eyes, nor the dark circles under them from lack of sleep. She also hadn't been able to ignore the emotion in them, something that both excited her and made her nervous. Was she really feeling what she thought she was feeling?

"While you were swimming amongst the mermaids, we discovered that the trans rocks and the *Gull*'s logbook were taken while Grant was out of his cell," Col said with a frown.

"How did he get free?" Erica demanded.

"He almost killed the warrior Honi, who was on post. Honi had just relieved Lolli from his shift," Col said with a shake of his head. "Grant hit Honi so hard, the poor lad did not know what day it was."

"What did Grant do with the items?" Caylee asked.

"He hid them, and we haven't been able to find them," Bryce explained as he finally sat next to Caylee.

"We have time to search." She laid a hand on Bryce's arm. "Why don't you get some sleep."

"I think we all need to catch up on our rest," Erica said as she stood. Brett followed her closely.

When the room emptied, Caylee remained where she was and studied Bryce closer. There was a twitch under his right eye, and he stared out at the room, deep in thought.

"What bothers you?" she asked, her hand still on his arm.

"Why did he take the rocks?" He turned to look at her. "The book, he would know we would need it and maybe use it to barter with. But the rocks?"

"You worry he will use them to go back to Castle Pines?" Caylee asked. Suddenly she too was worried Grant would use them to escape back to the mainland.

"But why? Why would he want to return?" Bryce asked.

"I never told my cousin it was Grant who had betrayed me and my family," she said suddenly, full of fear.

"But did he know that?" he asked as he covered her hand. When she shook her head no, he nodded and smiled. "Let's leave this for another day. Tomorrow we will deal with it."

"So, are you going to tell me that you missed me?" she asked as she looked at him through her eyelashes. Her face went warm when he continued to look at her.

"Tell you?" His eyes went soft as he leaned closer, then stopped inches from her lips.

"What I think your eyes have been telling me since I woke up on the rocks," Caylee whispered back.

"Tell you that I love you?" he asked, still hovering inches from her lips.

"You know you want to tell me." She smiled when he narrowed his eyes at her. "Saying it will make you feel better."

"Will it?" he teased.

"I've been told that."

"Hmm." He leaned back an inch, a thoughtful look on his face.

She laughed, then grabbed the front of his shirt, yanked him closer, and kissed him.

The next two days were spent in anticipation.

Caylee spent as much time with Bryce as his duties allowed. She soon discovered that being captain of the ship didn't leave as much time as she'd hoped.

In the early mornings, he had seconds to stand with her

on the deck and watch the sun rise. Then he was off to his cabin for his duties. He had time around lunch and spent a few minutes with her eating, then he was off again doing rounds. Some of those rounds were spent in the ropes draped around the sails, high above the deck. Since the sheer height made her head spin, she chose to remain below deck while he was climbing the rope ladders to and fro.

In the evenings, he had more free time. Usually, he would seek her out before dinner and eat with her and the others. Then he would ask her for a walk above deck. The first night, he showed her a private corner of the ship where the rigging was stored on the quarterdeck. After he had kissed the breath out of her, he then showed her a private spot on the main deck.

"I feel there are far too many secret corners on this ship," she teased him before they finally settled near the railing along the port side.

"My dear, I feel there aren't enough," he teased back.

The third morning she awoke to a cold room. They all dressed quickly in their new warm gear. Caylee laced up her thick boots, and once done, Tonkee handed her a warm fur hat.

"Kayla said there is frost on the rigging," Tonkee said, her long red hair tied back and squished under a blue wool cap.

"Is the deck slippery?" Erica asked with concern.

"No. The men kept the fire baskets lit the whole night," Tonkee replied, speaking of iron baskets with ash pans under them to catch any spark that might burn the ship's decking.

"How about we eat breakfast and then play cards in your new boyfriend's cabin?" Erica teased.

"As long as there are cakes for later," she joked.

Breakfast was quickly eaten, and she noticed all the crewmembers were now wearing their winter gear, including the funny little cook, whose coat barely buttoned over his large belly. Once above deck, she paused at the first fire basket to warm her hands. She had forgotten her gloves in her cabin.

"Look!" Tonkee exclaimed.

Turning, Caylee saw the water in front of the ship was foamy with waves. Then her eyes registered that it wasn't foam but ice. All three rushed to the front of the ship and gazed at the odd sight the ship was fast approaching. Soon, large slabs of ice floated past the bow of the ship. Huge white shapes bobbed in the water.

"Icebergs," Bryce said from behind them.

"Bergs?" Erica asked, taking a tentative step away from the banister.

"Soon, they will get larger. If our luck holds, they will not block our path completely," he explained.

"What will we do if that happens?" Caylee asked, sticking her cold hands deep in her new coat's pockets.

"Then, we walk," Bryce said with a frown.

Grant wiped the blood from his lip and cursed his captors. The wound had reopened each time he drank or ate, which fueled his hatred for all those on the ship, including his fiancée.

His last attempt to whisk Caylee away to Pon Hellz had failed, just like his first attempt, when the nymph had blown him away from Caylee. He had tried to reach for her hand then. His other had been wrapped around his medallion; the one Io Maltesea had provided him. The one that would take him from this world and into the other.

His second attempt had been thwarted by the nasty crew of the foul ship. He hadn't even gotten close to Caylee then, but he had managed to hide the stupid rocks and the book.

A smile caused his lip to bleed more, but he didn't notice as his thoughts turned to the struggle this might cause. He knew the loss of the trans rocks would hinder the wizard's communication with the mainland. But more importantly, the loss of the book might wreck the mission to find the Trillium.

Unconsciously, Grant's hand went to his shirt front where the medallion still lay under his tunic. The guards had searched him for the stones and book, but they had not robbed him of his most prized possession.

He studied the two guards outside his bars, and his smile grew wider. When he needed to, he would escape again by using what small magic he held, then he would get his hands on Caylee.

22

DUA SACRO

Bryce studied the island with trepidation.

Large ice chunks crashed against the sandy shore with each wave. They bobbed around his ship, but the weather he could see on the island looked different, warmer.

The air around his ship was freezing. His breath blew out in puffs of vapor, and his coat did little to keep out the cold. Even standing in the wheelhouse, he felt the chill. Yet on the island, the breeze barely blew the tropical trees that grew in a large grove just beyond the beach. Beyond the forest sat a high mountain. Its peak reached far into the sky and was covered at the very top with snow.

They had sailed to the tip of the eastern side, where a large river flowed out from the trees and the water met the ocean. He had called for his men to lower the anchor, but they had not yet lowered the boats as the feeling of unease could be felt by all on board.

"We need to start before lunch," Col stated, causing Brett to turn and look at the wizard. "I think I should go first."

"No, we all go," Caylee said, and Bryce heard the authority in her voice.

"But if there is danger..." Col stated.

"Of course, there is danger, but this is why we have come, to gain access to the Trillium," Caylee stated. "And I have no intention of waiting another day. I need to find my family."

"We should limit the landing party," Bryce suggested, his face grave as he studied Caylee. "The wizard should go, but I think no more than twenty will land on shore, in case there is trouble." He held a hand up and continued. "Trouble we require assistance getting out of."

"I want Erica to stay," Caylee said with a nod.

"Agreed, but I think the seer, Svlain, should go," Bryce urged. Col nodded his head in agreement.

"I think the others should be the dragon warriors," Col added.

"Agreed, but I fully intend on being in the party too," Bryce said darkly. He was pleased when he saw Caylee and the wizard agree.

"Gather your supplies. I will get the warriors ready. Caylee, you may want to inform Erica," Col said before he left abruptly.

"She won't be happy," Caylee said, then she followed her wizard.

"Eno, I am going to bring Chaos," Bryce said to his second in command. "If I don't return, you know what to do," he said as they walked to his cabin.

The bird was waiting for him, red feathers bristling and eyes wide in excitement.

"Another adventure?" Chaos asked as Bryce packed an overnight bag.

"There might be danger," Bryce said over his shoulder towards the bird.

"I have not been disappointed yet." Chaos flew to land on Bryce's shoulder with ease.

Two small boats were launched and the landing party of twenty made their slow way towards the shore. They had to navigate around floating ice while the waves continued, threatening to blow them into the large ice chunks. When they made the shoreline, everyone had to shed their cold-weather gear within twenty feet of shore. The air was not just hot, it was stifling and humid.

"It feels like Midzark," Svlain said as she laid her warm coat on the branch of a nearby tree. "Except the air is moist here."

It was agreed they would follow the river. The missing logbook from the *Brown Gull* had spoken of how the crew had followed the river up into the forest. It had explained that at its end sat the mirror they were searching for.

"We should have only a day and a half march inland," Col said as he peered into the thick trees. "But during this time, I want everyone on guard."

Bryce hoped the seer would have a vision that might help guide them to the Trillium, but as of yet, the nymph had remained quiet. Erica and Brett had argued when Caylee asked them to remain behind on the ship. However, in the end, both had agreed to stay aboard. Svlain's husband, Zain, hadn't consented and, after quietly talking to Col, was granted the right to join the group.

When they entered the forest, the sounds of the ocean disappeared. The trees were tall, and their large leaves cast dark shadows on the forest floor.

"Where are the animals?" Caylee's question had Bryce

and the others casting around. "There aren't even any bugs," she said with a shiver.

"Maybe the cold surrounding the island kept creatures off," he said thoughtfully.

"But what about birds?" She cast a look at Chaos, who still sat upon Bryce's shoulder.

There was no answer to her comment, so the band continued their march into the heart of the island. Long after lunch, they stopped for a break. The forest floor was covered by underbrush, but it was sparse and there weren't many roots.

No path was found, but the shore of the river was wide, and only once or twice did they have to veer from its edge to skirt obstacles. Small waterfalls or rocky outcrops were all the hurdles they met. Their pathway was easy; however, the constant climb inland was steep and when they stopped, everyone rubbed their thighs to try to relieve sore muscles. They started their trek again and had just reached a curve in the river when a large boom sounded far behind them.

"What in the hell was that?" Bryce demanded, turning to look back down the path they had just taken. "That sounded like a cannon."

"No, that sounded like magic," Col corrected.

They stood there for several minutes, each trying to see down the river or through the trees. When no other sounds came to them, Col advised they continue their march.

"What if my ship is in trouble?" Bryce asked. His worry for his ship and crew almost had him heading back down the river at a run.

"Eno is there. He's a good second in command," Caylee advised.

"We cannot turn back now," Col urged.

When Bryce did concede, he did so reluctantly. Their

march continued and the ground got steeper. They still heard nothing from either animal or the ship far behind them.

"Look, you can see the ship from here," Caylee said as they climbed around a small but strong waterfall. The rocks were stacked high on either side, and the group had to scramble along the river's right side using the stones as steps.

"What is that smoke?" Pren asked as they all climbed up on the rock.

Bryce almost cut his palm in his haste to reach the higher ground. Thin plumes of black smoke drifted from the front of his ship.

"Cats! It's on fire!" the warrior Lolli exclaimed.

"Look, they must be putting out the fire now," Tonkee said, pointing her long arm out at the scene. "See, already the smoke is less."

"But what happened?" Caylee asked, turning her head to study Bryce.

"He has escaped again," Svlain said quietly. "He will come for you," she squeaked. Then she fainted and her husband caught her.

They made camp that night along the banks of the river as the large yellow moon, Lazerith, was rising in the east. The ground was rocky here, and the only level ground they could find was a dirty, muddy bank. However, Col and the others used their short knives to cut some branches from the nearest fir tree. They layered the branches under their bed rolls to keep themselves from rolling around in the mud.

Zain had revived Svlain after her vision, but she had been weak and unable to travel at a fast pace. Therefore, their travels had been slowed.

"We knew it wasn't going to be a day trip," Caylee told Svlain as she handed her a cup of tea.

"But I am slowing you down," Svlain complained as the others continued to make camp around them.

"But now we know Grant is loose," Caylee advised her. She couldn't help but look out into the darkness beyond the camp's fire.

"How did he get loose?" Tonkee hissed as she maintained her protective position next to Caylee.

"His magic," Svlain replied to Caylee's shock. "He told us as much. Remember, he said his grandfather was Kriston's brother, which makes Grant a royal."

"I'm a fool!" Caylee hissed when the realization struck her. "His royal magic." She shook her head as a shiver of repulsion passed through her.

"Remember, he fooled us all," Svlain said as she patted Caylee's hand.

Dinner was a pot of stew that the cook had made on board and Kayla, who was the best at heating and cooking in their group, had warmed up over the fire. The cook had also packed bread and cakes, and a large breakfast for the morning.

After the meal, everyone settled down amongst the pine branches to sleep, except the two guards on duty. Caylee had set her bed near the fire, but soon realized it was far too hot to sleep. After a few minutes of tossing and turning, she sat up and moved her bed further from the fire.

"Here, why don't you try this spot," Bryce advised and stood to evict Dovic from the place next to his bed roll.

"Hey, I was going to sleep there..." Dovic complained, but he quickly moved off when Bryce hissed at him.

Smiling, Caylee looked down at him in doubt. His handsome face was the picture of innocence and the smile he gave her was charming.

"My mother warned me about men like you," she said, her bed roll still held in her arms as she narrowed her eyes.

"I promise, I will behave."

"Captain, you haven't behaved the whole time I've known you," she said with a laugh. She threw her bed roll down a few feet from his so that her head was near his, but the foot of her roll was in the opposite direction. This would allow her to talk to him, but ensure she was safe from rolling right into his arms that night.

"Tell me," she said after she had settled down. "I heard a rumor." She stopped and studied him. He lay on his stomach, his head propped in his hands as he faced her. His dark brows were drawn together in concentration, but his lips were still curved in a smile. The firelight flashed on his black hair, and her fingers itched to run through the locks.

"Ask anything of me, my lady," he joked.

"Bryce, I heard that, I mean, is what you told me about your parents true?" She saw the laughter leave his eyes.

"Why do you ask?" he replied.

"Erica heard a different story than what you told me, and Svlain another." Caylee tilted her head. His eyes narrowed. "And I asked cook, who told me a different story than the one I heard from Jap."

"And let me guess, Eno told you another story," Bryce said with a sigh.

"Why the deception?" she asked, trying to keep the hurt from her voice.

"Have you told all your secrets?" Bryce asked. He rolled over to lie on his back and looked up at the stars and moons.

"I will tell you my darkest secret if you tell me the truth." Her whisper had him quickly flipping back on his stomach to look at her.

When he said nothing and continued to stare at her, she took a deep breath then reluctantly told him of her encounter with the large cats and their demise.

"I was so scared and sick by what I had done that it was almost six years before I ever used my magic again," she admitted, fearful of how he would react to her news. But she wanted to hear his secret more than ever, and if sharing her hardship would prompt him to tell her the truth, she thought the risk was worth it.

"And is this why you are a vegetarian?" he asked.

"That, and I find it hard to eat a creature I have had conversations with," she said with a weak smile.

"Caylee, my parents..." He started, then he shook his head and tried to start again. "My mother wasn't the most loving person."

She remained silent while she watched his internal struggle. When he finally seemed to resolve it, he scooted closer until their noses were almost touching.

"My mother was a woman named Reta. She worked in a tavern in a small village on the southern edge of Malic. The name of the town has changed since I left, so it does not matter what it was once called. But the tavern was foul and did not cater to families, if you know what I mean." He drew quiet for a second and she reached out to trace a finger along his cheek bone. Her actions drew his eyes back to hers and for several minutes they sat in silence. Then he continued.

"My mother told me when I was about ten who she thought my father was," he continued. "But it turned out she was wrong."

"Oh, Bryce," Caylee started, but he placed a finger over her lips to quiet her.

"Let me finish," he urged. "The man I thought was my father was a sailor. He came into our town twice a year and told great stories of adventure and dangers. Stories I listened to with envy. He was kind to me and my mother when he was in town. But he would always leave again."

Caylee saw the hurt in Bryce's eyes from the firelight. She kept quiet this time and patiently waited for him to continue.

"It was two years later that I discovered that this man wasn't my real father. Because that is the year my magic manifested." He whispered the last two words so quietly that she doubted, at first, that she had heard him correctly.

"Your—" she began, but once again his finger came to her lips.

"Yes." He slowly took his hand from her lips and studied it as sparks emitted from his fingers. "You see, there were three royal families in the region. Most had lost their wealth. Two ruled as stewards to King Malic, while the third was a real bastard. He traveled through the region and used his magic to scare people or bully them into giving him what he wanted. When my magic manifested, I confronted my mother, who then reluctantly told me about Rouen." Again, he fell quiet as he continued to study his hand, now empty of sparks or magic. "Euan Rouen was a large man with more magic than brains. He took one look at me and laughed."

She reached out and grabbed his empty hand and held on. His eyes didn't meet hers now but kept looking at his hand, as if shocked to find hers there.

"He knew you?" she finally asked, and he shook his head.

"No, but my eyes gave it away, that I was his." When he looked up, his tan eyes glowed in the firelight. "I wasn't the only child, and I would not be the last."

"What did you do then?" she asked.

"I left home, and I never went back," he said with a weak grin.

"You were twelve!" she said, shocked to learn he had been on his own at such a young age.

"I was twelve, but I was never young. I was never innocent, and I had already been on my own for years before that." He smiled for the first time since telling his story. "The first thing I did was sign up as a cabin boy on the first ship I saw." Now his smiling face turned whimsical. "The *Fat Lady*." He sighed.

"The..." she started, but then paused, full of doubt.

"*Fat Lady*, yeah. It was a barge that ran up and down the Mazel River. It stank of fish and the crew swore like, well, like sailors." He laughed and continued to tell her stories of his younger escapades.

When she fell asleep, it was with Bryce's hand clasped tightly in hers and a smile on her lips.

23

THE POWERS THAT BE

There was no sign of Grant the next morning, and Caylee was glad about this. But still, the fear that he would show up at any minute hung over the group.

The mountain loomed ahead of them as they marched along the river, and Caylee replayed in her mind the conversation with Bryce as she walked. She now knew why he had told so many different stories about his parents. She would have done the same. Yet the thought of a young Bryce being on his own saddened her.

"Heads up," Tonkee said from behind her. Caylee had to quickly duck to miss a branch, and even then it brushed her temple. "Watch where you're going," Tonkee scolded.

"Sorry. My mind was on something." Caylee's words had Bryce turning back and looking at her for a second, then he turned and continued walking.

Their path was steep, and the river was now flowing over rocks as waterfall after waterfall hindered their way forward. Her legs burned from the constant climbing, and they went through their drinking water before midday.

"How much further?" Bryce asked.

"I wish we still had the book," Col said as he shielded his eyes from the sun. "I think it cannot be much longer now."

Caylee pushed a strand of hair back from her face and glanced upwards. The waterfalls were small, more like dips in the river than anything. However, suddenly she realized she was hearing a deep beating that pulsated into her entire body.

"What is that noise?" she asked as everyone stopped to listen.

"I think it's a big waterfall," Pren said as he looked up. "There, a break in the trees." He pointed to their right.

The opening led to a small lake. Its shoreline was spread out and free from trees, and on the far side sat a giant waterfall. The water fell from the top of a massive cliff and into a hill of snow at its base. The liquid disappeared into the ice and then flowed out of a cave closer to the lake. The cave was over ten feet tall and half as wide. Mist rose up where the water hit the ice.

"It's an ice cave," Caylee said in awe.

"This is something the book failed to tell us." Col frowned as he studied the area. "I do not like this."

"Is this the Trillium?" Bryce asked, a frown on his lips.

"I do not know," Col said with a shake of his head.

"Well, there is one way to find out," Caylee stated as she started forward.

"Hold on!" Bryce and Col both shouted as they rushed to join her.

It was easy to skirt the lake, but as they drew near the ice, the air temperature dropped, and they all wished for their coats again.

"Here, one at a time. No, not you first," Col scolded as Caylee tried to go to the front of the line. "Stand behind the captain," he scolded. "Pren, next to me and Tonkee, take up the rear."

"I want—" Caylee started, but she was unceremoniously pushed backward in the line.

"Ugh!" she said as Bryce reached for her hand and smiled.

"I keep forgetting you are a princess," he said with a laugh. "Until you try and boss people, that is."

She stuck her tongue out at him, and he laughed again. Once they started into the cave, however, all laughter stopped. The cave was long and dark. The ice made the air cold and there was an ominous feeling inside that made everyone edgy. Sounds echoed inside the tunnel and the dripping of the water, which ran down the middle of the cave, was deafening.

Twenty feet in, Caylee was so cold she didn't think she would ever feel her face or hands again. Ten feet past that and she knew blood had stopped flowing.

"The falls are just ahead," she heard Col say. She felt the mist of the water.

"Ugh, we have to walk through it," Pren advised them.

"Cover your head!" another voice shouted, and Bryce tugged at her hand.

"Hold on, we are about to get wet." He pulled her forward.

The sound of falling water grew louder. She saw the falling water seconds before she was pulled into it. Worried the water was as cold as the ice, she held her breath, fearful she might just freeze to death. As the falls washed over her, she sucked in a deep breath in shock. The water was warm and heated her as it doused her entire body.

"It's warm!" she said with a laugh that immediately died on her lips when she passed beyond the water.

Beyond the ice cave sat a vast hollow. The chamber had been carved out of bear rock and ice by the falling water. The air here was hotter than the cave, but still not as warm as the rest of the island. Her smile faded as she looked towards the center of the space.

Grant Worthington stood dead center of the cavern with his arms wrapped around Erica. He had a very sharp knife to her friend's throat.

"Grant!" Caylee shouted as the others stood stock-still with their weapons drawn. None were willing to rush the man and risk the woman's life.

"We have come to the end," Grant said. His pale green eyes narrowed as he tightened his hold on Erica. "Come on over, slowly," he hissed. "If you come with me, I will not hurt her."

Caylee saw the lie in his words but had no choice. She felt Bryce's hand tighten on hers, but she shook her head no and released it, then took a step towards Grant. She raised her hands, palms out, a broad smile on her face.

"Grant, how did you get here?" she asked sweetly.

"I have the book," he sneered. "There was a shortcut."

"A shortcut." She shook her head. "That would have helped. Grant, please release her. She is turning purple."

"She deserves it. She has meddled in my affairs long enough," Grant hissed.

"No," Caylee said and took another step towards him. "She has only done what I asked. It's not her you want, but me." She saw Grant's arms relax a little with her words.

"You need to come with me," Grant stated and, in his distraction, he almost dropped the knife as he reached into his shirt. The medallion he pulled out was small and glowed bright red.

"What is that?" Caylee asked, her eyes no longer on her friend nor Grant. A red mist swirled around inside the pendant, and she immediately understood what it was he held.

"Come closer," Grant urged her as he pressed his thumb on the glowing orb.

"NO!" Bryce shouted, and he raced forward towards Grant.

Seconds later, Caylee felt Erica's wind magic blast her backward. "Stop!" Caylee shouted once, then her body slammed into the ice wall and her world went black.

"Caylee," a moan sounded, and Caylee fought to open her eyes as the pounding in her head threatened to shatter her skull. "Caylee, wake up."

It was Svlain who was speaking. She and Zain were bent over her, trying to revive her. Zain had a bag of smelling salts under her nose while Svlain sat near, softly speaking her name.

"I'm awake." She jolted upright, which caused her head to spin once before it settled back to normal. "Bryce!" she shouted.

"He is gone," Col said as he knelt next to her. "The mist took him and Erica."

"Grant!" Caylee hissed, and they all nodded. "I'll kill him."

"You have to find him first," Col said, helping her to her feet.

"The Trillium?" Caylee asked and studied their surroundings.

"I do not know," Col said with a shake of his head. "I cannot find it."

Caylee turned and studied the rocks at the base of the cliff. There wasn't any mirror there. In fact, there wasn't anything there except rocks. Turning, she studied the ice, but its surface was muddy and unclear. No mirror there either.

She was just about to give up when she glanced back towards the cavern they had arrived by. The tunnel was a dark slash, a black square behind the shining water of the falls. Yet it wasn't the cavern she was now seeing, but a movement. Unsure what she was seeing, she pulled her short sword and moved into a defensive stance. The others followed her posture, but it appeared they didn't know where the threat was as they faced everywhere but the tunnel.

"There, do you see that?" She pointed towards the tunnel.

"The cavern?" Col asked and shook his head. "There is nothing there, it is empty."

"No, I see movement." She took a step closer. As she drew nearer, an image materialized in the clear water of the falls they had passed through. The tunnel's darkness behind helped the image grow sharper. Her mother's figure stepped out from a dark doorway, and Caylee dropped her sword in her excitement.

"Mom!" she gasped. The image shifted and her father followed. "Dad!"

Her parents stood in the doorway momentarily as faint light hit their faces, which were set with determination. Her father moved to place a hand on her mom's back as he led her out of the doorway.

"Where are they?" she asked, and the image shifted. Now she was looking at her parents' backs. The land beyond was outlined in the image, causing her breath to catch in her throat.

There was a volcano, which was a massive triangle of red and black, rising high before her parents. Black ash and red lava spewed from the enormous mountain. It clogged the air and lit up the night sky. It was horrific to witness, and dread filled her as the vision showed, in great detail, a valley that lay at the mountain's base.

Then the vision shifted, and Caylee saw Charlotte and a dark-haired young man step out of the doorway behind her parents. His face was familiar, but Caylee couldn't figure out how or from where she knew him.

"Charlotte!" Caylee shouted and almost rushed at the water, but hands held her back.

"No, it is just an image," Col told her as he held her tight.

The image shifted again, and Caylee cried out as a white stag stepped from the door. The stag had hair that shone in the faint light. Its golden hooves and white mane were beautiful, but it was the single golden horn that sat in the center of its forehead that took her breath away.

The unicorn turned its golden eyes towards her and, through the vision, she heard a voice inside her head whisper, "*Hurry, child.*" Then a small object flew at her and the image was gone.

EPILOGUE

Zander watched the ship glide through the water far below his dragon, Bree Nu. A smile passed his lips and he turned to study his wife, Rey, who was yards from him on her own dragon, Fru En. He waved and pointed down towards the ship as she nodded and pointed back to the dragon tribe's island. Understanding, he nodded once and banked back towards land.

Zander and his wife had arrived only the night before, understanding that they were arriving a whole day earlier than the ship was expected. But Zander wasn't waiting patiently in Castle Pine for his twin to return home. Instead, he had flown out as quickly as possible, with a full regiment of guards of course, and his bride.

It had been a whole month since he had been whisked away to Earth, and his family had been shattered. A month and eight days. Caylee had contacted the castle only two nights ago, using the trans rocks they had found in Grant's hiding place under the ship's main decking. She told of Grant's betrayal and his attack on Erica and the ship's captain.

They had spoken several times about each other's adventures, but Zander had refrained from telling his sister about his marriage. He wanted to save that for when they were face-to-face.

"Did you see her?" Rey asked after they had landed.

"Yes, she was standing in the front of the ship, waving," he said with a smile. He helped her off her dragon's back. "She was there!"

"Let's go to the harbor and greet her," Rey urged. She grasped his hand, then she gave it a solid tug.

After their guards landed, they all made their way down to the harbor. The locals had all been excited when the royal guards, along with the army, had landed on their small island. Now, with the impending approach of another royal, the crowds started to gather at the docks. Before the ship drew into view, the area had the feeling of a parade.

"Zander!" Caylee had shouted the second the gangplank had been lowered. Then she threw herself at her brother.

The hug was long and fierce. The two twins cried and hugged until Rey cleared her throat next to them as the crowd shouted with excitement.

"Rey, it's Caylee!" Zander said as tears ran down his face.

"Rey!" Caylee shouted and threw herself at the dragon warrior.

"Actually, it's Princess Rey now," Zander said with a smile. "I married the girl."

He saw shock and excitement cross Caylee's face before she threw her arms around his wife's neck again. "Sister!" she shouted with a laugh, and she planted a kiss on Rey's cheek.

"Zander, we need to talk," Caylee said with excitement as they finally turned to walk up the pier towards the crowd.

"Later, when we are alone," he said and with one arm around his wife and the other around his sister, he walked into the crowd.

Later turned out to be hours. First, they had to make their way past the crowd and towards the dragon warriors' village. Then there was a feast and party, during which none of them were ever left alone. Col presided over the party and, with Svlain and Zander's help, held most of the questions about their travels at bay. Brett was there, but after a few minutes, he made an excuse to be alone.

"Leave him, he has other things to worry about than a party," Caylee told Zander.

"But I haven't seen him in forever!" Zander said with a pout.

"Erica and he are engaged, but Zander, we need to return home as soon as possible," Caylee told him. "I know where our parents are."

"You do?" Zander demanded as he grasped her hands tightly.

"Yes, Erica and Bryce, Captain Bryce Rouen, are with them," she stated.

"Was that his ship you came home on?" Zander asked, his brows drawn together as he remembered the vision he'd had while on Earth.

"Yes, I love him, and he loves me. But Zander, Grant betrayed us, and he has them, he has our whole family." She squeezed his hands tightly.

"Where are they?" Zander demanded.

"A place called Pon Hellz. I know how to get there now," Caylee said with a frown.

"What?" Zander asked. "How?"

"Oh, Zander, I was a fool. The answers have always been in the same place. It was there all the time." Caylee frowned up at him as Rey drew closer to them.

"Where, Caylee?" Zander asked again.

"Home." Her words echoed in his ears and hope at recovering his family suddenly bloomed inside his chest. "The doorway is the red mist in Mom's drawing room."

BOOKS BY J.J. ANDERS

The Scholar

The Warrior

The Queen

The Fallen

The Hidden

The Gifted

The Exiled

The Betrayed

The Lost

JJ Anders is the pseudonym used by the powerhouse writing duo of NY Times & USA Today bestselling author, Jill Sanders and her identical twin sister, Jody. Hailing from the Pacific Northwest, these two talented ladies have merged their creative forces to craft an amazing new fantasy series that will leave you begging for more.

With over forty bestselling romance books and counting, Jill alone is a force to be reckoned with, boasting thousands of glowing reviews with a cumulative 4.5 star rating. Jody's powerful imagination and newfound love of writing has spawned the thrilling new world and enchanting characters of Genoa. As a furious reader and devoted mother, Jody's passion for storytelling reaches full bloom by teaming up with her talented twin to bring her magical stories to life for the enjoyment of readers everywhere.

www.ingramcontent.com/pod-product-compliance
Lightning Source LLC
Chambersburg PA
CBHW051256210726
48287CB00002B/523